EVERY TIME HE DIES

EVERY TIME HE DIES

By Tara East

ISBN: 978-0-6485815-0-5

Interior book design by Eight Little Pages

For Ele & April. Miss you.

AUTHOR BIO

Tara East is a Doctoral candidate with degrees in Journalism, Editing and Publishing and Creative Writing. Her articles on writing, literature, gender and culture have appeared in Writing from Below, Queensland Writers Centre, The Huffington Post and The Artifice and her fiction has appeared in TEXT journal and October Hill Magazine among others. Home is with her partner, Ashley, and their mini-schnauzer, Sadie. She maintains an active writing blog at www.taraeast.com.

CHAPTER 1

Daff

Eighteen months ago

December 31, 2014

Daff heard her heart like a gunshot: click, crack, boom. Typical cop's daughter. She wasn't raised on sentimental bush poetry, read out loud while the family picnicked together on warm summer days. She was shown how to kick a guy in the nuts, scream like thunder, call 000 and hide under the bed. When she was a kid, there'd been weeks when her father couldn't kiss her goodnight because some junkie had stabbed him with a needle and the test results weren't back yet. So, when Daff looked at Tom, she didn't hear lub-dub, lub-dub; she heard click, crack, boom. Which made sense. He was a cop too.

Sitting in McGee's Irish Pub, Daff swirled the remains of her first and last pint of Guinness. The famous stout had lost its frothy head twenty minutes ago: Happy New Year. Before leaving home, she and Tom tossed a coin for the unprivileged role of designated driver. It had been their tradition for the past three years. Daff lost, again, but she wasn't entirely put out. Tom tended to be a happy drunk, and that goofy smile he'd get after a couple of pints offered its own intoxicating effect. Click, crack, boom. These days, Daff wished she'd paid more attention; that she'd taken the time to memorise the finer details of that broad grin.

McGee's was your typical Celtic affair: dark wood booths, doors and bar, low lighting and burgundy walls. They'd scored a pair of hard wooden stools at the bar, lit from above by a panel of coloured glass that announced the pub's best sellers: Kilkenny and Guinness. Around them was McGee's latest marketing strategy, a retro-themed New Year's Eve bash.

Daff pulled at the cinched waistband of her new olive dress, thinking bitterly of how much it was living up to its name; no wonder women gave up the fit and flare style for pants and blouses. She combed a finger through the back of her dark hair and tried in vain to re-secure the drooping victory roll. Around the room, others had gone with simpler styles: hair parted to the side, pushed back over one ear and neatly secured with a plastic flower. Tom looked good though, despite his initial resistance to Daff's suggestion that they make the special trip to the Sunny Coast and attend the party. His pressed khaki slacks, brown plaid shirt and fedora gave his already lengthy six-foot-two frame a streamlined look. Click, crack, boom. The only inauthentic accessory was the black and red adventure watch Daff gave him a week earlier. He'd been lusting for that watch—the new beaut thing—since a constable in his department got one. The smile on his face when he'd unwrapped that present made the last eight months of saving worth it. Though it clashed with the retro outfit, Daff felt a pleasant warmth at seeing him wear it.

"What's the time?" Her eyes darted towards Tom's wrist.

"Twenty to twelve."

The combination of a late night and a sole drink resulted in the usual ultimatum: food or home. Tom gallantly ordered two burgers.

Daff watched as a party of four in a nearby booth fought over the bill. Eventually, a tall man with tartan suspenders snatched the receipt, flipped his mates the bird and dashed towards the counter with his three friends in tow. Her back ached and she was sick of repositioning her legs every few minutes. Seeing her chance, Daff slipped from the stool and into the freshly abandoned booth.

"Nice grab, darlin'." Tom slid into the open seat opposite her.

Daff glanced towards the swinging double doors of the kitchen, willing them to open and deliver her burger. Instead, she was met with the scowling black looks of several unashamed patrons; apparently, she wasn't the only one hungry for a decent seat.

"We should have won best dressed. That Marilyn look-a-like? Pfft! And that gangster guy? He was just over the top and the suit didn't even fit him."

"Amateurs. The judges are obviously wankers. Couldn't they see the brilliant authenticity of our costumes? The standard fifties suburban couple." Tom waved his hand through the air as if he was cleaning a window. "Who could be more deserving of a two-week gym membership and Woolworths gift card?"

"Very short sighted." She smiled, despite her grumbling stomach.

A waitress dressed as an American diner hostess appeared and slid their burgers onto the table. "There's your meals, babe." She popped her gum, gave Tom a wink and sashayed back into the crowd.

Daff eyed her plate, suddenly wary about the establishment's hygiene practices, but she was too hungry to be cautious. She plucked a chip and took a swipe at the tomato sauce that oozed from Tom's burger, another one of their traditions.

Tom dragged his plate back and leaned forward, protecting his midnight dinner. "So, what are your plans for the New Year?"

"Move in with you?" They'd talked about it extensively, so Daff didn't know why it came out like a question rather than a statement.

"Eh, steady now. Bit late in the game, Daff, seeing as how you've already dropped half your library onto my living room floor. The bathroom door won't even close now, all them damn bras you've left on the handle." Tom continued with a wink. "But I'm surprisingly okay with that."

Three years and he could still make her blush. With half a burger lining her stomach, she was ready to gulp down the remains of her Guinness and attempt another swipe at Tom's sauce.

"Don't be greedy." Tom pretended to smack her hand away, while subtly pushing his plate forward. "Come on, I want another goal. What are you going to do this year? Quick, quick," snapping his fingers, "Time is money, baby."

"That doesn't even make sense!"

"And yet you stay."

Daff tried to hide her responding smile, but failed. "Well, I do have other ambitions: finish my degree, keep an orchid alive …"

"Life on the edge, eh?" Tom dropped his burger and pinched a handful of chips into a bouquet of potato. "You'd look pretty hot in a white lab coat. Get some hipster black frames, some heels, and you'll be sorted."

Daff put on her best American bimbo accent, twirling a free lock of hair in her open hand. "*Oh my god, babe!* Killer uniform was like, *totally* on the top of my pro list. Like, right above my passion for science, criminology and desire to help mankind."

"I've always thought you were a bit shallow."

"Thanks."

Tom picked up a coaster, spun it between his hands and looked out the window into the darkened car park. "How much longer do you have left? Six months?"

She nodded.

"Might be able to buy our own place soon."

Daff straightened, burger and rib jabbing forgotten, "Have you heard, already? Did you pass?"

"No, I haven't heard, but the lecturer said I was amongst the best in class." He kept his face neutral, but Daff could see the pull at the corner of his wide mouth.

"Tom, this is a big deal. Why didn't you tell me sooner?"

"Nothing's happened yet and until I get a letter in the mail … I didn't want to get your hopes up."

"Well … Congratulations!" Daff raised her empty glass, and Tom clinked his own against it.

"Usually, you congratulate someone *after* they've passed."

"Tom, you're gonna be a great detective." She leaned across the table, her hand joining his. It was warm and familiar, so like her own.

He gave her a wink. "Thanks, *sweet cheeks*. I got a lot to live up to."

"Don't bother comparing yourself to Detective Sergeant Jon Lawrence." She added mockingly. "You'll never win." Though she'd tried to keep the tone light, a shadow crept over the conversation. Thoughts of Lawrence, her father, inevitably led to thoughts of her mother, Ruth. If the cancer hadn't eaten the life out of Ruth then their divorce may have.

Tom traced the back of her hand with his thumb, his eyes softening. "Sorry." He hesitated, his mouth nervously shaping the words. "Your old man put himself down as available for on-call again this year. That's three Christmases in a row."

A hand curled around Daff's heart, squeezed. *He's not my old man.* "Stop, please. I don't want to ruin tonight."

"You're really sticking with this, aren't you?"

Designated driver or not; if someone offered her a second Guinness right now, she'd take it.

"Listen, if I pass, maybe I should look into transferring to another station, or we could leave the city all together."

"No," she shook her head. "I like Brisbane, it's my home; yours too. We're not going anywhere. Besides, it would be stupid for you to leave the Valley and start somewhere else; Lawrence only has a few years left." *Two, exactly.*

"Okay." Tom withdrew his hand from hers, pulled his phone out and opened a real estate app. They weren't in the market, not yet, the gesture was pure indulgence, but Daff welcomed the distraction.

She could feel her chest unwind as Tom scrolled through an assortment of renovated Queenslanders, low brick homes and fibro houses. A future bloomed before her: Tom passing his detective certification and sharpening his teeth at the Valley Station, working his way up to senior detective, then sergeant. She'd complete her studies, apply for internships and carve out a career in forensic toxicology. They'd get married, have kids, and buy a house with a big yard so Daff could build her ideal garden. She could plant citrus trees and a vegie patch, a hedge of red robins and mock oranges, and in winter she could fill the beds with petunias, marigolds, pansies and gerberas. She liked that Brisbane had the culture of a city with the feel of a country town. They'd both grown up here, and now they could make it their own. Her younger self would have found the idea of marriage, kids and a mortgage strangling, but life with Tom was an exhale. A relief, a salve to the awfulness of the past few years.

Tom's eyes narrowed, losing their focus as he grinned his infectious grin. Daff knew a good opportunity when she saw it. She grabbed the keys to his Mitsubishi Lancer and announced that it was time to leave.

Daff bundled her inebriated constable into the passenger seat and started the engine. His snore drowned out the grind of the four-cylinder tin can; the motor pushed to its limits as Daff headed towards the Sunshine Motorway and settled in for the hour-long drive back to Brisbane. She switched off the radio to welcome the New Year in peace as Tom's breath filled the tiny cabin, a slow rhythmic exhalation of complete relaxation, complete trust. A metronome reliable enough to tap your toe to; she found herself sinking into it. With a full stomach and a pint of drink, her eyes became heavy, looking for a moment of relief. Her hands relaxed out of the mandatory ten-two position as a black SUV came up alongside her and cut into her lane, its brake lights blinding. Daff jolted. Sleepy hands fumbled. The Lancer skimmed the divide between clean asphalt and untamed bush. The front wheels folded. Flip. Tree. Crack. Darkness.

The digital clock blinked steady: 2:13.

Time passed until the sky became light: flashes of white, blue and red. That's what Daff remembered best, how easily those halogen lights had wiped out the constellations. Paramedics tried to resuscitate Tom at the scene. At 3:36, life was pronounced extinct. Thomas Luke Pease joined the night sky.

CHAPTER 2

Detective Lawrence

Thursday June 30, 2016

Detective Lawrence examined the older victim first. The blonde woman was in her forties and wearing a denim miniskirt that she should have retired a decade ago.

There was that word again: retired. Lawrence's sixty-fifth birthday was three months away. A fact confirmed by his drooping grey eyes and drawn basset hound face. Once a copper hit pension age, it was all over, you never had to set an alarm or don your blues for a beat shift again. Of course, it had been a long time since Lawrence had worn his blues on duty. He'd been clocking on for forty-odd years; that kind of time deserved respect. Last week though, a constable in her thirties made a Hitchcock reference while poking him in the paunch. Lawrence didn't see the resemblance—he still had most of his hair—but the message beneath the comment brought an unexpected blow: he was a fat old man on the cusp of retirement, his ex-wife was dead and his only daughter refused to speak to him. When he walked out of the station for the final time, no one would be waiting for him.

The blonde was propped on a chair in the corner while the second victim, a brunette, was dumped face down on the floor. The Sundowner Motel, or the Sun, as Valley dwellers called it, had managed to hold onto its position on Edward Street despite the suburb's improving reputation. When Lawrence moved here in the eighties, Fortitude Valley was the wallow in which the dregs of city society settled: junkies, dealers, bikers, strippers, working girls. You could still find them, of course, but now the place was filling up with trendy cocktail bars and restaurants, high-end boutique stores and luxury car yards. You were less and less likely to get your teeth knocked in. Lawrence thought you could make an argument about progress, but the two Jane Does before him offered a strong counter point.

Lawrence heard the crime scene photographer cough dryly and he moved aside so the fella could get on with it. The crumpled Moroccan-inspired bedspread matched the dark saffron walls—dated, even by the detective's humble standards. The bedside lamp furthest from the door was on. The padded chair at the breakfast bar was pulled out and there was space beside it for a second seat. The carpet was worn, flattened and spotted with a decade's worth of suspicious stains. If anyone ever slept in this dump, Lawrence thought, they probably kept their jeans on.

The photographer sniffed, unwrapped a Butter-Menthol and moved towards the adjacent bathroom, the second victim momentarily forgotten. Lawrence crouched beside the woman sprawled on the floor, knees protesting as he leaned over his stomach. She was tall, small framed and had long dark hair. She could be in her early twenties, but gauging a young woman's age was tricky business; fourteen-year-olds could look twenty-five, some twenty-nine-year-olds looked nineteen. Unlike the first victim, this lass was fully clothed: leather jacket, jeans, boots.

Boots? She wasn't staying here, then. Maybe she'd interrupted things, Lawrence thought, that's why he'd killed her. Lawrence didn't know for sure that it was a *he*, but experience and statistics made for a safe bet. There was a large blood stain beneath the victim's head, her throat sliced open. *One victim choked, the second attacked with a knife.* He ignored the cramping in his knees as he leaned forward to get a better look at her face. The mouth was wide, nose narrow and eyes pale blue. *Daphne.* Lawrence shot up with such force that he lost his footing, half falling against the nearby cupboard.

Daphne.

"You good, detective?" The camera man asked, emerging from the bathroom.

Lawrence nodded, his throat too thick to talk; he turned and left the way he entered.

Outside it was cold, and for that he was thankful; hopefully it would knock some sense into the old noggin.

It's not Daff, he thought while sucking in another mouthful of morning air. The nose was too thin and the eyes too big. Really, the poor girl in there didn't look anything like his daughter. He took another breath, slow and steady, and reassured himself again, *it's not Daff.*

Lawrence gripped the loose barrier of the landing and leaned out over the near-empty car park wishing for nothing more than a Wini-Red.

You stubborn old goat, Ruth's voice echoed in his head, *how long are you gonna wait before you call her?* Ruth had been gone for near on four years. Cancer. Now that was the real stubborn goat, he thought. Still, he could hear her nagging him now just as clearly as she had when she was alive. He squeezed the railing like he was making orange juice. It hurt how desperately he wished things were different. Days could bumper together, filled with a hundred easily forgotten regrets; the big ones, though, they stay with you.

Ruth had confronted him after she'd received her diagnosis. She said she knew something had been going on and that she wasn't prepared to spend the remaining days of her life living a lie. So Lawrence had told her everything. He knew the affair would cost him a wife, but he hadn't expected to lose a daughter.

A red Toyota Corolla pulled into the car park. Lawrence released his grip. At least McPhee had gotten his voicemail, but the blighter didn't have to come in his own car; he could have stopped at the station first. He'd completed his certificate a month back, gaining the new title of Detective Senior Constable McPhee. Lawrence still thought it strange to see him in plain clothes instead of his blues. *It should have been Tom.*

A flicker of rage rose from his gut before he could snuff it out. Tom had passed his certification, but never collected his gold badge. Lawrence shook his head, forcing out all thoughts of his estranged daughter and her deceased partner. He gripped the railing and watched as McPhee crossed the asphalt, his red handlebar moustache making him stand out like a bikie at a CWA meeting. The VLAD laws had been in effect for eighteen months; considering the state's recent crackdown on illegal motorcycle gangs, Lawrence thought the moustache was more odd than ironic. The two had been partners for the past six months; retirement never looked so good.

Now that he was outside, Lawrence noticed a lingering smoky scent. Junkies loved to mask their drug use with incense; Lawrence couldn't walk past a new-age shop without that musky scent conjuring up some memory of a former bust. Between the acrid smoke and the motel's seedy reputation, Lawrence made a mental note to follow up with the forensic physician; make sure that the blood samples were checked for drugs. Meth was big right now.

McPhee had mounted the steps leading to the second-storey landing. "Mornin' Detective."

Lawrence nodded in reply. They were lucky to have arrived first; emergency services had already left and it wasn't often they beat the forensic crew. The crime scene unit usually had first dibs, but Lawrence was in no mood for waiting around until Sergeant Peter Murphy and his team showed up.

"Let's get this over with it." The detective stepped back towards room eight, his partner behind him.

"Jesus, that's a bit brutal." McPhee's hooded eyes ran over the brunette on the floor before drifting up towards the blonde. Snapping on his gloves, he crouched by the body on the floor, careful to keep his shoes out of the tacky pool of blood. From this angle, the victim's face was concealed beneath a splay of dark tendrils. Lawrence's breath hitched: how easily that girl could've been Daphne. A few moments ago, he'd thought it was.

"She's young," McPhee murmured. "I'd say early twenties." Being in his late twenties, McPhee was in a much better position than Lawrence to perform such crackpot analysis. "She's got some bruises on her neck too. Must have been strangled before …"

Lawrence slipped on his gloves and pulled back the duvet. Though the sheets were rumpled, they were clean, at least to the naked eye. He peered over his shoulder towards the half-dressed blonde. Hopefully the guy hadn't used a rubber and there'd be a few seminal stains on the sheets. He quickly scanned the room again, but could see no evidence of incense having been burned. If they'd taken the time to clean that up, it was unlikely they'd left the murder weapon behind.

McPhee stood up and edged towards the older victim to get a better look. "Maybe it's a mother-daughter tag team type deal."

"Maybe," Lawrence murmured as he slid open the bedside table drawers, but there was nothing in there except a copy of the *Good News.*

"Weird, isn't it?" McPhee peered at the purple bruising around the woman's neck. "If the guy had a knife with him, why did he strangle this one?"

Lawrence glanced at the body in the corner. He'd read enough pathologists' reports to know what this one would say: thyroid gland haemorrhaged, hyoid bone fractured, small abrasions on both sides of the throat. Death by asphyxiation. "Maybe it was personal. Either he knew her, or she reminded him of someone. If he was high, then there's probably no logical reason to it at all."

McPhee stepped over to the cupboard and pulled it open. "No luggage or personal effects. I'm pretty sure the blonde didn't show up at the hotel door in nothing but a bra and skirt."

"He probably took her shirt with him, nothing else was left behind. We'll find out from reception who booked the room, if it was in her name or his." He didn't bother adding that at the Sun, most guests booked under fake names and paid in cash.

"I'm guessing the brunette walked in," McPhee's eyes traced over her. "Maybe our guy was just finishing up with the blonde and this one arrived too early. If our guy was using meth or on speed, he'd be able to go for hours."

"We can't rule out that the women were staying here, not yet. Forensics will run the bloods, check for signs of sexual assault. Dr Cardwell might even lift some DNA skin cell samples off her," Lawrence indicated the blonde with the swollen throat.

"You might want to check this out, Detective." The photographer emerged from the bathroom, sticking his thumb over his shoulder behind him.

Lawrence gingerly stepped around the body on the floor and entered the bathroom. His eyes went straight to the bath, half expecting a third victim, but the shower curtain was pulled back and the tub was empty. No towel hung on the rack and he hadn't seen one in the room either. If the murderer had been high, he still had enough sense to minimise the chances of trace evidence. Maybe he'd done this before. When Lawrence turned towards the vanity, he hardly registered the bare counter and untouched toiletries.

The room froze. He stopped breathing. His stomach dropped. *Fuck.* He'd thought the club had wised up, that this kind of shit was over. Lawrence took an unsteady step forward. They'd left their symbol on the mirror: a circle drawn in blood, slashed by a diagonal line. The crude design was no bigger than his hand and, though the blood was smeared thinly, the symbol was still clearly identifiable. Given the towel factor, Lawrence knew it would be a match to one of the victims.

"Isn't that—" McPhee squeezed into the tiny bathroom beside his superior.

Lawrence nodded. "Yup. Road Dogs' club logo."

"You interrogated the maids or guests yet?"

"Questioned, not interrogated, and no I haven't."

McPhee leaned forward to get a better look. "You reckon Murphy can lift a fingerprint out of that?"

"Maybe, the dragging could have ruined the print though. Still, there's a chance that some DNA was left behind."

Lawrence stepped around McPhee and headed back out onto the landing.

"Where are you going?"

"I don't want to be here when forensics arrive. Murphy will chew my arse out." Lawrence headed down the external staircase. The sun was out now, lighting up the bitumen of the car park, and Lawrence was glad. With only a few more months of active duty left, he'd tried to forget about the Road Dogs, to let it go, but here on this sunny Queensland winter day he'd been given another shot.

CHAPTER 3

Daff

Thursday June 30, 2016

Daff pulled her orange scarf tighter. The sun had set half an hour ago and Golden Beach would have been in complete darkness if not for the glow of the bonfire. Standing by its flames, she could almost ignore the cool evening air, but when the wind picked up it stung her cheeks. Even in Queensland a mid-year beach visit could be lousy.

She should have stayed at home, she should have told Peta, "No, I'm not coming. Go by yourself."

Thursday night was laundry night. Daff liked to get the domestic duties out of the way before the weekend; that way she could spend Saturday and Sunday tending her garden. The coriander had gone to seed; the basil was covered in its delicate white flowers—they'd need to be removed—and the geranium cuttings were ready to be transplanted. They'd look good in the small garden bed by the front stairs, Daff thought.

Peta was chatting to one of the other meditators and in the firelight, she looked more golden than usual. It was easy to forget how small she was—her personality was a formidable compensation for her lack of height. Phrases of their conversation travelled through the evening air: *transcendental, heart chakra, emotional freedom technique*. Daff fought the urge to roll her eyes. She really should have said no. But Peta was a master at convincing people they wanted to do something they absolutely did not want to do.

Despite the ridiculousness of the evening, and the winter chill, Daff had to admit that it was nice to be outside. She was pleased to have worked her way into a permanent embalming position at Dean & Clayton's Funeral Home, but the mandatory cleaning chemicals were so powerful that the air inside the mortuary was almost devoid of smell. There was no trace of bodily fluids or chemicals but, although there were no windows, the air wasn't stagnant. It smelt more like a Tupperware container that had been sealed for too long: confined emptiness.

It was a hard day. She'd spent most of the morning preparing the body of an elderly woman, Margret Underwood. The funeral had been organised in a rush, scheduled for the next day. Deceased for twelve hours; the rigor mortis had already reached its peak. Margret had been found on the toilet; her body slack against the wall, arms and legs curled protectively towards her torso. Lots of people died on the throne, particularly if they had a pre-existing heart condition like Margret did. Bowel movements could drop a person's heart rate and cause cardiac arrest, Daff knew.

She tried to shake out the rigor mortis by massaging the woman's muscles, but Margret remained in the foetal position. If Daff waited seventy-two hours, the muscles would become pliable again; but time was a luxury and the funeral was scheduled. Daff explained to the family that their Aunt Margret had settled into a position that was comfortable for her and she should be allowed to remain in it. Perhaps they would consider buying the coffin three sizes up? The one designed for a six-foot frame. The hardest part of the job was dealing with grieving families; handling corpses was nothing.

More people gathered around the fire; Daff counted fifteen. Some looked perfectly ordinary, wearing jeans, jacket and a scarf like herself. A few had small touches of ironic enlightenment: mala beans or Tibetan-inspired pullovers. Then there was the guy wearing purple slouch crotch pants, his dreads bound into a fat bun on the crown of his head and his ear lobes stretched to the size of a chicken's egg by black plastic plugs. Most were gathered around a woman wearing a teal beanie and white jumper. When the pair beside her began a discussion over their mutual devotion to Kundalini yoga, Daff decided it was time to go. She'd taken three steps, when the woman in the white jumper announced that it was time to begin, inviting everyone to gather around the fire.

Peta broke away from her conversation and pulled Daff down beside her. "No escaping now."

This time, Daff openly rolled her eyes. "I'll be wearing Birkenstocks in no time."

"Shhhhh." Peta's eyes flicked over the foot attire of each attendee.

The group settled into a circle around the fire. The woman in the white jumper sat on a folded towel and thanked everyone for coming.

"Close your eyes," she began. "Take a deep breath in through your nose and out through your nose. Focus on the expanding movement of your chest and belly as you breathe in and feel how they shrink when you exhale."

Daff wondered if they had sat too close to the flames as her cheeks prickled and puckered with the heat. The meditation guide invited them to imagine a staircase that lead to a door. Restless, Daff felt a cramp twist around her left knee, and an irresistible itch spring up on her chin. She twitched her leg and scratched her face.

"Resist the urge to move!" The guide cautioned. "Breathe into any areas of discomfort and allow the breath to move the blocked energy."

The guide's blatant lack of anatomical knowledge was laughable. *Your breath can only go into or out of lungs*, Daff thought, *it can't relieve a cramp in your knee*. Just as carrot juice can't cure cancer. Her chest constricted as an image of her mother arose: she was in the kitchen, healthy and alive, making a pot of tea. Daff swiped the memory away as if it was a picture on her smartphone. A gust of wind swept up the beach, making her hot cheeks tingle against the sudden cool. Her nose started to run and she sniffled quietly.

"If you find yourself thinking about the events of the day or what you'll do when you leave here, your plans for the weekend or your greater life purpose, allow these thoughts to pass through your mind without judgement. This is the voice of your ego. Release the thought and return to your breath."

Despite the instructions, Daff's mind began turning over each of these forbidden subjects. *If we aren't supposed to think about our day, the weekend or our lives at all, why bloody mention it?* Daff thought, suddenly tired. Then she scolded herself. She'd already given up laundry night—that sweet, pleasurable routine—and she may not believe in this woo-woo stuff, but she also refused to spend the next hour in a state of annoyance. Instead, she resolved to find enjoyment in this rare moment of inactivity. This week, it would just have to be Friday night laundry.

The guide continued her spiel about a beautiful garden and meeting your inner-child by a lake, but Daff had already tuned her out, focussing instead on the crackling fire. The sharp snaps of the heat against the night's dropping temperature were accompanied by the overtones of a rising tide and the clicks of crickets and other small insects. Her world become a small dark globe filled with the unpredictable cadences of nature.

A sliver of light crept beneath her sealed lids like a rising sun. At first, she thought it was the light from the fire, so she shut her eyes harder. But instead of disappearing, the glow grew until Daff could see nothing but its golden blaze.

A small voice at the back of her head told her to open her eyes … but the light was so warm, so dazzling; it could take your breath away.

A shadow appeared in the distance like a ball held underwater and then suddenly released. *Open your eyes*, the voice insisted again. Uneasiness swept over Daff, but she kept her eyes shut, couldn't turn her focus away from the figure in her mind's eye. The black shape sharpened and began to take form, morphing into the silhouette of a slim figure; loose dark hair flowing against the brilliant light. The shadow moved forward, growing larger. There was something familiar in its details, the way the shadow moved, the ratio of its parts, but she couldn't identify it. If she could wait just another moment, then maybe she'd remember.

The figure edged closer, its hand outstretched, beckoning. A familiar sense of affection drew around Daff, plucking at the edges of her mind until a thread loosened. Daff struggled to maintain her breath, her ribs pulling towards one another in a way she knew was impossible. Beads of sweat rolled down her temples, cheeks and neck to gather in her scarf.

Mum? Daff gasped, illogically stretching out her hand, her heart thumping against her ribs.

"Slowly, start to become aware of your body," the guide's low, drawn-out voice broke through, shattering the light and the figure sealed within it. "Gently, wiggle your fingers and toes. Feel your consciousness returning to your body."

Daff's eyes flew open and she snatched back her outstretched hand, hoping no one had noticed. Her breath was unsteady, her eyes watery. She rubbed them with the back of her hand and sniffed, if anyone asked, she'd brush it off as the symptoms of a winter cold. That wasn't your mother, she scolded herself. Stop being ridiculous.

A hand suddenly came down on her knee. Her body jolted; a small shriek escaped her. She looked up at the owner of the offending hand.

Peta's eyes were wide. "What's wrong?"

Daff managed to brush off Peta's inquiry until after the guide had thanked everyone for coming. The fire was put out and Daff turned, following the group as they slowly headed back up the beach towards the car park.

"I'm not ready to head home yet." Peta stopped and pointed down the beach in the opposite direction. "Come on, let's walk a bit. Then we'll go."

Daff hesitated, but when she failed to come up with a plausible objection, she reluctantly agreed. They walked along to the sound of the incoming waves and the squelch of their winter boots in the soft sand. Eventually, Daff stopped and slipped off her shoes and socks, more willing to put up with the cold sand than the awkwardness of walking in boots. They talked about small things: work, plans for the weekend. When the beach abruptly ended at the side of a small grassy rise, the pair had to choose between continuing up along a walkway and onto the footpath or turning and heading back. Daff was retracing her steps when Peta finally got to the point of their moonlit walk.

"So, what happened during the meditation? You seemed pretty upset."

Daff shrugged, but the gesture was lost in the dark. "Nothing happened. In the end, I wasn't even listening to the guide—just to the sound of the fire and the waves."

"Why were you crying then?"

Daff didn't want to describe the strange dream; it felt both too private *and* insignificant. There wasn't a lot to say anyway. She'd seen a shadow and thought of her mother. Grief was a string of endless mental tricks: memories summoned without reason, seeing your loved one's face imprinted on a stranger in a crowd or catching an imagined whiff of their perfume. Peta would make the dream significant. She'd turn it into a powerful insight, a mystical breakthrough, a shard of spiritual guidance or a moment of genuine mediumship. It wasn't that; it was a dream. Daff was tired. She'd had a busy day at work and for a few moments, her mind had been allowed to wander and relax. It was a dream.

"I wasn't crying. My eyes were watering because I'm getting a cold."

Peta draped an arm over her friend's shoulder. "My God, the lengths of your denial. It's been almost two years since the accident, Daff. You must know why I brought you here?"

The memory of a darkened highway, the car's headlights arcing across a line of trees and the crack as its bonnet hit home kicked the air out of Daff's lungs.

"It's been eighteen months and I'm fine." Daff shook off Peta's embrace. *Why did she have to bring up the accident?* "I've dealt with it."

"How? You've never talked about it, not to anyone. Not even me. I'm not even really sure what happened that night. And then you just upped and left the city, you don't know anyone here on the coast, you still won't talk to your dad, and I worry about you. You've completely isolated yourself, Daff. You gotta talk to someone or this stuff is going to rot away inside of you."

Leaving Brisbane had never been her idea; it had been Lawrence's. They'd spoke once since the accident. Lawrence had showed up at her apartment with a cash-filled envelope and told her she needed to leave the city; it was time to start somewhere new. Daff knew that was bullshit—he was just sick of the guilt. But he'd been different that day. The look in his eye was desperate, pleading.

Of course, she hadn't told any of this to Peta. She strove to keep her voice level. "I really don't see the point in talking about it. The accident happened and he's gone. I just want to forget about it. So drop it. It's none of your damn business anyway."

Peta stiffened, stunned into silence, and Daff instantly regretted her words. "Look, I'm sorry. I'm tired." She dragged a hand across her brow, hoping the action would wipe away the image of the shadow's outstretched hand. "It's time I headed home."

The pair continued back along the beach in silence. Daff was staring out at the dark waves, sucking in the sting of the salted air when her bare foot came down on something cold, flat and hard. *Broken glass*, she thought instinctively, and she brushed a hand across the sole of her foot, waiting for the sting of an open wound, but there was nothing. She knelt down and gingerly swept at the sand until her hand skimmed a smooth small circle of glass. Daff excavated the object from its shallow grave and draped it across the palm of her hand.

Peta stopped, noticing her friend's sudden alarm. "Shit! It's not a needle, is it?"

"No, no, it's a watch." Daff's eyes strained under the moonlight. A large round face attached to red silicon bands: a man's adventure watch. Her hand convulsed and the watch fell back onto the beach with a soft thud. It looked just like *his*, she thought—but that was impossible. Embarrassed, she picked up the timepiece and slipped it into the pocket of her jacket.

"Taking it, are you?"

Daff nodded. "I'll put a post up on the community Facebook page, see if anyone claims it." The lie came out so quickly Daff almost believed it herself.

Peta held out her hand. "Give it here for a sec."

Daff felt herself become rigid, like a child stubbornly refusing to share a new toy. Her cheeks flushed with the irrational reaction, and she slowly pulled the watch from her pocket and placed it in her friend's waiting hand.

Peta clasped the watch and stood silently for a moment as though she were in prayer. "Okay, all done." She handed the watch back to its new owner.

"What the hell was that?"

"You should never take a foreign object into your home without cleansing it first. That's just asking for bad juju."

Daff ordinarily ignored such baiting, but if it distracted Peta from her original line of questioning, she was willing to be hooked.

"What do you mean *cleanse*?"

"Everything contains energy; even you, *Miss Science,* can't deny that. Our personal objects have energy too—*our* energy. I just removed any energy that may have been left by the watch's previous owner."

Daff fought the urge to gag. She wasn't about to resurrect this old argument. "Whatever makes you happy."

"You can also do it to people," Peta continued. "You can cleanse away the negative emotions, feelings or energies that have become trapped in somebody, particularly when trauma has been involved."

"Still not talking about it." Daff stepped out onto the car park, relieved to see her powder-blue VW Beetle in sight.

***

Daff cursed herself when the security light failed to turn on. She must have forgotten to flick the switch when she'd left earlier that afternoon; her narrow, partially renovated worker's cottage looked drab in the moonlight. It took three attempts to slide the key home and unlock the door. Daff flicked on the hallway light and walked into the lounge room, dropped her bag on the low coffee table with a thud and sagged into her armchair.

Of course, she could have sat in any chair; they were all hers now. The silence of the house was stark after the symphony of insects, crashing waves, and chattering hippies at Golden Beach. An hour ago she'd longed for home, but now there was nothing to drown out the ringing in her ears. Tinnitus. Another gift courtesy of the accident; a constant reminder of all she'd lost that night.

Peta's words slipped beneath the insistent hum. *You've completely isolated yourself.* As if Daff had chosen these losses.

On days when Daff finished her work early, if a service was on, she'd slip into the chapel and take a discreet seat at the back. There was such relief when the service broke up and the family stood, clinging to one another to keep themselves together.

A week after her mother's terminal diagnosis, Lawrence had come home from work, pulled up a chair at the kitchen table—the table Daff had eaten breakfast at her entire childhood—and told Ruth he'd been having an affair with an officer from Gaming and Vice. They'd separated immediately, though Ruth had insisted he come over for weekly visits and the pair had maintained a strange, conflicted friendship until her death. When Ruth's funeral had ended, Daff had walked past Lawrence as if he was stranger. Which he was, really. She had cut him out of her life and didn't even notice the absence. You can't miss someone who was never there.

Daff wriggled restlessly in the chair, hoping the action would break her spiralling thoughts. She felt a weight shift inside her jacket. Remembering her discovery on the beach, she pulled the watch out of her pocket, wiped the black face with her thumb and brushed away the remains of gritty sand. It was still ticking. She closed her eyes, focussing on the sound, hoping it would override the buzzing in her ears.

"What an exciting life you lead."

Daff leapt from the chair, banged her knee on the coffee table, and half fell, crouching on the floor. A man, an intruder, loomed above her at the opposite end of the table. She instinctively slipped the watch back into her pocket as a chill rolled through her body.

"Who the hell are you?" She'd expected to sound tough, but the words fell out in a whisper. She stood too quickly, her head spinning as she extended to her full height. Though she was tall for a woman, it made little difference; the intruder was over six foot, lean and broad. If he attacked her, Daff thought, she may not be able to stop him. He was dressed in blue jeans and a plain black t-shirt. Outside, it was easily below ten degrees; why was he wearing short sleeves and no jacket?

She fought to keep her face strong and fierce as her fight or flight responses kicked in. Her heart was in her throat, in her ears. It would do no good to become hysterical, but panic had its advantages. Every sensation was heightened: the creaks of the house, the trace of her own floral perfume, the sweater's prickly material against the gooseflesh of her arms.

She needed help. She should call for help.

Jim and Mary are away. Daff cursed the ill-luck. The Andersons, her only neighbours, had ducked up to Rainbow Beach for the night. Yesterday, Jim had popped his head over the fence and ask her if she would feed their dog, Molly, while they were away.

Daff glanced at her handbag that sat on the table between them. She cautiously leaned towards it, hands shaking, hoping to reach her phone before the man attacked her. "If you don't leave *immediately,* I'm going to call the cops."

He stood there with his eyes wide and mouth loose, his expression crumbling with relief. "You can see me?"

Daff tried to slow her breathing as her heart beat a double tap. This man was either high or suffering from a mental disorder. His dark brown eyes made it hard to distinguish pupil from iris, yet Daff sensed that he was clean. She liked the second option less; crazy people were harder to predict, harder to manipulate. At least, that's what Lawrence had told her. She swiftly snatched her bag and stepped aside, putting the couch between herself and the intruder. With her eyes locked on him, she fumbled through the contents of her bag.

"Finally! Someone can see me!" He barked a dry laugh. "You don't understand I've been—"

"Don't take another step," Daff held up the phone as if it was a weapon. "I'll call the police if you don't leave."

Daff didn't wait for a reply. She tried to dial 000, instantly regretting the security screen lock.

The man walked *right through* the couch and stopped in front of Daff. "I don't think that's such a good idea."

Daff took a step back, and the phone slipped from her grasp and clattered onto the floor. No scream escaped her throat, yet her mind unravelled as it sought some explanation for how this man just broken the laws of physics. *I'm seeing things. It's not possible.*

"I'm not going to hurt you; I actually can't hurt you." He held up both hands as if he was stopping traffic. "There's nothing to worry about."

"Sorry, but that's not very comforting." Daff lurched for the phone, but the intruder stepped forward, blocking her path. Turning, she sprinted for the kitchen and yanked open the cutlery drawer. She drew out a heavy carving knife and braced the arm that held it against her chest. *You're less likely to be disarmed if you keep your weapon close,* Lawrence had said, years ago, while eating breakfast and recounting the break and enter he'd attended the night before.

The intruder stepped into the kitchen, his hands still raised, and Daff stepped back to keep her distance. "Get out of my house!"

"I can't," he said. "I need your help."

"You need money? Fine. Take my wallet."

"That's not what I need, I don't have much use for money these days."

None of what he said made sense, Daff thought, but he sounded lucid and he seemed to be in control of his movements. She assessed him again: tall, slim, but not skeletal. His skin was fair, but vitamin D deficiencies resulted in low-levels of serotonin, not madness. His floppy dark hair fell across a slightly crooked nose. Someone had broken it. He was a fighter. Daff knew how much strength was required to plunge a knife into a human body—that she could do—but overpowering him was another matter. Her best chance of survival was a surprise attack. "How many times do I have to ask you to leave my house?"

"I'm sorry, but I can't."

"Why?"

"You have my watch."

How does he know about the watch? Daff shuffled back, banging into the refrigerator. The intruder stepped forward.

"Don't come any closer." Daff pulled the watch out of her pocket with her free hand. "Take it!"

She threw the timepiece at his chest. He didn't even try to catch it. It should have slammed into his breastbone and fallen onto the floor, but it didn't. The watch was a thread passing through the eye of a needle. It sailed through him as though he were no more solid than morning fog. The watch clattered onto the floor behind him.

"What are you?" Daff asked. "Get out of my house, I'm warning you."

The man's face turned to steel and he crossed the kitchen in three quick strides. "Or what? You'll kill me?"

This was it, the moment she'd been waiting for. Daff lunged, throwing the full weight of her body forward as she plunged the knife into his belly. She knew exactly what it would feel like, or what it *should* have felt like. It took strength and conviction to slice through layers of skin, muscle and organs. She waited for the impact, but it never came. Instead, she slammed her shoulder into the lino of the kitchen floor, her head connecting with the corner cardboard. The knife flew from her open hand. Screaming, she clutched her forehead as she looked up at her assailant.

"You can't kill me," he loomed over her. "I'm already dead."

CHAPTER 4

Detective Lawrence

Thursday June 30, 2016

Lawrence stared at the desk calendar that should have been replaced three years ago. The A3 pad now doubled as a coaster and notebook and was dotted with circular coffee stains and random conference call scribbles. Though the motel had emailed him a copy of the register, Lawrence had rewritten the guests' names onto the useless calendar; he enjoyed the physical act of striking off each name as he spoke to them. It was no great shock to find that room eight was paid for in cash and booked under the name Jane Smith.

When he asked the receptionist, a teenage girl, to print out a copy of the register, she'd looked nervous. At first, Lawrence thought this was a natural reaction considering that the coroners van was parked in front of the reception's sliding glass door; still, he hadn't expected her to deny his request, claiming their guests' right to privacy. When he explained who he was, she'd shrugged and said she'd have to clear it with management, her mother, first.

Folks have always been hesitant to talk to cops, but it had worsened in the past ten years. He put it down to the news and social media. Coppers captured on video saying the wrong thing, losing their temper, pulling people over for violations they hadn't committed. He'd read a study a few weeks back that ranked Australia as the thirteenth-least corrupt country in the world. And it was harder to pull off dirty deals these days, which was a good thing, but this suspicion, this hatred, this belief that coppers were willing to manipulate the law for their own gain—that they were power hungry, cruel, above the law—lingered.

Police had always been *other*, separated from the public so as to maintain their authority. When he'd started in the seventies, the job had banded them together. They ate together, drank together, slept with each other. Lately though, Lawrence had noticed that the "boys" club—*mateship*—no longer existed; younger cops kept to themselves. Lawrence worried what the station would look like in another decade—how much more distance would grow between officers and the people, and between the officers themselves.

Lawrence had spoken to ten people that morning, eight over the phone and two in person: a couple who had slept in and hadn't checked out of the Sun yet. So far, no one could recall hearing or seeing anything unusual. McPhee walked passed Lawrence's cubicle, placed another cup of coffee onto the detective's desk. Lawrence took it with a mixture of gratitude and guilt; it was his fourth that morning.

"You think that's good, wait until you see this." McPhee waved a manila envelope in front of Lawrence.

"What's that, your resignation?"

"You wish, *Hitch*." McPhee cocked an eyebrow. Lawrence replied with a cold stare. McPhee cleared his throat and continued. "Crime scene examiners found the girls' wallets in the dumpster out the back of the motel. Both had drivers' licences so I was able to pull up some of their details."

He dropped the envelope on top of the makeshift list. Lawrence exhaled, not realising he'd been holding his breath, and flipped open the envelope's flimsy cover. Before Lawrence had a chance to read the victims' names, McPhee impatiently pointed at the words listed under occupation. "They aren't pros!"

Lawrence nodded; though neither had explicitly voiced this possibility at the crime scene, he knew they'd both been thinking it. It was an easy assumption to make considering the older woman's state of undress and the motel's reputation.

Lawrence spread the files across the desk, read the victim's respectably short histories and checked each headshot against his memory from that morning. The blonde who'd been propped in the chair was Sarah Miller and the brunette, whom he'd momentarily mistaken for his daughter, was Beth Dawson. Looking at the photographs, Lawrence thought both women were on the edge of blandness: wallflower types. Their hair colour was natural, clothes ordinary, and they wore little to no make-up. They looked normal, nondescript, but most victims usually did; too many cases featured ordinary folks meeting violent ends. He'd take a gang-related crime any day; at least those blighters had known and accepted the risks of their lifestyles.

No copper likes to think they've become jaded or lost their sense of empathy, Lawrence thought—*but you do.* At least a little. You get used to seeing dismembered bodies, walking through morgues, delivering death notices and having folks lie to your face. You come to expect the worse and you start to think of that as normal. These cases though, they still got to Lawrence. They reminded him that no matter how invisible you are, no one is ever really safe.

He tapped the screen of his smartphone and thought of Daff. Ruth's warning was still fresh in his mind: *the longer you wait the harder it will be.* Growing up with a cop for a father hadn't been easy for Daff. He'd been strict with her, sure, but she didn't know what he knew. She hadn't seen the things he'd seen, and that's how it should be.

Threats were nothing new to cops, but after Tom died, Lawrence knew it was time for Daff to leave the city. The lad's death was ruled an accident, but Lawrence suspected otherwise, even if he couldn't prove it. The truth was she was lucky to have him for a father and he didn't need to apologise for anything. Lawrence flipped his phone over, slapping the case file on top. "So, if they aren't sex workers, who are they?"

McPhee pointed at the smiling blonde, "Sarah Miller, forty-five. She's a midwife up at the Mater. No kids, no criminal record, not even a speeding ticket." His finger moved to the brunette, decked out in cap and gown. A graduation photo. "This one is Beth Dawson, nineteen. She was a business student at one of the universities. Single. No kids."

Lawrence rubbed his cheek, his once-taut jaw was now slack. Aging: it happened gradually then all at once, but he didn't *feel* any older. Though, he had to admit that caffeine, routine and bills seemed stronger motivations these days than civic duty, so maybe he *had* changed. Maybe it really was time to retire. Lawrence glanced at the photographs again and picked up the image of Beth Dawson, thinking that aging was a privilege that neither victim would get to experience.

"Different in age, career and lifestyle. What's the connection?"

Though Lawrence had directed his question to the open folder, McPhee was the one who answered. "Actually, they've got more in common than you think."

Lawrence looked up at the constable, who was waiting for his cue. When he didn't get one, McPhee carried on.

"Sarah Miller recently married Henry Ernest, the Road Dogs' president. I wouldn't have pegged her for a bikie chick, but I guess people can surprise you."

That they can. It wasn't uncommon for professional women to become romantically involved with active criminals. Perhaps they had become bored by the predictable trajectory of their careers, the familiarity of their suburbs, and developed the quiet restlessness of those who can afford the luxury to live without struggle. Then again, maybe the outlaws picked them. A pretty white-collar wife complemented their false personas as ordinary citizens. Both assumptions could be right.

He was about to relay this valuable insight to his constable when McPhee produced a second manila folder and dropped it on the desk. Lawrence didn't need an invitation; he knew Henry's history, he'd typed half the reports in that file, but he opened it anyway.

The file's thick contents opened with a mug shot of a medium-sized man with a long white beard, bulldog eyes and sinewy arms covered in bled-out tats: a textbook image of a bikie. Henry had been the sergeant-in-arms for the Jackals until he'd had a punch-up with the club president, Jim Cole. Though the reason behind the feud was unclear, Lawrence assumed there'd been a disagreement over some internal running of the club. Maybe Jim had wanted to increase distribution or import different illegal substances; who knew?

What Lawrence *did* know was that the Jackals had splintered: Henry had taken half the crew with him and started his own club, Road Dogs. With Henry's former connections, the club had started dealing from day dot. Though the gang was small, they'd been steadily building a solid reputation in the Valley, with most of the members having a history of assault and petty theft. Unfortunately, the Jackals survived the split and the two clubs were edging towards a turf war, both looking to monopolise the Valley's nightlife.

The Road Dogs' club patch, a circle slashed by a diagonal line, had become a regular sight around the Valley until the VLAD laws banned the wearing of club vests. Lawrence had tried to snuff them out then. Established international clubs were enough to deal with, he didn't need local idiots complicating things. Between glamorised TV versions of *The Life,* true crime novels and media coverage of the VLAD laws, Lawrence thought it was lucky there weren't more of them.

"I saw your name on a couple of the reports. Looks like you tried to set something up just as I was starting here. What happened?" The fold-out chair squeaked as McPhee took a seat.

Lawrence closed the file and leaned back in his own chair, facing the constable. "I got called out to a B and E one night, some young lad trying to sneak out an office window with the owner's laptop pegged under his arm. Only the windows had been painted shut twenty years before during a dodgy reno, and the owner caught him trying to shoulder open the glass pane."

The boy was eighteen. His pupils dilated. When Lawrence asked him what he'd taken and who'd sold it to him, the boy answered in a nervous jumble. "If I tell ya who and what, you're not gonna call my mum, eh?" Before Lawrence even had a chance to start a negotiation, the kid cut in. "It was coke, officer. Road Dogs sold it to me."

"We got the kid to set up another meeting," Lawrence continued, "waited an hour and half, but no one ever showed up."

Maybe something had happened and the dealer couldn't make it, maybe someone had tipped the club off, or maybe one of the members had seen Lawrence waiting in his unmarked vehicle and decided to bail. The next day, Henry paid Lawrence a surprise visit at his unit. The fact that the old bikie had found the copper's address was concerning enough—Lawrence barely slept a wink the following week—but it was the pres's message that turned the detective's stomach into liquid. After that, Lawrence decided to redirect his attention back to homicide. Let the Road Dogs be someone else's problem for a while.

"How's Beth connected to the club?" Lawrence took another swig of his coffee.

"Don't know. I'm guessing she was trying to get on with one of the boys. I haven't delivered the death message yet; do you want to do it?"

Lawrence nodded and stood up, shrugging on his jacket. "Yeah I'll do it. I want to talk to Henry first though, before he has enough time to come up with a decent alibi."

"How long until the pathologist's report comes back?"

Lawrence shrugged. "Could be six or eight days, maybe longer, maybe sooner." Usually it would be the former, but he'd put in a request for the Sundowner bodies to be a top priority. The last thing he wanted was to be sitting in the corner at his retirement party, discussing the ins and outs of this unresolved case. The request would probably go ignored though. Not enough resources, not enough staff, not enough fucks left to give.

Without asking, McPhee followed his superior as he made to leave the office. "You reckon Henry did it?"

"Don't know for sure. He doesn't have a history of assault." *At least not on paper.* "But until we have a motive it's hard to say."

"It's not enough that the club symbol is drawn on the mirror?" McPhee slipped through the station's glass door and pulled his own jacket tight as he stepped out onto Brunswick Street.

"Nope, it's circumstantial. The symbol proves nothing. If both victims are already linked to the club, why risk leaving trace evidence by drawing that symbol?"

"You reckon someone outside of the club killed them—like the Jackals? Maybe drew the symbol as a way to frame the Road Dogs?"

"Maybe, but it would've been more convincing if they hadn't have drawn it."

"I thought Road Dogs had a feud with the Jackals?"

"They do." Lawrence pulled the keys out of his pocket and unlocked the car. "Both clubs have been dealing in the Valley and they've knocked heads a couple of times."

The station had received a call just last weekend to come and break up a brawl on Constance Street. A Jackals member had been carted off on a gurney after taking a Road Dogs' baseball bat to the face.

"It's pretty bold to go after a pres's old lady though. Jackals may want to push the Road Dogs out of the Valley, but murdering a couple of the club's women is a stupid way to go about it."

McPhee got into the passenger seat as Lawrence pulled out onto the street. "What do you mean?"

"Henry Ernst isn't gonna give up his turf because his wife died. If anything he's gonna want revenge. He's gonna want to wipe the Jackals out."

"You reckon Henry killed his own lady so he had an excuse—a reason to start a turf war?"

Lawrence shrugged. "Clubs aren't supposed to target the family members of rival clubs, though it does happen. It *may* have been the Jackals. We'll have to talk to their president too."

"Right. And where is their clubhouse?"

Lawrence felt his cheeks reddened and he hesitated. "I'm not sure. Can you google it?"

CHAPTER 5

Daff

Thursday June 30, 2016

Daff grasped the edge of the kitchen bench. Her head was a spinning top, her vision doubled; an unfortunate time for a concussion. She gingerly pulled herself up, extending her arms and legs, worried that she may have sustained a fracture. She was relieved to find there were none.

"How did you do that?" She looked up at the man who was now blocking the exit to her back door. "You didn't duck or turn. You didn't even flinch …" *as I plunged a knife into your stomach.*

"You don't look so good, maybe you should sit down."

Daff rested her full weight against the kitchen counter. She wanted to sit down, but not while this stranger was in her home.

"I'm telling you for the last time, get out of my house!"

"You don't get it: I can't hurt you, okay?" He crossed his arms, rooting himself to the spot. "And I'm not leaving, because I need your help."

"I'm not going to help you—you're insane! Get out!"

"I can't!"

A cold shiver ran down Daff's back. Whispers of Lawrence's hard-earned advice echoed in her ears, *Even if your life is under threat, you need to stay calm. You can be compliant to a point, but don't let them take you to a second location. If that happens you're screwed. Talk to them, try to get them to see you as a person, try and make a connection. If you see an opportunity, take it.* That advice worked for hostage situations, rapists, serial killers. She hadn't been hurt or threatened yet, but it didn't change the fact that he was an uninvited stranger.

"What's your name?"

The man's face went blank. *Good*, Daff thought, *that question took him by surprise.*

"I can't remember." He released his arms. "That's why I need your help."

Daff took a step back, edging closer towards her phone. "Okay, that's good, that's great." Her voice came out shrill even though she was aiming for calm. "I can call someone to come get you, I'm sure there must be someone who is looking for you, worried about you."

"You still don't get it." The man looked suddenly exhausted. "No one can help me except for you. You're the first person to see me in three days."

"What are you talking about?" Daff hoped the conversation would distract him as she reached down to clutch her phone.

"I *think* I might be dead."

Daff shot up, her head spinning with the unexpected movement. She clutched her forehead. She didn't want to hear it. Not the first time that he'd said it, and not now. But she had to know. "What did you say?"

"I'm dead. At least, I think so."

I must be hearing things, Daff thought, *maybe seeing them too.* It was the only explanation. She rubbed a clammy hand across her brow and tried to remember if it had been sage that the hippie woman had waved around at the beach. The watch had gone through him; *she* had too. He must be some kind of hallucination. It was the only explanation. Pain laced through her left shoulder and she wondered why the fall hadn't broken the vision. Maybe it hadn't been sage, but something stronger?

"You're not dead. You're standing in my kitchen. I can see you, I can hear you. You're very much alive."

Without warning the man's eyes became slits. Daff resisted the urge to flinch as he marched towards her, swiftly raising his hand and bringing it down in a wide arc. Daff raised her own to block the blow, but the intended slap flowed through her like a running creek over stone. Her muscles quivered as reality failed to meet her expectation, as if she'd lifted a brick that weighed as much as a feather.

"What are you?" Daff flittered through the possible explanations. "I'm hallucinating. You're not real." She turned, having decided she was no longer under threat, and switched on her phone.

"I am not a hallucination. I don't know what happened to me, but I do need your help."

Daff hit the phone's small green app, her hands shaking as she tapped the first name on her list of recent contacts. Peta lived in the city, on Sandgate Road; Daff tried to calculate how far along the motorway her friend could have travelled in the twenty minutes since they parted. Her heartbeat was high, but Daff couldn't tell if she was experiencing delayed shock or if her nervous system was simply reacting to the hallucination. *He is a hallucination*, she repeated to herself. *Nothing more.* At least she knew he couldn't hurt her. Daff pressed the phone to her ear, the ringing tone drowning out the hallucination's yammering.

Peta answered within a few rings. "Miss me already?"

"Peta, something's happened. I need a ride to the hospital."

Daff said she'd explain everything once Peta arrived. She'd given her friend a spare key when she moved in six months ago, so Peta could let herself in. She arrived thirty minutes later. Daff was stretched out on the couch, a cushion firmly pressed against her ear.

"What are you doing?" Peta said.

"So, this is the sheila that's gonna drag you to the asylum," the hallucination said. "She's pretty short, I reckon you can take her; you seem to know your stuff. Did you used to do Karate? That block looked classic *Karate Kid.* So, are you going to introduce us or are you sticking with this whole 'hallucination' bit?"

"He won't stop talking," Daff sat up, peeled the pillow from her face and replaced it with kneading hands.

"Who won't stop talking?" Peta flicked her eyes around the room.

"You can't see him, can you?"

"Just you and me, good looking." Peta winked flirtatiously before pressing the back of her hand to Daff's forehead. "You don't have a temperature. Is it a migraine?"

Daff pulled away, made to get up, but then thought better of it. "I think I am having some kind of hallucination."

"This is a waste of time, I'm not a hallucination."

"What are you seeing?" Peta had adopted her nursey tone. Daff had rarely seen this side of her friend, the professional, serious, logical side. It was only last week that the pair had argued over the effectiveness of chemotherapy. Daff had defended medical treatment; Peta, ironically, believed the whole thing was a hoax. That's why she had become a nurse, she said, so she could create change from inside the system. This is how it had always been between them, the realist vs the surrealist.

"I thought he was a weirdo, that he'd followed me into the house. That he wanted money or … I couldn't tell if he was high or mentally unstable."

Peta stood up, whipping out her phone.

"What are you doing?"

"I'm calling the police."

Daff held up her hand. "No, stop." It was bad enough explaining this to her best friend; she didn't need any cops here. "Peta, no one is here."

Peta hesitated before snapping the phone shut and returning it to the back pocket of her jeans. Resuming her seat beside Daff, she asked her friend to start from the beginning.

Daff explained the strange man's sudden appearance and his insistence that she help him. "He said that I had his watch." Daff pointed to the object in question. The watch lay abandoned on the floor where it had landed.

Peta stood up, rounded the couch and picked up the timepiece. Now in the brightly lit kitchen, she could see it clearly. Her eyes widened.

Daff's throat tightened. Peta had been with her the day she had picked out and purchased Tom's watch. "You don't have to say it, I know. I recognised it too." She held out her hand as Peta dropped the watch into it.

"Is it his?"

Daff turned the watch over in her hands. She'd chosen an inscription for Tom's watch, but never taken it to the jeweller. The back of this watch was plain too. She rolled it over and examined the heavily scratched glass face; Tom's, barely a week old at the time of his death, had been in perfect condition. Of course, eighteen months had passed since then.

"No, it can't be," she confirmed. "He was wearing it on the night of the accident; he was probably buried with it." Even as she said it, a shadow of doubt crept over her. "That's why I need to go to the hospital." *Because I'm unravelling.* Daff braced herself for one of Peta's lectures: *I told you that you needed to talk about it. I told you that you were repressing your grief/ trauma/ anger. Now look at you. You're a mess.*

"You don't need to go anywhere. What you need is a big glass of water and some sleep."

Daff shook her head; hydration and rest weren't going to fix this. She tried to explain again, this time slower and with more detail. She told her friend that the man didn't know his own name, that the watch had gone right through him. That she had gone right through him too.

"Then he said, *you can't kill me, I'm already dead.*" Daff looked past Peta towards the man in question. He stood beside the bookcase, his arms folded protectively over his chest.

Peta glanced over her shoulder, following her friend's gaze. "Can you still see him?"

Daff nodded, pinching the bridge of her nose; the headache was worsening. "Yes. Look, this isn't right. That's why I called you, I don't think I should be driving."

"Maybe you're not hallucinating," Peta turned, her wide eyes soft, and hesitated. "Did you see that fella with the dreadlocks at *Circle* tonight?"

The image of a tanned guy wearing a pair of ridiculous purple pants surfaced in Daff's memory; he'd looked annoyingly serene sitting cross-legged on the opposite side of the bonfire. She shrugged. "Yeah?"

"That's Taylor. He offered to take me for a drive once, and even though I think dreadlocks look better on chicks, I went. He owned a light green vintage EH Holden; it had the white top and everything! I'd never been in a car with bench seats before. Every time he took a corner, I'd slide right across it. We took *a lot* of corners." Peta's voice drifted off as she recounted the joyride. Daff could imagine the carefree way her friend would've accepted the ride, like getting in cars with strangers was no big deal.

"Anyway, Taylor's a barista at a café in Mooloolaba, so I knew there was no way he could have bought a car like that. So, I asked him and—"

"Land the plane, Peta."

"I *am*." The crease between her brows deepened. "Taylor said he inherited the car when his grandfather passed away. Apparently, they were really close. How sweet is that? Anyway, Taylor reckons that as soon as he got that car, all this weird stuff started happening in his house: footsteps down the hall, the light blinking in the bathroom. Said it gave him the heebie-jeebies. So, one night, Taylor gets this urge to drive by his grandpa's old house and as he hooks the corner into their street, for a split second, Taylor swears he saw the old guy sitting shotgun."

"So … you're saying that if I need to go to the hospital, I should call Taylor?"

"No, Daff, what I'm saying is maybe what you're seeing is a spirit. The spirit of the person who belonged to this watch."

The hallucination straightened, suddenly alert. "I like her," indicating Peta. "You should listen to your friend."

She shouldn't have mentioned the man; of course Peta would come to a woo-woo conclusion; never could she find the answer in the logical, the realistic, the scientific. When they were teenagers, Peta used to slip crystals into her bra, hang dream catchers over her bed, mess around with Ouija boards and fill her diary with channelled messages from her spirit guides. Unfortunately, most of these practices had rolled over into adulthood. The bookshelf in her current apartment was filled with metaphysical and esoteric books as well as the medical tomes she'd used during her nursing degree. Daff still didn't understand how Peta had graduated; maybe she'd channelled all the answers from her spirit guides.

The only way to win this argument was to use Peta's logic against her. Daff struggled to keep her voice even. "Well, now, that's impossible. After all, you cleansed the watch before I brought it home. Remember?"

"It doesn't always work like that, this stuff isn't finite," Peta shrugged. "Maybe his connection to the watch is too strong."

"Oh Jesus, Peta," Daff pushed her friend's hand away. "You must be kidding me with this crap. You can't just twist the rules around to suit your own agenda. You think he's a ghost: fine, but can't we argue about this in the car?"

"I'm not taking you to the bloody hospital." Peta's face hardened. "You could have called a taxi if that's what you wanted, but you didn't. You called me. And I think you know why, because this *man* isn't a hallucination, he's a ghost."

The man dug his hands into his pocket, his eyes narrowing. A moment ago, he was relieved to have Peta onside; now he looked uncertain, guarded.

Oh, don't be ridiculous. He's just a projection of my own emotional state. Daff buried her face in her hands. "I didn't call you over here for a séance. Be reasonable. Please. This is my health we're talking about."

"Exactly. Why do you think I took you to *Circle* tonight? You've been suppressing what happened to Tom, to you. You're lucky the trauma has manifested in the way that it has."

Daff swallowed her bitter reply: *yes. I'm very lucky.*

Standing up abruptly, she ignored the web of pain that shot across her eyes. "There's no such thing as ghosts." She snatched the car keys off the coffee table. "And if you won't help me, I'll do it myself."

Daff had taken three steps before Peta stopped her, swiftly removing the keys from her friend's grasp. "No. Nurses gossip, and your reputation is having a hard enough time as it is. Give it the night. If it doesn't right itself by morning, then I've got another idea."

There wasn't much of a reputation to ruin, but the idea of describing these symptoms to a group of strangers made Daff break into a cold sweat. "Fine."

"No late-night outings either, at least not without me." Peta slipped the car keys into her pocket. "I'll crash on the couch tonight, just in case you want to talk."

Daff shot her a dark look. Wordlessly, she turned and headed down the corridor towards her room. Peta knew where the spare blankets and pillows were; if she wanted to spend the night, she could help herself.

"Ghosts are real." Her friend called from the lounge room. "Though, I've got to admit, I'm pretty surprised *you* can see them."

"One." Daff whispered to herself. *And the fact that you can't see him*, she thought, *only further proves my point: things are not okay.*

***

Daff knew how dreams worked. It takes ninety minutes to move through the first four stages of sleep; once you reach the REM phase, your subconscious mind begins processing the day's events by melding them with imaginative storylines. Daff hadn't visited a labyrinth that day, so she wasn't sure why she was dreaming about one. She also didn't know why she was running; she hated running. Her feet pounded the wet earth, flicking the thick soil up and back onto her calves, spotting her skin like rain. Her arms stretched out before her, the hands needy and grasping. The knotted walls of the maze grew higher.

Somehow she knew, the way that you do in dreams, that her only hope of escape was to find him. Tom stood sentry at every corner, entryway and intersection, disappearing into the greenery whenever he was within reach. Panic stripped her mouth dry, so that when she called out his name her voice shook the air like a death rattle. She kept going. Calling and running, around and around, in an endless loop until, at last, he stepped out from the dense hedge and clasped her wrist. She winced against the blinding white light and felt herself falling. Dropping, she braced for impact; her drumming heart was a distant beat as though the vital organ had been drawn from her chest and suspended mid-air. Click, crack, boom.

The labyrinth melted away and Daff took in her new surroundings. At least *this* memory made sense. Peta was driving; her golden hair was shorter back then, brushing her shoulders, kissing the black fabric of her plain dress. Daff didn't know Peta even owned a black dress. She plucked at her own outfit, a smock: loose, drab, ugly. The cheap material made her skin itch.

"Doing okay there?" Peta flicked on her indicator, turning in to the funeral home. The car park nearly full. When Daff made no reply, Peta did. "Sorry, stupid question."

Daff shuffled in her seat and readjusted her already smooth collar. "I haven't seen them, since … you know … before."

"You can't hold that against them. The shock of *everything*—I can't even imagine what they must be going through." Peta stopped abruptly and risked a glance towards her shaken friend. "Then again, I guess I didn't have to look too far for inspiration."

Daff shook her head. The thoughts that had consumed her during those endless days in the hospital returned with a lashing speed that sliced the tender memory of that night clean open. Besides Lawrence, Peta had been her only visitor. She'd arrived with yellow carnations and a steely determination to *do something*. Even though there was nothing to be done.

Three days later, Daff was released. The Pease family—Tom's family—had never come, and she couldn't bring herself to go to them. She imagined herself knocking on their front door. She could hear the rap of her knuckles on the wood and feel the soft wool of Mrs Pease's cardigan as they embraced. Then the vision slipped. Mrs Pease vanished and the front door closed and Daff knew that her presence at this once-happy family home was no longer welcomed, because Tom was dead and she wasn't.

They found a space at the back of the lot and Daff popped her door open. The funeral home's lawn was scattered with people gathered in small circles of three or four. Some guests circulated between the groups like they were networking at a cocktail party. With Peta by her side, Daff crossed the plush lawn. She spotted the boys from the Valley Station immediately, their official uniforms an authoritative contrast to the other guests in black. Some of them she knew, others were only vaguely familiar faces. Lawrence wasn't among them. An officer that Tom went to the academy with, who Daff had cooked dinner for once, saw her, nodded and looked away. She'd been the driver. Now, Tom was dead. A young constable was distributing pamphlets with Tom's photo on the front. An order of service. Daff took the folded sheet without opening it.

Edging closer to the building, Daff saw Todd and Karen Pease. Just last week she'd sat opposite them during Christmas Eve dinner at their home. Karen, who always corrected Daff whenever she addressed her as *Mrs Pease*, had cooked a roast with all the trimming. Twirling through the kitchen in a flurry with the sleeves of that soft cardigan pushed up as she washed lettuce leaves and dirty bowls, unaware that this was the last time she'd reprimand her son, slapping his hand as he reached for a steaming potato before the serving dish was even placed on the table.

There'd been no breeze that night; the guest fanned themselves with their napkins between mouthfuls of cooked food. They'd teased Tom and her with talk of marriage, grand babies and the adorable house for sale, "Just a few blocks over."

Now that son was dead.

"Stay here," Daff freed her arm from Peta's, wanting to offer her condolences alone.

Karen and Todd stood together, their backs to the lawn as they talked with a small group of friends. Reaching out, Daff smoothed Karen's arm. She expected Mrs Pease to turn, embrace her in a sharing of grief. Instead, Karen looked at Daff with flat eyes, her mouth pinched, as if she'd cut open an apple and found its rotten core. Daff's lips quivered, searching for the right words when a strong, gentle voice cut across the crowd. A woman in a grey suit and angular blonde bob emerged from the glass doors.

"Please, come in, take a seat. We'll be starting soon."

Daff and Peta sat at the back of the hall. Too soon the slideshow and eulogy were over and guests were invited to approach and bid their final farewells. Daff's shoulders burned with the glare of an entire room as she approached the casket. The pressure in her chest increasing with each step, she was convinced that her ribs were on the verge of cracking.

She stopped in front of the coffin, confused. It was too small; too narrow, too short. There'd been a mistake: Tom was much too tall and broad—too big to fit into such a small case. Daff felt certain that if she turned around right now, Tom would be standing at the back of the hall, high-fiving his mates and congratulating them on pulling off such an epic prank. Daff didn't turn around. Tom wasn't at the back of the hall or in front of her; he wasn't in the damn room at all.

She pressed her fingers into the cold solid lid until her prints were embedded in its gleam. "Sorry."

She didn't return to her seat beside Peta. Instead, she lingered by the exit, just in case she needed it. She watched as a parade of family and friends wove between the rows of seats, the aisle and front platform. Her heart in her ears blocked out the melancholy tune that played from the speakers: click, crack, boom. Click, crack, boom.

Smoothing her palms over the itchy dress, she decided to wait outside until it was over. Turning to leave, she heard the squeak of a door opening behind her, and a woman stepped out from a side entry. The funeral director. She did well, Daff thought. Her opening delivery had been clear and steady, drawing the crowd together and advising them on how to navigate this river of grief. At last, someone had told them what to do, and it was simple: listen.

Her angular bob and solid grey suit gave her the appearance of an anchor, of dependability—of gravitas. Her official duties done, she scanned the hall quickly and turned back towards the door, paused, and looked up in Daff's direction.

"You must be Daphne." Her smile was gentle as she stretched out her hand.

Daff hoped her own was dry when she shook it. "How did you know that?"

"I helped the family with the slideshow."

Of course, the Peases had included a photograph of Tom and her from Christmas. The two of them were smiling towards the camera while tugging on opposite ends of a bon-bon, unaware that one day this memory would be projected onto a screen, hung high above a coffin.

"I shouldn't be here." Daff had been thinking it all morning, but in the presence of this stranger, she finally said it out loud.

"You absolutely should be," the woman replied. "Thomas would want you here."

Tom, Daff corrected, and she woke suddenly from her dream, her eyes flying open as the memory of Tom's funeral dissipated in the morning light.

Daff worried that she wouldn't sleep. It hadn't occurred to her that dreaming could be worse. She thought the hallucination might keep her awake, determined to prove himself as anything other than a hallucination. It didn't, but when she sat up and wiped her still-damp eyes she flinched at the sight of him in her mother's wicker chair. As a child, Daff would settle into Ruth's lap and together they'd read story after story until the chair ceased to be comfortable. She'd given away most of Ruth's possessions—the memories they summoned were just too painful—but she'd chosen to keep that chair. She imagined those tales woven into the rattan lengths and wondered if the current occupant could hear them.

When she rose, he offered a mumbled pleasantry, which she promptly ignored. Engaging with a hallucination would only make things worse, strengthening the neural pathways, offering a more supportive foothold. Entering her narrow ensuite, Daff briskly washed her face with cool water and dressed comfortably in jeans and a long-sleeve pullover. Sleep had solved nothing; the hallucination was as clear as he had been last night.

She would not be going in to work today. She would make a cup of tea, wait until her preferred medical centre opened and make an emergency appointment with her GP. Despite her better judgement, she'd taken Peta's advice. Now it was time to do what she thought best. Daff opened the bathroom door, ignoring the man who sat in Ruth's beloved chair, and crossed the room towards the hall.

Peta had slept on the couch, and her pillows and sheets were now haphazardly folded and dumped on the coffee table. Daff could hear the kettle whistling in the kitchen. Her chest deflated. She'd hoped to have more time to gather her thoughts; instead she would have to enter the kitchen and announce her plan.

"Good morning." Peta filled the fat white teapot to the brim. "Did you sleep okay?"

Daff lied and said that she did while pulling two cups out of the dish rack; she'd no interest in making idle chit-chat this morning. "He's still here. I'll be making the earliest appointment possible. This can't go on."

The man had followed her into the kitchen. Briefly catching Daff's eye, he shook his head. She noticed that his black shirt was unrumpled and that his floppy hair was still straight despite having spent the night sleeping in the wicker chair. Then she remembered he was a hallucination and of course imaginary fabric wouldn't wrinkle.

"Don't worry, I've already taken care of it. I've made an appointment for nine."

Daff instinctively checked her wrist, though she couldn't recall having put the watch on. It was a little after seven; how had Peta made an appointment? Medical centres weren't open until mid-morning.

Peta eyed the watch, though she said nothing. "I've booked you in with the best. She comes highly recommended." She spun the teapot clockwise twice and counter clockwise once before filling the cups. The subtle scent of bergamot drifted through the air and Daff gingerly accepted the warm drink.

"Thanks, but I think it's best that I see my usual GP. Someone who knows my history."

"Oh, she's not a GP. She's a psychic."

Daff choked on the tea, spluttering. "Excuse me?"

"I found her online page last night and I sent her a private message explaining everything—don't worry I didn't say too much, you know, it can get in the way of accuracy—and she said she could fit you in first thing this morning."

"You booked me it for a psychic reading. That's your great solution?" Daff involuntarily glanced at the man; looking for moral support, before remembering that he was the reason she was in this predicament. "Cancel it. This is ridiculous."

"I'm not cancelling it. What have you got to lose … or are you afraid that she may agree with me, that your man is not a hallucination?" She leaned against the counter looking pleased with herself.

"I'm not a hallucination." The man stopped in the doorway, one foot in the kitchen, one foot in the dining room.

"Fine. I'll see the psychic, but I'm making an appointment too."

Peta nodded as though she'd expected nothing less and smiled into her teacup.

Daff refilled her own and glanced out the kitchen window towards the Andersons' back verandah. Molly, their caramel-coated cocker spaniel, was draped across her dog bed, looking utterly bored. Her food dish and a plastic tub of dog biscuits were resting on top of the barbecue in the corner.

Crap. Daff downed the remains of her tea, dropped the cup in the sink and told Peta she'd be right back. She felt a light tingle pass over her skin as she walked through the man and back into the living room, grabbing her winter jacket off the back of the couch. The Andersons were due back that afternoon; Molly wasn't likely to starve, but Daff still felt a pang of guilt. Unlocking the front door, she drew her jacket tight as she crossed the concrete footpath that connected the verandah steps to the front gate. The morning sun was soft as it brushed the wet grass, turning the dew drops into liquid jewels. Suddenly, the hairs on the back of Daff's neck stood up. Looking over her shoulder, she saw the man following her down the front steps. He hung back, his hands buried in his blue jeans' pockets like she was dragging him on an errand he didn't want to do. *He's not real,* she assured herself as she slipped out her gate.

Molly bounded down the backstairs as soon as she heard Daff unlatch the front gate. Daff slipped into the yard while trying to make sure the dog didn't escape it.

"Good morning." She brushed the dog's thick soft coat as Molly jumped up and dotted Daff's jacket with wet paws. She didn't hear his approach, so she was startled when the man suddenly appeared beside her. Ignoring him, she gave the dog one final pat before heading towards the back stairs that led up to the verandah. Her foot hit the bottom step when she noticed Molly hadn't followed. Stepping back, Daff peered into the front yard. The dog was standing in front of him, her tail wagging madly as she sniffed his outstretched hand.

Daff filled Molly's dish, maybe a little *too* much, and gave her a scratch behind the ear before returning home. Despite the cool of the morning, a light sweat covered her brow. She must have seen a cat, Daff thought as she unlocked her front door. That's what Molly was looking at, why she was wagging her tail. *The dog can't interact with my hallucination.*

She hung her jacket on the hook by the door as she inhaled the sweet and spicy scent of fruit toast; her stomach grumbled. The hiss of the running shower filled the small house, but she was thankful to have a minute alone. Well, almost alone. The man was constantly within eyesight. Entering the kitchen, Daff saw that Peta had left her a slice of toast on the cutting board. She took a swift bite of the crisp bread and carried it back to her bedroom, closing the door behind her.

"You saw that, right? That dog could see me; it sniffed my hand."

Daff turned towards the voice; the man had followed her in and was standing between her and the sealed door. Though she'd silently repeated the same mantra since the moment she'd woken that morning—*you're not real*—he was still there. She pushed open the bedroom curtains and took another bite of her toast as though he hadn't spoken.

"Look, I get that this is all a bit weird and it's a lot to take in, but this hasn't been easy for me either."

She flicked the doona into place and snorted despite herself.

"I know your friend has made an appointment for you, but frankly, I think it's a waste of time. You just need to talk to me. We can figure this out."

Picking up the pillows off the floor, she rearranged them at the head of the bed, fluffing the ones that had flattened during the night.

"Daff, that's your name, right? I need help." He hesitated for a moment. "Please, I can't stay like this."

Daff felt a memory beginning to unfurl: a night's sky spotted with stars. She quickly pushed it away.

Despite her best attempts to pretend he wasn't there, it was difficult to ignore someone talking directly to her. The shower was running; if she spoke to him now, no one would know. Besides, what difference would it really make to entertain this apparition of her own imagination? After all, Peta may be right. The vision could be the result of unexpressed trauma. She'd certainly experience enough of *that* in the past four years between the disintegration of her relationship with Lawrence, Ruth's passing and the accident. These events had sucked the air from her lungs—but a person can live for three minutes without oxygen. And, by some miracle, or force of will, she was still standing.

If Daff could get him talking, maybe she'd be able to uncover the source of her own subconscious wound. She'd deal with it, rid herself of this delirium without the aid of medical treatment and save herself the embarrassment of describing this bizarre symptom. It was the most efficient solution.

"You really can't remember your name?"

The man shook his head: a confirmation that stumped Daff. If her unravelling mind were capable of constructing such a precise hallucination, surely it was capable of throwing in a little backstory?

"What do you remember?"

"Before you picked up the watch, not much." He raked a hand through his hair as if the memories of his past had been displaced there. "I was on the beach for about a day."

"Did anything happen? Do you remember someone dropping the watch?"

He shook his head. "Nothing. It's not like I woke up on the beach, though it was kind of like that. I was just there, suddenly, and I can't remember what came before it. There was no one around until the sun came up. Fit chicks and retired dudes walking their dogs mostly. None of them could see or hear me."

"Why did you stay there?"

"Because I can't leave the watch. Your mate's right, I'm bound to it. The furthest I can get from it is twenty metres or so."

"Oh." The word hung in the air like a lantern, though it lit nothing. Daff turned and looked out the window as the morning breeze carried a handful of dry fig leaves across the lawn, their cycle complete. That's the thing about time: it only moves in one direction. She examined the watch again. It looked strange on her; the large face made her wrist appear small and delicate in comparison. Daff couldn't recall having ever been described in those terms. "What do you want to be called?"

The man huffed and folded back into the wicker chair. "I don't want to be called anything, I want to find out what my *actual* name is."

"What about Frank?" Daff offered while a small voice in the back of her head scolded her for beginning this conversation.

"I don't see how giving me a name is going to improve anything."

Daff shook her head. She wasn't offering christening as a solution, but she couldn't go on referring to him as 'The Man' either. Besides, now that she'd got him talking, she felt like she was onto something; that maybe this manifestation of her imagination would reveal why he was here if only she could keep him talking. The small voice at the back of her head cautioned her against this interaction, but she quickly silenced it.

"Everyone needs a name." Daff straightened so that she could properly survey him, so that she could find the name that would equal his appearance. He was right. *Frank* was the name for a short man with Italian heritage. This man was much too tall and much too pale-skinned for such a name. His face was open and cuffed by loose, straight brown hair, dark brows and eyes. He had the look of a solidly middle-class white man in his early thirties. "What about Mick?"

He looked at her as though she'd kicked a dog. "No."

Surprised that she'd become so involved, Daff shook her head and tried to transfer this task back to him. "Well, it's going to be your name; do you have any suggestions?"

"Stanley?"

She'd known a Stanley once, a constable who spoke in the third person and snorted instead of laughed—a most unfortunate trait for a police officer. Daff bit her lip and suppressed a grin at the memory. She snuffed out this urge to chuckle by quickly listing the most depressing things she could think of: credit card interest, failing economies, global warming, losing one's mind. It worked. "Was Stanley your grandfather's name?"

"I don't remember my grandfather's name. It's the first name I thought of that sorta felt right."

Daff nodded, though she didn't understand how feelings had anything to do with the choosing of a name. "Yes, but it's a bit old-fashioned. What about something a bit younger, like Seth or Bailey?"

Without bothering to reply, the man knelt down beside the pile of books that squatted by the wicker chair. "There must be a decent name in one of these?"

Daff crouched beside him. She had travelled up to Toowoomba for the summer book festival earlier in the year. It was called a festival, but really it was a beefed-up second-hand bookshop. A warehouse lined with trestle tables that were stacked up with foam boxes of neatly packed books. You could 'rent' a shopping trolley and load it up until the wheels buckled. Daff had let her eyes drift across the exposed spines, waiting for a cognitive connection: a title or author she recognised. Like most readers, over the years she'd compiled a mental list of *Novels to Read*, nineteen of which she found that day. Her final purchase, however, was a wild card. A twentieth book. It was the title that caught her eye, just as it did now.

"This one." Daff lifted a handful of volumes from the top of the pile and placed them on the floor. She slid a hand across the title: *A Good Way to Go*. It had sat untouched on the floor of her bedroom since the day she bought it. Daff pulled back the cover, opened it at random and scanned the print.

"Here!" She stabbed the page with her index finger. "Liam. That's a pretty good name."

The Man nodded either in approval or surrender, then shrugged. "I don't see what difference it's going to make, so sure, Liam it is."

Daff, pleased by her small victory, plonked the book on the pile and returned the top tier to its former position.

There was a light tap on the door, and Peta called from the other side. "Come on Daff, we'd better get going. I'll drive."

Even though it was early, the main street of Maleny was packed. Bikers who'd been out for a morning ride, cyclists and backpackers filled the cafés. Apparently, no one worked on the coast. It was always busy here. Daff was glad it wasn't raining though; even in winter the Sunshine Coast Hinterlands had its damp days. Eventually, Peta got through the congested business centre, took a left and pulled up two blocks down.

"There it is," Peta pointed towards a two-storey red-brick unit block on the right. The windows facing the street were filthy with dust, and the metal railings that encased the four small balconies were rusted.

Daff took in the gnarled bushes that filled the forgotten garden bed and the dead lawn. It must have been the only sliver of land in Maleny that wasn't green. "This is supposed to make me feel less crazy?"

"I'm an optimist," Peta grinned. "Did you bring the watch?"

Daff held up her wrist, the watch's glass face catching the light. Liam had come too, not that he had much choice in the matter.

Peta led the way up the central staircase to the second floor and rapped on the door of unit four. If Daff was going to bail, this was her final chance. The muscles in her long legs twitched, ready for flight, yet she remained transfixed to the spot. The corridor was a waiting room filled with an air of anticipation and dread. She tried to think of an excuse, some reason to leave, but the door opened before she could. The owner was a short woman with flaming red hair that framed her face like a nimbus. She wore a floor-length purple gown, and her mouth was bracketed by deep crevices.

"This is the woman with all the answers, is it?" Liam leaned against the door frame like he needed a rest.

"Hello," for a moment Daff thought the woman was addressing *him*, but it was Peta who replied, introducing herself and Daff. The woman stepped back, smiling gently. She told them her name was Lauryl and invited them in.

The unit was styled after its owner with ornate fabrics draped over couches, windows and doorways. It was dim inside. Lit only by Himalayan salt lamps and a sliver of natural light coming through an opening in the heavy curtains. Fat crystals and card decks weighed down a round table in the room's centre. Lauryl motioned towards the table's empty seats but Daff hesitated. She didn't want to sit down at the ridiculous table with the ridiculous woman who would confirm the ridiculous idea that Daff was communicating with ghosts. *Ghost*, Daff corrected herself. *Hallucination*, she corrected further.

Daff loosened her scarf, feeling suddenly hot. Despite the building's external appearance, the décor of Lauryl's apartment suggested that the woman made a decent living. She might be well-known. *What if someone sees me leaving this apartment?* The last thing Daff needed was for people to think she believed in this woo-woo hippie crap. Then she remembered that the only people she knew on the coast were the staff at Dean & Clayton's Funeral Home and she wasn't likely to run into any of *them* here. She watched as Liam busied himself in front of an extended sideboard that was covered in bells, crystals, bowls and other mystical knickknacks. He reached towards a small carving of the Buddha, but his hand went through it like a fish through water. Daff took her seat at the table.

Lauryl's eyes flicked from Daff to Peta. "Is this a couples reading?"

Peta flicked a flirtatious glace at her friend, "She wishes."

Liam barely concealed his laughter.

"Peta's here for moral support," Daff glared at her former lieutenant-turned-traitor. "Though she's leaving a lot to be desired."

Ignoring this dig, Peta continued. "I'm not totally averse to the idea, mind you. Love is love, right?" She waggled her eyebrows.

Daff smoothed her palms down her jeans, right heel tapping. She should have been more forceful last night; she shouldn't have let herself be so easily persuaded. Liam was right, this was a waste of time. "Can we please just get on with this?" *Before Peta marches head-on into an equality debate and how we're all connected and if we could just work together a little bit harder we could achieve peace on earth.*

Lauryl shuffled the cards and mumbled an incantation to the angels, asking for protection and guidance. Daff fought the urge to roll her eyes and march headlong out of the front door. A movement on the other side of the room caught her eye. Liam.

He was still examining the small sideboard whose surface was covered in trinkets. In the centre of this haphazard arrangement was a large crystal skull lit from within by a tea light candle. He reached for the object, and again, his hand passed through the thick glass as if it was vapour. Daff pinched the bridge of her nose. He looked so real, so solid, and she had to remind herself that he was the one carved out of air. Pressing her feet into the burgundy Persian rug beneath her, Daff swallowed her misgivings and made her decision. She was staying.

Lauryl smacked the deck with a closed fist before fanning the cards in a perfect semi-circle. "Pick three cards and lay them face down on the table."

Daff's eyes ran over the spread. "Which three?"

Peta did a poor job of stifling her giggles.

"No, no," Lauryl waved a finger in the air. "You have to use your intuition. Let your guides lead your hand to the cards that are right for you."

Daff wasn't sure what the woman meant by *intuition.* Eventually, though, she decided it was simply a sappy term for instinct. Reaching out, she plucked three cards and slid them towards the reader. Lauryl gathered them and the rest of the deck up, and reshuffled and re-spread the cards.

"Pick again. This time, close your eyes. Open your hand and run your palm slowly over the cards—without touching—until you feel a tingle or a warmth. That is the card for you. Then do it again until you have all three."

"This is just embarrassing." Liam folded his arms over his chest.

Daff told him to shut up, then her cheeks flushed as she explained to Lauryl who the comment was directed at. Embarrassment rose up in her like a new balloon, but she closed her eyes and did as instructed. She knew the tingle across her palm was not from mystical origins but nerve compression. She knew the man was not a ghost but the result of some mental trauma. It was schizophrenia or a brain tumour. She pushed three cards across the velvet table cloth. Lauryl nodded and flipped them face up.

"I can see why you wanted a reading my dear, you have a lot going on."

"Well that's a line," Liam snorted behind her.

Lauryl leaned forward and tapped the first card on the left. At the top was the number thirteen in roman numerals, at the bottom was the word *death,* and sandwiched between was a skeleton on horseback, dressed in armour and waving a flag.

"I work in a funeral home—I'm an embalmer," Daff shrugged as though that explained everything.

Lauryl waved a hand. "Don't tell me anything personal. It will muddle up the messages from Spirit. Besides, *Death* isn't about death. This card represents change, but it's in your past position. That tells me that a significant event, a change, that occurred in your past is still affecting you now."

Daff didn't know how to respond to this vague statement; should she nod, shake her head or remain neutral? Lauryl moved her pointed finger to the central card: *The Tower.* Two figures were pictured falling from a high brick pillar, and a bolt of lightning was striking the tower. Daff wandered how Lauryl had become so well-known with such miserable-looking images; no promises of fame or fortune here.

"The Tower. Wow! You only pulled three cards, but two are major arcana."

Daff had no idea what that meant. Lauryl explained that a tarot card deck has seventy-eight cards: twenty-two major arcana and fifty-six minor arcana.

"The major arcana represents life's big decisions, events or changes: marriages, births, health, careers and spiritual awakening. The minor arcana is simpler; more grounded in day-to-day advice. The fact that you have two major arcana in both the past and present position tells me that you're going through a major life change right now."

The urge to get up and leave returned. This lady was churning out every cliché in the book: significant event, major life change. Daff wouldn't have been surprised had Lauryl said *I see a tall dark stranger* … only that would have been true! The woman had built a reputation on watered-down gypsy advice so generic it was laughable.

"The falling figures," Lauryl continued, "represent the beliefs that we must release in order to move forward. The lightning is destroying the tower, so that you may build a new one. A new you. Filled with the new beliefs that will serve you better in the future."

"Thank you, Lauryl," Daff stood up and dropped a twenty on the table.

Liam rolled his eyes, "I would have given her a ten."

"But I haven't read the final card!" Lauryl protested, her eyes cutting towards the orange bill. "And readings are a hundred!"

Daff turned and made for the door; Peta followed without a word.

"I don't need a full reading. I got all that I needed." Daff suppressed the need to quip that twenty dollars for five minutes of generic advice was a pretty good deal. Instead, she reached for the door knob.

"Wait! There is a presence, an energy attached to you."

Daff paused, her breath hitched, "Who?"

"The entity's connection to you is very strong. It's here now, in this room." Daff turned, ignoring Liam and looking only at Lauryl; she would give nothing away.

The woman had let her eyes relax; her gaze was unfocussed. "It is a feminine energy. Yes! It is a female; she is standing on your right side."

Liam, however, was standing bedside Lauryl on the other side of the table. "I reckon you can still get that twenty back."

The psychic opened her eyes, looking pleased. "She grieves for you."

The vision of a golden light and a shadowy figure flashed before her. "I'm sorry, but that means nothing to me." Daff opened the door, stomped down the stairs and didn't look back.

Lauryl stood on the platform outside her front door. "Please don't write about this on Facebook!"

Daff didn't hear her; she'd already pulled out her phone and dialled the number of her local GP.

Daff poured the boiling water into the two black mugs. The ride home and much of the afternoon had been spent in silence. Looking through the window above the kitchen sink, she could see the final embers of a winter sunset. The clear, cloudless sky had turned into an expansive golden scape. If she waited another ten minutes, the first of the evening stars would appear, blinking through the shadows. Daff turned from the window and wrapped her cold hands around the steaming pot. Small comforts. She'd gained nothing from the psychic reading. Lauryl couldn't see the future any more than Daff could see her own hand in the dark. With cups and teapot cradled against her chest, she shifted into the lounge room with the steely intent to take hold of the situation.

Peta's leg dangled over the arm of the couch, her phone casting a faint blue light over her face as her thumb swiped the screen again and again.

Daff slid the mugs onto the coffee table. "I've made an appointment with Dr Greene at Leichardt Medical Centre."

Peta looked up from her phone, her eyes wide. "You're giving up just like that?"

"Giving up? I tried your psychic idea, against my better judgement, and it didn't work. I'm going to see a doctor Peta; I'm not messing around with my health any longer."

"You're not sick." The corners of Liam's lips pulled down.

"You're not crazy," Peta affirmed. "Clearly Lauryl's a phoney but she's the first psychic you've seen. The real deals aren't that common, Daff. Come on, give it another go. I've found this woman, a mobile reader who'll come to your house."

Probably to check you out, Daff thought, *see if you have anything worth stealing.*

"The last woman you found online was useless, why is this one going to be any different?"

"Because I didn't find her online. I've been texting that woman who led the meditation at *Circle* last night; she swears by this woman, says she is the real deal—fully legit. Her name is Melissa Sweet and you can't object because I've already booked in for an appointment, today."

"Peta! Jesus!" Daff wondered if this was what an aneurysm felt like. "I didn't ask you to do that. I don't want some stranger coming into my home. Especially one with such a ridiculous name." *Melissa Sweet? No way is that real.*

"What's there to lose? You have your doctor's appointment now, if you don't like what Melissa says, you can still go see Dr Greene."

Peta was firm, and Daff couldn't ignore the simple fact that her symptoms didn't match any logical diagnosis. She wasn't suffering from multiple visions, or hearing different voices—it was one voice, one person. Schizophrenia did not run in her family, there were no records of any mental illness—not even the common ones like Alzheimer's or depression. The strongest drug she had ever taken were the painkillers you could buy off the shelf at the supermarket.

"When's she coming?"

Peta's grin looked ghoulish in the blue light. "In about twenty minutes."

CHAPTER 6

Detective Lawrence

Thursday June 30, 2016

McPhee's attempt to google the Road Dogs address brought up stuff-all. Originally, their clubhouse had been in the Valley, and though they still frequently dealt there, the rivalry with the Jackals had eventually forced them to relocate. Lawrence dodged the hassle of obtaining a warrant by calling in a quiet favour with a bank contact at one of the country's Big Four. It wasn't regulation, but sometimes you just needed to get things done. Within an hour, they had been given the public address of an auto repair shop. Apparently, Henry Ernst had been approved for a small loan late last year.

"What's the shop address again?" Lawrence turned onto the Ted Smout Memorial Bridge, heading towards Redcliffe.

McPhee rattled it off without checking his notepad. "So, are we delivering a death message or taking Henry in for questioning?"

"We'll tell Henry about Sarah and ask him a few questions, but we got no reason to take him back to the station, yet." Lawrence squinted against the stark midday sun. He hadn't had lunch yet, and the thought made his stomach grumble, or maybe it was just nerves. This death message could open up a channel Lawrence had spent eighteen months keeping closed. He'd made a deal with Henry, if you could call it that, kept his nose out of the Road Dogs business and kept Daff safe. The conversation with Henry that day felt a decade old, yet Lawrence still hated to think about it. Now, just three months shy of retirement, he somehow wound up as lead investigator in the murder of Henry's wife. After what happened with his own wife, Ruth, Lawrence supposed this whole ordeal was rather karmic. Though the more cynical part of him would describe it simply as bad luck.

"Come on, it's always the husband."

"Maybe." Lawrence replied, though it sounded more like *yeah, it usually is.* He took a right after hitting the Esplanade and a left a few blocks back after that. The street was a strange mixture of residential and commercial buildings, both in need of renovation. He spotted a dirt road halfway down the street; if you didn't know any better, you could mistake it for a track down to the beach. The temperature in the car dropped instantly as they passed beneath the road's considerable canopy, where the thick branches of fig trees collided. The overhead sun scarcely penetrated the dense foliage, making it look later in the day than it actually was. A large industrial shed squatted at the end of the road. Lawrence switched off the ignition and pulled on the parking brake.

The view through the windscreen reminded him of a stereotypical outback photograph, the kind that depicted dilapidated shearing sheds or abandoned farm equipment, left to decay beneath searing sun and summer storms. The kind of photographs they hung in tourist galleries. The kind of galleries he used to take Daff to during weekend trips to the Sunshine Coast Hinterlands.

"We going in or did you bring me here to hold hands and make out?" McPhee unclipped his seatbelt, but made no further move to get out of the car.

"Not my type, buddy." Lawrence tried for a jiving tone, but it fell flat. Flinging open their car doors, the two police officers crossed the dirt parking lot.

Lawrence rapped his plump knuckles against the sliding steel door. Chips of paint flaked off and drifted down onto the cement slab that stood in for an entertainment area; around them were a handful of cable drums, each turned on their side and littered with empty beer bottles. A black sign picturing a car wheel crossed by two spanners—the design eerily reminiscent of a skull and crossbones—hung above the door. The club's supposedly legitimate business's name was printed in red letters: *Beachside Motors.* Though it was lunchtime, the place looked deserted, like they'd packed up early and called it a day. The knock continued to go unanswered. McPhee pressed an ear to the corrugate, winced against the unexpectedly cold steel and shook his head. "Should we wait in the car?"

Lawrence nodded, unable to decide if he was more disappointed by the unanswered door, or the chore of continuing to make small talk with his partner for the next twenty minutes. Their footsteps sounded hollow as they weaved between the makeshift tables and headed back towards the vehicle. A metallic shudder and piercing scrape echoed behind them; Lawrence glanced over his shoulder.

A young man in his early twenties stood in the crack of the door. His dark eyes narrowed as they shifted from Lawrence and McPhee to their unmarked vehicle. Despite their plain clothes, the pair looked like cops.

"Afternoon, we're looking for Mr Ernst. Is he in today?" Lawrence knew all the members of the Road Dogs, or at least he used to. The lad looked European, maybe Greek; his shaved head and sleeveless t-shirt showed his dark skin and backyard tattoos to great effect. His hands were clean. *Not a mechanic.* Lawrence fluttered through his mental rolodex but failed to find a match. *He's new. Maybe a nom—a would-be club member.*

"Who's asking?"

Lawrence waited a beat before answering. "Detective John Lawrence and Detective Timothy McPhee."

"Timothy?" The *maybe* nom cut his eyes towards McPhee and smirked. "Ernst is in a meeting."

"The matter is urgent."

The muscle in his clenched jaw jumped but before he could say anything else, a rasping voice from inside the shed cut him off.

"We're out." A tall man dressed in jeans, filthy work boots and a loose black tee clapped the lad on the back. "Gates is in the toot. Stand-by, Jakey-boy, case it needs a scrub after."

The lad grimaced but made no objection as he disappeared back into the workshop, supposedly to tend to this unpleasant bathroom errand. The man filled the gap left by Jake and then some. At least Lawrence recognised this one: Gary Thompson, the club's treasurer. Members called him Suicide, not because he practised any dark acts himself –well, clearly not that kind anyway—but because he rode a vintage Panhead complete with original suicide clutch.

"Lawrence," Thompson slipped his grubby hand into the pocket of his jeans and widened his stance, an action that only further emphasised his pronounced belly.

"Gary," the detective refused to call any of the members by their nicknames, *especially* Suicide. "Ernst in today? I need to speak with him."

"What about?" The biker lifted his chin slightly. A scuffling of feet and the piercing sound of grating metal erupted from behind him as the sliding door on the opposite side of the workshop was opened. The warehouse filled with easterly light and bodies. A crew of ten men appeared, picking up tools and rags, switching on a generator and the kettle—their combined hum signalling a return to honest work. *Are they all members?* Lawrence scanned their faces. Some he recognised, others he didn't. A middle-aged man with an impressive beard and arse sat precariously on an overturned milk grate with a chicken sandwich in one hand and a tattered manual in the other. Clearly, they didn't shut up shop for lunch. Not that anyone did, at least not anymore. The lad, Jakey-boy, had said Henry was in a meeting. *A club meeting.* As though the thought had summoned him, the bikie club president strolled out into the buzzing workshop.

Ignoring the rotund bouncer before him, Lawrence called out. "Mr. Ernst."

Ernst's shoulders stiffened and he turned sharply towards his name caller, eyes narrowing slightly. The heels of his riding boots clicked as he crossed the concrete work floor, albeit at a leisurely pace. Seeing that his role had come to an end, Gary pushed the roller door clean open, gave a nod to the club president and the shadow of a sneer to the coppers before slinking back to whatever it was he ought to be doing.

Ernst came to an abrupt stop in the entryway, his face carefully blank, yet wary. The man's small but distinct belly emerged beneath the coarse netting of a long white beard; he stood there, glaring at the coppers while working a rag over his blackened greasy hands. A breeze from the east cut through the workshop, ruffling the remaining hairs on Lawrence's head, and carried with it the scent of degreaser, petroleum and instant coffee. For one irrational moment, the detective wished the doors had stayed closed.

"Detective Lawrence." Henry dug a cigarette out of his breast pocket and wedged it between his lips. "Who's the ranga?"

Ernst lit the smoke, releasing the drag in Lawrence's direction. The detective inhaled, instantly regretting his decision to quit, and waved a hand to spread the fog. "This is Detective Senior Constable McPhee." McPhee inclined his head, but made no comment; his face turned a shade darker than his hair.

"Mr Ernst, it'll be better if we can talk in private. Do you have an office we can use?"

Henry grinned around the cigarette, his gold-capped canine catching the sun. "You got a warrant?"

"We're not here to search the premises, Mr Ernst. Can we come in? It's best if you take a seat."

Ernst lifted a tawny hand, partially covered in faded ink, and buried his thumb deep into his left nostril. "Here's fine, Detective."

Heat rose in Lawrence's chest and he took a deep breath. He couldn't make Henry sit down. If the knucklehead wanted to talk to a cop in the entryway of his business, then that was his decision. Releasing the breath, and his agitation along with it, Lawrence felt a little better. He tried to see Henry not as a drug-dealing bikie, but a man who was about to find out that his wife was dead. There were a few chairs scattered around the cable drums on the verandah; if Henry turned out to have a heart, he could sit on one of those.

Seeing Lawrence hesitate, Henry chuckled, grabbed the handle of the sliding door and began to guide it home. "Well, it's been great seeing ya Detective, but I don't talk to pigs."

Lawrence expected resistance, but that didn't mean he liked it. The only effective tactic for a zip-lipped suspect was shock. It may not be a professional tactic, but it worked. "Mr Ernst, I'm here to notify you that—"

"Call my lawyer, I didn't break my parole!" Henry stopped the door mid-track.

"This isn't about your parole, Ernst. I'm afraid I have some bad news. Your wife, Sarah Miller, has been killed."

Henry's jaw clenched and the sinewy muscles of his arms pulsed as he gripped the door's frame. Lawrence watched the disbelief spread across the old man's face like ink onto paper. He recognised the face of grief by its vacant eyes, creased brow and soft mouth. Lawrence had seen it clutching the doorways of houses and apartment buildings from Logan to Caboolture. It appeared in hospitals and shopfronts, at crime scenes and churches, at his own desk, and in his own home. Something was different this time: there was an edge to Henry's reaction, a cautious flick of his eyes and a pulling of the brow. He was nervous.

"I can't begin to imagine how you're feeling, Mr Ernst." Lawrence felt the bile rise in his throat. "May I say how sorry we are about the murder of Sarah Miller. We'll do everything in our power to discover what happened to your wife and bring justice to the person responsible for this."

"Where?" Henry raised his head, but he didn't meet the detective's eye.

"I'm sorry, I don't understand."

Henry shifted and looked directly at the detective. "Where was she murdered? What happened?"

Lawrence knew Henry was watching for a sign, a twitching lip, a sudden scratch: outlaws had a nose for bullshit. They were suspicious of everyone, especially outsiders, especially cops. Lawrence hadn't planned on lying, but he couldn't risk showing his hand either. "She was the victim of a violent crime. Her body was discovered at the Sundowner Motel earlier today. Forensics are still working on the cause of death."

Henry gripped the handle again, his eyes misted over. "If that's all you can tell me, then fuck off."

The door dragged and clipped as it rolled across the tracks, but Lawrence wasn't done. "Henry." Lawrence hoped the personal address would jar the bikie president enough to buy him a few more questions. "Where were you last night?"

"Here—where else?"

"Can anyone verify that?"

The biker smiled. "Yup, Tramp was here too."

It took Lawrence a moment to remember Paul Sinclair, the club's sergeant-in-arms: their number two. The nickname was inspired by Tramp's lifestyle. His residential address was the workshop; he slept on a crib out the back. Having a member live in the clubhouse wasn't only cheap security, but good security. Tramp earned his patch and title because he was a fighter. In fact, he'd been thrown in the paddy wagon along with a handful of other members following the scuffle last weekend in the Valley. It was easy to imagine Tramp wielding a baseball bat. Lawrence shuddered and absently slid his tongue over the front of his teeth. They were still perfectly intact, unlike the teeth of the nom who'd been raced to Brisbane Private. "Jackals been giving you any trouble?"

Henry reverted to his outlaw persona; his momentary grief at becoming a widower gone. "Why would they? Road Dogs is a social club."

Henry had said the same thing two years ago, when Lawrence picked him up after a brawl in one of the Valley's less glamorous pubs. He'd delivered the line with all sincerity, even with a bloody handkerchief pressed against his nose. It was no more convincing this time. "When did you last see your wife?"

Henry's answer slipped out before the door slid home: "Talk to her sister."

"I understand it's hard, Mr Ernst, but I have some more questions about your wife."

His response boomed through the thin corrugate. "Then drag me to the cop shop. Arrest me, get a bloody warrant, or fuck off!"

"We need the sister's address." McPhee eyed his superior, but Lawrence decided not to push the issue.

He had nothing on Henry, not really. If he wanted to be a prick, he could pull the *trifecta*: a classic cop move. He could threaten to lock Henry up for offensive language, resisting arrest and assaulting a police officer. The crusty old biker would have had it a hundred times. Legally, he could detain Henry for the next eight hours, grill him until he burned, but with no real leverage, he wouldn't get Henry to talk.

McPhee slapped Lawrence on the shoulder before turning back towards their vehicle. The detective was surprised he'd been able to get through the interview uninterrupted. Perhaps his subordinate was finally learning. He would reward McPhee by giving him the task of uncovering the sister's details while saving himself the headache of scrolling police databases—or, worse, those internet pages people check multiple times a day. He turned to follow his partner and wondered if two months was enough time to stitch up the case.

CHAPTER 7

Daff

Thursday June 30, 2016

Melissa Sweet looked as if she had just jumped off the back of a motorcycle after partying all night at an AC/DC concert. This was mostly due to the iconic image printed on her singlet, framed beneath her leather jacket: Bon Scott's horned head and purring lip. All that black looked odd standing amongst the shabby chic, predominately beige, décor of Daff's lounge room.

"Hi, I'm Melissa. Daphne, is it?" The woman shot out a hand; her fingers and wrist strapped with metal.

"Yes, but I prefer Daff." She shook Melissa's outstretched palm. Relieved to see that the psychic wore no crystal necklaces or organic cotton fibres. Daff smiled involuntarily, and Melissa's returning toothy grin softened the harshness of her appearance.

"She seems nice." The newly-named Liam looked at the woman admiringly.

Melissa stepped back and lingered by the door. "Sorry to be so crass, hon, but I collect my cash up front. Don't take it personally, I've just been screwed over too many times."

Daff gave a stiff nod as she handed over two fifties which the psychic quickly stuffed into a concealed pocket inside her jacket.

"Where do you want to set up?" Peta glanced at the couch, but Daff was already walking towards the dining table. She pulled out a chair and indicated for everyone to take a seat. Melissa sat opposite her host while Peta took the seat at the head of the table. Liam moved in close, standing directly behind Melissa, facing Daff. He had noticed it too. She couldn't see him. Daff was about to call the whole thing off when the psychic spoke up.

"Your friend here," she inclined her head towards Peta, "tells me you have a problem with an earth-bound spirit."

"I don't know about *earth-bound spirit*, but last night I started to experience a …" hallucination wasn't the right word; not for this conversation. Daff decided to speak literally. "I can see someone. Someone no one else can see."

"Including you." Liam waved a hand in front of Melissa's face. She didn't flinch. "If you kick her out now, you can probably still get your money back."

Daff considered doing just that when Melissa piped up from across the table. "Did anything happen prior to you seeing this spirit?"

The image of a circular light and a shadowy figure flashed before her eyes and Daff shook the dream away. "The morning was ordinary, but in the afternoon, I went with Peta to the *Circle* meeting on Golden Beach—"

"Ange is the one who gave me your number," Peta interjected. Melissa's ruby lips lifted into a small smile.

"After the meditation I came back home … and I wasn't alone."

"You forgot about the watch." Peta pointed towards her friend's wrist. "Daff found a watch on the beach and she brought it home. We think the watch is haunted."

"We?" Daff scoffed.

"You better not be back on the 'I'm losing my mind' angle." Liam glared at her. "Not after putting me through the whole pick-a-name business."

Daff returned the stare. "Oh, I'm sorry, this must be really inconvenient for you."

Following the direction of Daff's glare, Melissa glanced over her shoulder and shuddered. "The spirit is here now, isn't he?"

"Yup," Daff answered.

"I'll get a better reading if I'm holding the watch." Melissa stretched out her hand, the morning sun bouncing off her silver rings.

Daff unstrapped the timepiece, hesitating for a moment before dropping it into the psychic's open palm. Melissa didn't close her eyes or allow them to glaze over. She didn't even look at the watch. Instead, she fixated on a chip in the surface of the table. Daff looked sideways towards Peta who appeared absorbed, and Liam who'd stood back watching sceptically.

"This watch has strong ties. I'm afraid your ghost man is bound to it."

Daff hadn't said it was a man. Did Melissa assume it was a man because of the style of watch or had she picked up on something?

Peta leaned in and asked a question, but it was drowned out by Liam's furious response. "Fuckin' wow, love! What are gonna tell me next? The sky is blue, grass is green, life costs money, so cough up the coin, sucker, while I continue to spin you shit." Liam flung his arm as if he was swatting a fly. "This chick doesn't know shit. She can't tell us who I am or why I'm here."

"Shut up!" Daff's hand smacked the table. Peta and Melissa glared at her in confusion. "Not you, him!" She pointed towards the open space behind the psychic. Liam stepped back, his lips pressed into a hard line.

Melissa raised an eyebrow before shrugging and returning her attention to the watch. "The man is young, late twenties, early thirties. He's tall, very pale, but his hair and eyes are dark."

Liam's face lost its edge and he crouched by the reader. Even in this position, his stature meant they were shoulder to shoulder. "Jesus, maybe she is the real deal—or a damn good guesser."

For a moment, Daff wondered why Liam shared her own scepticism. Surely if he *was* a ghost he had good reason to believe in the supernatural? Quickly remembering that he was a construction of her own mind, Daff returned to the task at hand. "Yes, that's correct. Can you see him?"

"Not the way you can, hon. It's more like a daydream. I see him with my mind, not my eyes."

Daff pressed further. "Why is he here? Attached to the watch I mean."

"Is it … unfinished business?" Peta asked.

Daff cringed, but thought *to hell with it.* If she was going to have this conversation she was going to have it, regardless of its absurdity.

Melissa nodded. "You got it. The only reason a spirit sticks 'round here is because there's something they didn't get to do or say before they carked it. The ghost is probably attached to this watch because it had sentimental value when he was alive." Melissa tilted her head to the side, looking at Daff. "Is this the first spirit you've ever seen, hon?"

Daff hesitated. She didn't want to be rude by saying she didn't *actually* believe in ghosts, but the psychic cut in before she could answer.

"You don't believe in spirits, do ya?"

Daff's eyes narrowed. It was a neat parlour trick, observing a person's expressions, analysing their body language and passing it off as psychic insight or mind reading. The odds of the prediction were a conservative 50/50. Dismissing the timing of Melissa's question, Daff straightened and confessed that she didn't believe in ghosts.

"She thinks she's hallucinating," Peta and Liam said in unison. Daff squirmed in her seat and shifted her gaze down to her clasped hands. Was she insane? If she really did think Liam was imaginary, why did she "name" him? How did he say the same thing as Peta just now? Did her subconscious mind know Peta well enough to predict what she would say? Had she merely constructed this hallucination based on her best friend's personality? No. That *was* too much of a stretch. Daff shook her head, clearing away the rabbit warren of thoughts.

"Why don't you think ghosts are real?"

"I ..." Daff fumbled. Simply saying their existence wasn't logical didn't seem enough. Truthfully, all scientific discoveries existed in the physical world prior to being proven. "If I can see it and I can touch it then it's real." She amended, "If I and *someone else* can see it or touch it."

"Well, the reading isn't over. I may convert you yet."

"Good luck." Liam snorted.

Melissa squinted, raised her hand and patted her chest. "Hmmm, I can feel a tightness here. I think his death was somehow connected to his heart."

Daff wasn't sure if Melissa was speaking medically or metaphorically, but Peta was the one who asked, "Like a heart attack?"

"Maybe. Though given his age it's unlikely." Melissa paused, as though she were trying to hear something. "His death was unexpected."

"Well, let's be honest, most thirty-year-olds don't *expect* to die." Liam rolled his eyes.

Daff was about to tell him to be quiet when Melissa blurted, "He's a bit of a smart arse, isn't he?"

Daff barked a dry laugh, and the thought struck her, "You can hear him?"

"Yeah hon, but not the way you do. I reckon you must be clairvoyant—that means you can *see* things that regular folks can't. You're lucky. I'm *clairsentient*—that means that I *know* things. Information pops into my head like soundbites." She raised a hand in defence, "Lotto numbers not included."

"You just … *know* stuff?"

"You got it. And I can talk to spirits the same way—through my thoughts. I don't have to speak out loud to them." Seeing the obvious questions bubble up on Daff's face, Melissa continued. "And you don't have to either, hon. You can chat up your guy using your thoughts and you don't have to look like a crazy while you're doing it."

Daff stopped herself from pointing out that this whole conversation was crazy.

"Are you getting anything else about how he died?" Peta steered the conversation back to the reading.

"Oh, right." Melissa drew her attention back towards the piece in her hand. "His death was unexpected, quick, violent." Suddenly, the psychic's eyes flew up and met Daff's. "It's gone, it all just went blank." She dropped the watch onto the table. "That's never happened before."

Daff shrunk back in her chair. Melissa was good. For a moment, she'd almost believed that the psychic rock chick was actually onto something.

"It's more than we knew before." Peta shrugged.

The psychic's brows furrowed, peeling her eyes away from the watch. "Hon, if you can see and hear your ghost man, why do you need me?"

"He's not my *man.*" Daff's face warmed with irritation. "And the reason why you are here is because he can't remember anything about his life."

Peta piped up, "We thought that maybe you'd be able to tune into him. See what he was doing before he …"

"Died?" Liam filled in the blank, though Daff was the only one to hear him.

Melissa shrugged. "Sorry hon, maybe I'm not allowed to know. Maybe this is something you gotta figure out on your own."

Daff closed her eyes. Too exhausted to analyse the validity of such a statement.

"Well, I guess I betta get going. Can I use your bathroom, sweets?" Melissa asked as she pushed back her seat, but before Daff could direct her down the hall Melissa sat down again. "Wait. Someone else is coming through."

"Someone else? A different spirit?" Peta asked.

Liam looked around the room. "I don't see anyone."

Daff couldn't either.

"Yeah," Melissa replied. "This one though, he ain't earth-bound. He's pointing towards his head like something …" Melissa scrunched her eyes, rocked back on her chair and gritted her teeth. Peta leapt from her seat and grabbed Melissa's hand.

"What's happening? Are you okay?" Daff stood, trying to recall a distant first aid course that had included instructions on how to reduce injury during epileptic fits.

Melissa's eyes became slits, as if she was staring directly at the sun. "It was a car accident. He died instantly. Blunt trauma to the head. There's a strong T sound."

Daff's knees went soft. The web of bone, muscles and tendons disintegrated as she sank to the floor.

"Tom," Peta whispered.

Daff's mind raced. Her thoughts morphing into a frantic, incoherent, jumbled mess; she reached out, trying to grab one, trying to focus her mind on something real and solid. Something she could tether herself to. She heard a scraping sound, followed by a metallic clink, then a warm hand pressed against her shoulder.

"Whatever happened that night, hon, it's in the past." Melissa's voice was smooth, honeyed. "Tom is okay. He's where he needs to be, but you need to forgive yourself, hon; what happened wasn't your fault. You gotta let it go. Tom wants you to let it go."

Daff couldn't do this. Not here. Not with this stranger watching her. She had to get up. She had to get off the floor, but Peta had already sealed her in an embrace.

"Listen, hon," Melissa continued, "this is why your ghost-fella found you, why you two are connected. You gotta help this man complete his unfinished business, and he's gotta help you face your grief."

Daff couldn't breathe, smothered by Peta's arms and the psychic's grip on her shoulder. She homed in on her ribs to feel the tension of her intercostal muscles as they reacted to the expansion and contraction of her lungs. In. Out. In. Out. Focus. Breathe.

A cough broke the silence and Liam cleared his throat. “So, who the fuck is Tom?”

CHAPTER 8

Detective Lawrence

Friday July 1, 2016

It was mid-afternoon when Lawrence fell into his desk chair. Beth Dawson's parents had come down from the Sunshine Coast and Lawrence had offered to pick them up from the motel and drive them to the morgue for identification. A task he was glad to have finished. That poor girl looked so much like Daff it hurt.

There had been the standard questions: what was your daughter like, did she have many mates, did she have a bloke? Their answers had been pretty standard too. She was a good girl, an undergrad at a Brisbane university, lots of mates—they were all good girls too—and no boyfriend.

The Dawsons said what everyone said: "None of this makes any sense." Lawrence wanted to tell them that it never does.

He'd contacted the university and explained the situation to administration, and within half an hour he'd had Beth's academic transcript and the contact details of her lecturers. Beth had gotten good grades and the lecturers described her as an 'enthusiastic participant' in their tutorials. That was the easy stuff to verify. It hadn't gone unnoticed that Mr Dawson wore a Rolex and Mrs Dawson a designer purse, but if Beth had some shady friends or boyfriends, her folks weren't admitting to knowing them. Mrs Dawson said she'd email through the mobile numbers of Beth's friends once she got home, and Lawrence hoped one of them would be useful.

As it turned out, Lawrence's priority request to pathology hadn't gone ignored. He figured it was some kind of pity favour: no one wants to retire on an open case. With the pathologist's external examinations completed and the body positively ID'd, Beth Dawson had been released and transported to a funeral parlour at the Sunny Coast, to be closer to her parents' home. He'd read the pathologist's report. Though toxicology found traces of methamphetamine in both Beth and Sarah's blood, drug overdose was not listed as the cause of death. Beth had her throat cut and Sarah was strangled; you didn't need to run a test for that. Lawrence had buzzed the forensics lab to check if any trace evidence had been uncovered. Officer Amy Poy answered the phone and testily informed him that tumbleweeds would be rolling over his desk before that particular report was finalised. Some things were coming together, but Lawrence still couldn't prove that Henry was the killer.

"You ready to go?" McPhee loomed over the desktop monitor.

Lawrence nodded, collecting his notepad, pen and keys. "I'm driving."

The pair had barely crossed over the Brisbane River when McPhee turned to his superior. "When you were talking with Henry yesterday … it seemed kind of personal."

Lawrence shrugged.

"Did something happen?"

"Nothing but the usual. Now shut it, I'm trying to work out the fastest way to Redbank Plains."

McPhee pulled out his phone. "Stay on the Clem 7, then take the Ipswich Motorway past Rocklea, you'll take a left onto Collingwood Drive and then you're just about there."

"Thanks Google."

Lawrence followed his constable's directions until he arrived at Willow Drive. "What's the number again?" The detective squinted, longing for his glasses, as he tried to read the tiny numbers on the letterboxes.

McPhee flipped his phone again. "Thirty-four A." He'd dug up Sarah Miller's sister's name, phone number and address in the time it took Lawrence to make a cuppa, the blighter. With a few clicks of the mouse, a case could plough forward or come to a halt. Either way, internet search pages had become standard workplace procedure and Lawrence wondered how many cases he could have solved had those 'engines' existed back when he was a constable.

He looked around. The estate was veined by thin streets with equally thin houses, each a replica of the one that came before it, though some were better maintained than others. McPhee spotted it then, pointing towards a cream duplex with maroon trim.

Lawrence pulled into the driveway. Like the automation of a cuckoo clock, a woman in her early fifties with wispy blonde hair piled high atop her head appeared at the front door. This must be Heather Miller. She was wearing a blue dress that Ruth would've described as tea length. *Jesus, the things you remember.* She raised a delicate hand to shade her eyes from the harsh morning sun, and a prickle of gooseflesh laced the detective's arms. The simple gesture hurtled him back in time to those rare Sunday morning when they would split a pot of tea on the verandah. Ruth was reading the paper, and as she lifted her head to deliver some snarky commentary about the decline of journalism, she shaded her eyes against an eastern sun.

Lawrence blinked fiercely until the vision of his deceased wife disappeared, yet the goose bumps remained as he stepped out of the vehicle, flashed his badge and attempted to slip into the role of dignified police officer. "Good afternoon, Ms Miller, we're here to speak to you about your sister—"

"It's about time you showed up." The impatient sharp tapping of the woman's court shoe filled the air. "I've been ringing the CBD station for the past day, but no one gives a rat's arse. My sister is missing. Do you know how much could happen in twenty-four hours? She could be lying in a ditch somewhere! Is that why you're here? Have you found her?"

Lawrence's stomach clenched as if anticipating a blow. It had been a long time since a woman had spoken to him like that. When Ruth called it quits, part of him was relieved to know they'd never fight again; funny how the things that drive you nuts are the things that you miss. A brisk breeze picked up. Leaves scattered across the path and Heather's dress moulded around the curve of her hips, her thighs. Lawrence wiped his hands along his trousers and tried to ignore the fluttering pulse in his neck.

"Detective?" Heather glared in his direction, though their eyes did not meet. She seemed oblivious to the stray curls the breeze had tugged free and that now fell flatteringly around her narrow chin. "It's near on twenty-four hours. So, are you here to follow up on my calls or stand on my front lawn?"

Lawrence took a ragged breath and forced his mind to get back on the job. No one had said anything about a Ms Miller calling the station. Who told her that she had to wait twenty-four hours to lodge a missing persons report? Must have been that new proby. *Candice? Was that her name?* Her field officer must have already taught her the fine art of dodging 'unnecessary' work. Lawrence made a mental note to drop a copy of the Handbook onto her desk when he returned to the station.

Death messages were never easy, but Lawrence could tell this one was going to be a killer; Heather Miller looked like a lady ready for a fight. He was about to confirm Heather's suspicions when he stole a glance at McPhee, who was drained of colour. For a moment, Lawrence pitied the younger detective, then quickly shrugged it off. He'll learn, he thought, everyone tackles these situations differently: denial, disintegration or dander.

"Maybe we should discuss this inside. Can we come in, Ms Miller?"

"Why not? Better late than never I suppose." Heather turned, left the door open, and walked back into the house.

As he watched her walk away, Lawrence's eyes naturally drifted downwards and noted that her backside was as curvy as her hips. Taken aback by this unexpected spark of desire, the detective tugged at his collar and tried to remember why he was here. The memory of Sarah Miller's inflamed purple neck flashed before his eyes. *Right.* With a quick nod towards his constable, the detective followed his best lead into her home.

Inside, a sliver of sunlight cut the lounge room and brightened two cream-coloured armchairs. At Heather's command, the officers took their seats while their host perched on the edge of a sofa opposite. Though she'd invited them in, she hadn't offerd them a drink. Clearly, Heather's invitation had been strictly cordial; she wanted them to deliver their news and get out.

Lawrence pulled a notepad from his shirt pocket and had a pen at the ready. "When was the last time you saw your sister, Ms Miller?"

"I'll be asking the questions, officer. I want to know about my sister—"

"What about her?" McPhee interrupted.

Heather looked at McPhee as if he'd suddenly materialised on her sofa. She turned back towards Lawrence. "Do you know if she's alive?"

Lawrence knew that once he delivered the death message, it would be hard to extract anything useful from the sister. Ethical or not, he could usually get in one or two questions before suspicion arose, but Heather was already on the defensive, and the thin cut of her lips told him that he'd be better off answering her damn question.

"Ms Miller, I'm sorry to say that your sister, Sarah Miller has been killed. We believe she's the victim of a violent attack."

"She was murdered." Heather skipped the jargon, white hands clasped in front of her.

"It's too early in the investigation to know that for sure." Even though it wasn't. "Heather—my apologies, Ms Miller, we have a few questions to ask you."

She nodded, slid off the sofa's arm and into the seat proper. Her brown almond-shaped eyes stood in stark contrast to her soft pale hair. They were framed by delicate wrinkles that hinted of a life of laughter. Lawrence liked that. Not that she was laughing now. Heather's face had fallen and her eyes hardened; this wasn't the face of grief. Probably delayed shock. Everyone handles these situations differently, he reminded himself. Realising he'd been staring, Lawrence cleared his throat. "Ms Miller, when was the last time you saw your sister?"

Heather tilted her head towards the corner of the room. Lawrence couldn't tell if she was trying to remember or if she was about to throw them out. He was about to repeat the question when her answer came. "Thursday morning. Seven-thirty. Before I went to work. I manage an art gallery in the Valley."

"Where did you see your sister?"

Heather looked baffled. "Here." She flipped her hand up as if holding an invisible tray. "She's been staying on my couch for the past week." She pointed to a pile of carefully folded sheets stacked beside McPhee's chair.

So Sarah and Henry had split up. Henry's warehouse was an hour away, his last registered address less than that. The close proximity alone would provide him with plenty of opportunities. Henry and Sarah's separation could be a motive, though, separation alone made for a weak motive—and thanks to Paul Sinclair, Henry had an alibi, whatever that was worth. Still, Henry *was* Sarah's husband and, as McPhee had pointed out, it's always the husband.

"Why was your sister staying with you?"

Heather gave a mock snort. "Because Henry's an arse. I can't believe she shared a bed with that animal." She straightened and delicately pressed a finger against her mouth to wipe away a thin layer of perspiration.

Lawrence felt his cheeks warm; he needed to stay focussed. "Have you heard of a motorcycle group called the Jackals?"

She said no, but the answer came too quick; too *anticipated.*

"Ms Miller, if you know anything, even if it seems insignificant, please tell us. It could help the investigation. If it's retaliation that concerns you, I can appoint an officer to your home."

Her pink lips pressed together; her eyes fixated on the space beside the detective's head. The silent interrogation made him nervous, and he wondered if his guess had been right. She nodded, softening beneath the weight of her decision. "I will take the extra security, thank you. Sarah mentioned that club, the Jackals, but all she said was that they didn't get along with Henry's … group."

She glanced sidelong towards a small table at the end of the sofa. Lawrence followed her gaze. The table held up three objects: a landline home phone (a sight that comforted Lawrence immensely), a plain lamp and a single picture frame of the two sisters smiling at the camera. He surveyed the walls quickly. There were no other photos, only large abstract paintings. Perhaps she'd never had children? Her hands had relaxed, resting on top of her knees, and Lawrence saw that the left ring finger was bare. This woman may have just lost the only significant member of her family, Lawrence thought. Everyone handles these situations differently, but why is she *so* composed?

Unable to decide whether her carefully concealed emotions were the product of an uptight personality or something else, Lawrence returned to his list of questions. "I'll arrange the security today. What can you tell me about your sister and her relationship with Henry?"

Heather sighed. "Sarah met Henry one night at the clubhouse. They hit it off and seven months later they were married."

"Wasn't she like forty? Bit old to be a bikie groupie." McPhee leaned in.

Lawrence felt his jaw flex and wondered how he would smooth *that* one over when Heather, graciously, continued.

"Sarah wasn't old. She knew that Henry was involved in … *unsavoury* activities, but she didn't care. She loved him."

"Henry doesn't strike me as the marrying type. How did that come about?"

Heather catalogued Henry and Sarah's love affair from their short-lived honeymoon period to their hasty wedding—a decision that came about when Henry's controlling ways coupled with Sarah's desperation: she'd always wanted to get married. Sarah had hoped the marriage would be the solution to all their problems. It wasn't. Shortly after exchanging rings, Sarah learnt that her new husband wasn't a one-woman man.

"The wastebasket full of unfamiliar French letters gave him away," Heather explained. The situation had come to a head last week during a barbecue at the clubhouse.

"Sarah caught him, red-handed, feeling up one of the club's little tarts … barely out of her twenties."

The Ernsts had a loud and very public argument before the meat had even been flipped on the grill. Sarah had announced that she would be filing for divorce; Henry had laughed and told her she'd better get going then. She'd shown up at Heather's place later that night.

"Did Sarah ever say that she felt unsafe around Henry?"

Heather gripped her knees, her body stiffened. Lawrence noticed she was afraid—but of Henry or the club? Perhaps police protection wasn't enough to ease her mind. Maybe Heather worried that blabbing to the police could lead to a body-bag of her own. Hell, the club could already have eyes on this place. If McPhee could track down her address, then members of an organised crime group could too. Lawrence leaned back, looked over his shoulder and out onto the open street. There were a few parked vehicles butted against the gutter, but none featured a balaclava-wearing driver.

Heather curled a hair behind her ear, decision made. "Sarah never said anything about that. As far as I know, Henry never threatened her."

Lawrence watched Heather carefully, waiting for the shuffle of a foot or a tightening around the eyes, but she remained composed, taut as ever. "Did you ever see signs of physical abuse, bruises maybe, or a change in Sarah's behaviour? Did she become distant in recent months?"

"No. Henry's a cheating dog and a son of a … but he never hit her. I can't say how he treated her in the privacy of their home, but Sarah wasn't changed by their marriage."

"Did she talk about her plans, what she might do?"

"She was planning on leaving town, obviously." Heather flipped her hands again. "She was thinking of starting afresh. Somewhere new. She even asked me to come with her—"

"Why was that?" McPhee asked.

Lawrence knew why. You don't just leave the president of the Road Dogs. Sarah couldn't flee Brisbane and leave her sister behind. Sure, maybe nothing would happen, but the threat would be there. The club would know everything about Heather: where she lived, worked, what car she drove and what hours she kept. If Sarah was going to leave, she would need to tie up all loose ends; her sister included.

Heather stood and began walking towards the door, "Thank you for coming by, Detective, but I'm afraid there's somewhere else I need to be."

"It won't take long Ms Miller, but I do need some more information—"

"Then you'll have to get it another time. I have an appointment." She checked her wrist watch and drummed her index finger against the glass face three times while boring a hole with her eyes in the void beside the detective's head.

Everybody handles grief differently, but Lawrence had never encountered a broad who accepted it *so* indifferently. Heather's polished shoe tapped a double time on the equally shiny tiles as she waited. Admitting defeat, Lawrence rose from the plush armchair and handed Heather his card. "This is my direct line. If you remember anything or if the club tries to contact you, call me."

Heather nodded, flicked the corner of the card and slipped it into a concealed pocket in her skirt before escorting them from her home.

Outside, the officers ambled towards their vehicle. "You think she's holding anything back?" McPhee dropped down into the passenger seat.

"Probably. Gang crime: everyone wants to see the guy arrested, but no one wants to be seen pointing the finger."

"Can you blame them?"

Lawrence glanced at his partner, then back towards the rendered house. Heather was alone: no man, no kids, no dog, and no security. Her sister had been killed in a dive motel; nothing could change that. Sure, she could give a statement, but court would move a hell of a lot slower than Henry Ernst would. She'd spend the next few years looking over her shoulder, wondering if today will be the day she winds up dead in a motel room. Lawrence turned on the ignition and released the stiff parking brake.

"No, I don't blame her."

"I've got a cousin like that." McPhee smoothed his unintentionally ironic moustache. "Heather probably has a milder case of it though."

Lawrence eyeballed his constable, "What are you talking about?"

"You … don't think Heather was a little … unusual?"

"I've met stranger. I thought she was nice. Sort of." The detective shrugged and pushed the vision of Heather's figure-hugging dress from his mind.

"She's an aspie, or at least, I think she is. She reminded me of my cousin is what I am saying. Who knows? Maybe I'm wrong."

"In what way?"

"Huh?"

Lawrence suppressed the urge to thump his co-pilot. "In what way did Heather remind you of your cousin?"

"Oh. The lack of emotion, minimal eye contact, the tapping."

"That's it?" The detective tried to recall the colour of Heather's eyes and realised he couldn't.

"Well," McPhee waved an open hand in the air, "sometimes you just know, right?"

"Right." The pair drove across the Story Bridge in silence. Relying on instinct can be dangerous, but it can also throw you a crumb when you've got little else to go on.

They were a few blocks away from the station when Lawrence took an unexpected left-hand turn.

"Where are we going?" McPhee clutched the car's door handle.

"To the Jackals' clubhouse."

"You know where it is?"

Lawrence nodded; when he couldn't find McPhee earlier that morning, he'd asked one of the constables to look it up for him.

When Henry split from the Jackals, the club was reduced to eight members: small compared to the Road Dogs' fifteen. So, Lawrence wasn't entirely surprised by the clubhouse's small size when he pulled up in front of a small house on Hill Street. The place was a two-storey fibro with a low brick fence and three Harleys parked in the driveway. Minus the bikes, it looked like any ordinary residential house. Looking around at the other occupied houses in the street, Lawrence was surprised that the station hadn't receive any noise complaints. He'd just gotten out of the car when a short man with a bad neck tattoo appeared on the narrow front porch.

"Whacha after, old man?"

"Detective Jon Lawrence and Detective Tim McPhee. I need to speak with your club president. Is he in?"

The short man hesitated for a moment, then nodded. When he turned, Lawrence noticed that the back of his vest was bare. *He's a nom.* Someone trying to get into the club. The lad looked barely twenty, so young and so keen to live a life on the fringe. Maybe times were getting tougher? Lawrence thought. Then he scoffed: a crim was a crim. *After we leave, he'll probably get a good touch-up for letting us in.*

Lawrence could feel eyes on him as the dying lawn crunched beneath his feet. The lad opened the door for the detectives and Lawrence felt his armpits grow damp as he entered the dimly lit lounge room of the makeshift clubhouse. The musty couch stood guard over a coffee table covered in ashtrays, rollie packets and beer bottles. The wall between the lounge room and kitchen was cut out, making one giant room.

Three weather-beaten men sat around a circular kitchen table littered with tools and mismatched bike parts: clutches, sprockets, air filters. A fourth man stood by the sink with a rag half shoved into his back pocket. He was of medium height, with a closely shaved head and a goatee. Lawrence hadn't met the president, Jim, before, but he'd seen him around the station once or twice when he'd been thrown in the watch house after making a nuisance of himself on a Friday or Saturday night. The fellas around the table looked up as Lawrence and McPhee stepped into the open kitchen; their eyes tightened but they stayed on task: scrubbing filthy sprockets with toothbrushes and cleaning air filters.

"Something the matter?" Jim pulled the rag from his pocket, rubbed it over his blackened fingers.

"I'm Detective Lawrence and this is Detective McPhee from Fortitude Valley Station. We're here to ask you a few questions. Henry Ernst's wife, Sarah Miller, was murdered yesterday. You know anything about that?"

"Nope."

"You fellas ever heard of a girl called Beth Dawson?"

The nom who had let them in materialised behind the detectives. "Did you say Dawson?"

"Did you know her?" McPhee lifted his chin so high the whole kitchen could see up his nose.

Jim glared at the nom who promptly folded his arms over his chest. "The name sounded familiar, but nah. Sorry, officer."

"If you know something, lad—"

"I don't know her." The nom spoke through clenched teeth. Jim stepped forward and the men at the table straightened. The room shrunk by inches.

Lawrence's eyes narrowed before he addressed the men at the table. "You heard of her?" All three shook their shaggy heads. "I heard one of your boys was carted off to Emergency last weekend after running into some of the Road Dogs' lads. You guys got a beef going?"

"There's nothing going on between Road Dogs and us and we don't know anything about Henry, his missus or that other bird. So why don't you just fuck off?"

Jim straightened, pulled a smoke from inside his leather vest and lit it, his silver rings clinking; for a moment Lawrence could easily imagine what it would be like to take one of those in the cheek. The tallest man at the table shifted and Lawrence flinched, thinking he was pulling a piece from his pocket, but it was just a spanner. The windows were closed, making the stench of tobacco and degreaser suffocating.

"You nervous, detective?"

Lawrence met the bloke's gaze before looking at the counter behind him. The kitchen bench was as cluttered as the table, lined with cereal boxes, scraps of paper, receipts, coins and random junk. There was even a silver dog dish, only this one wasn't filled with dry biscuits, but a fist full of weed.

When Lawrence failed to respond, Jim followed the detective's gaze and grimaced.

"Interesting choice of dog food, boys." Lawrence said, swivelling back towards Jim. "If you don't start talking, then I'm going to have to get a search warrant, or maybe I'll just give my buddies over at Gaming and Vice a call. This place will be ripped through in a couple of hours. I wonder what else they'd find …"

The edges of Jim's mouth drew down and his hands curled into fists.

McPhee pulled his phone from his pocket and hit the voice record app. "Where were you last night?"

"Here." Jim withdrew his cigarette, stubbing it out with unnecessary force. "We're always here."

"I'm gonna need an official statement, from *all* of your boys. They all here?"

"Nope."

"Then call them."

"Sure, *Chief*."

Lawrence pointed at the nom who was attempting to become invisible. "You first, outside."

Even though he'd gotten them to cooperate, Lawrence didn't want to stand in that kitchen for another minute. It was too hot, and as illogical as it sounded, to remain inside the clubhouse was to give them the upper hand. The detective turned, headed towards the door and told McPhee to take his pick. They were going to be there for a while.

CHAPTER 9

Daff

Friday July 1, 2016

Peta had offered to stay, but Daff assured her she'd rather be alone. Well, as alone as she could be. The accident happened eighteen months ago, but Melissa Sweet's reading compressed that year and a half into mere moments, bringing the memory of that night too close: the slide of the car, her head hitting the steering wheel, the damp morning air and Tom gasping his final breath. Click, crack, boom. Daff thought she knew how to navigate this river of grief, how to move with the current while keeping her head above it, but these memories and that reading were threatening to drown her.

After Peta left, Liam had questions that Daff wasn't prepared to answer. He'd told her he couldn't leave the watch, that he was bound with a twenty-metre radius of it. Remembering this, Daff tossed the watch into the laundry basket at the opposite end of the house. She needed time to think, to adjust. Last night she was convinced she was losing her mind, that Liam was a fabrication caused by suppressed trauma. Now she thought she might be losing her mind for entirely different reasons.

Tom wanted her to forgive herself for the accident.

Tom, who was dead, *still had wants.*

Liam's a ghost.

Ghosts are real.

And Daff was supposedly responsible for uncovering Liam's real identity and returning him—to what? The afterlife?

Daff cursed herself for attending the meditation circle with Peta. If she hadn't gone, if she hadn't picked up that damn watch, then none of this would be happening. She'd still be swimming.

The watch.

Daff flopped into the wicker chair in the corner of her bedroom. It was in this chair Ruth had read her daughter stories; now Daff felt like she was telling them to herself. She'd pocketed the watch on a whim because it looked so similar to the one she'd given to Tom. Even Peta recognised it. The similarity of the watches was a coincidence, but the thought caused a silent dread to settle over her shoulders. There was a vague memory of a zip-lock bag filled with Tom's personal effects. Had the watch been in there? Had he been buried with it? She couldn't remember. Those weeks following the accident were shrouded in fog.

If she hadn't have stepped on the watch at Golden Beach, she never would have met Liam and none of this would be happening. Melissa had made it sound like Daff had no choice but to help Liam, but that wasn't true. If Liam was bound to the watch, if he couldn't leave it, then all she had to do was get rid of it.

Daff's shift started in an hour. She didn't have much time. Looking out the window she could see her three wheelie bins neatly lined up alongside the verandah railing. She could toss the watch, but the rubbish wouldn't be collected until Monday. There was incineration. She could take the watch to work and slip it into a casket before it was shipped to the crematorium, but she knew the day's work plan, having checked it before she left yesterday. Only two bodies were on the plan and neither was being cremated. Plus, there were too many unknowns with that option. Incinerating the watch may free Liam of its hold on him … or he could vanish along with it. Both options made Daff feel slightly squeamish.

She could sell it.

Daff snatched her handbag off the edge of the bed and headed towards the laundry. There was a pawn shop on Bulcock Street; if she left now, she'd be able to sell the watch and still make it in time for her shift. Liam was leaning up against the washing machine when Daff entered the small room.

"You doing okay, Daff?"

The question went unanswered as she flung articles of clothing aside, looking for the watch.

"So, that reading was pretty heavy, eh? I'm really sorry about what happened to your friend."

Daff felt her breath hitch. She found the watch and tossed it into her handbag.

"Are we going somewhere?"

Though the house had held onto the chill from last night, it was warm when Daff stepped outside. She slung the handbag onto the passenger seat, giving Liam no choice but to sit in the back. She then pulled out and headed towards the city centre.

It was eleven-thirty on a Friday. Usually, Main Street would be bustling with pedestrians and Daff would be forced to park a block or two back in one of the residential streets, but time was on her side. A green Range Rover pulled out in front of her and she was able to snag the thirty-minute parallel park. The pawn shop was on the opposite side of the street and a few shops up. She grabbed the handbag, avoiding Liam's gaze and crossed the dappled street without looking.

A car honked. "Jesus! You trying to get yourself killed?" The ghost fell into step beside her. "Okay, clearly you're upset. I think you should go home, I don't know that you should be—"

Daff turned into the entryway of the pawn shop before he had a chance to finish. Its glass door was held open by a cast iron cat whose upturned face pointed towards that black and white sign that read OPEN. The shop was a storage container of unwashed winter blankets, incomplete sets of glassware and lived-in furniture. It was stale and dim and dusty. A man in a baggy button-up short-sleeve shirt was behind the counter. Curly white hair poked through his open collar, encompassing his arms and jaw, everywhere but the crown of his head. He sat in a fold-out camping chair, his feet propped on top of a nearby box, ankles crossed.

Liam stepped in front of her. "What are we doing here?"

"Browsing, buying or bartering?" The man looked up from his magazine.

Daff stepped around Liam and headed towards the counter while she pulled the watch from her handbag. "Bartering."

She dropped the watch into his upturned hand.

He licked his thumb and gave the already clean glass a quick wipe. "Does it work?"

"It is working." She indicated the ticking hand, noting the clouded appearance of his eyes and wondered whether the man had actually been reading his magazine.

"There's a scratch on the glass. That'll affect the price." Maybe his eyes weren't so bad after all.

"You're selling the watch?" Liam's voice was tight but controlled. "Don't do this, please."

"I'll take whatever you think it's worth." Daff wanted to explain that the money was irrelevant; it was freedom she was after. "I'm decluttering, and rather than throw it out I thought I'd pass it on to someone else who could use it."

"Your husband knows you're getting rid of this?"

Daff glimpsed at Liam, who was looking at the watch. "I don't have a husband."

"Good. 'Cos once you trade it in that's it. No takesy backsies." The man slid the watch onto a book that lay open on the counter and began scribbling some notes onto the clean page. A ledger, Daff thought. A very casual one.

"Look, I don't really know what's happened this morning, but please don't do this, Daff. I need your help. I can't stay like this."

The man turned towards the register, pulled out a twenty and held it towards Daff. "That's the best I can do, lovey."

"Don't take it. Come on, Daff. Please."

She hesitated.

The man sighed. "You drive a hard bargain lovey, I'll give ya twenty-five." And he slid a pink note on top of the orange one.

Daff took the notes, thanked him and headed for the door.

"Are you kidding me?" Liam followed, his control loosening. "You're seriously leaving me here? I can't believe you're just gonna pike out like this." Daff stepped out onto the street, knowing that Liam wouldn't be able to follow her for much longer. "Daff come on, you can still get the watch back! *Please!*"

She crossed Main, got into the car and pulled out. Her eyes fixed upon the traffic and the pedestrian crossing, though she saw none of it; all her attention was on Liam standing on the footpath, shouting and cursing and pleading as she slowly drove past. White knuckles. Sweating palms. One night, a hundred years ago (or three), Tom told her that when he was a teenager, his old man forced him to put down the family dog, Max, who had been deteriorating before their eyes for the better part of a year. Said it would be character building. Tom had never cried so hard in his life. Killing Max was one thing. Hopping back into the Ute, his dad driving because Tom's whole right arm was still rattling from the kick back, and driving back into town while his loyal kelpie remained behind to rot beneath the ghost gums was the "shittest thing" he'd ever done. Daff flicked on the indicator, wiped her nose with the back of her hand and told herself not to look back.

Daff swung into her usual park, third on the right of the rear entrance, and killed the ignition. The lot was near empty with only two other vehicles parked: the receptionist, Nancy's red Getz and the cleaner's grey panel van. Daff entered through the rear door and found Nancy in the tearoom rummaging through the fridge for her lunch.

"Afternoon." Daff stuffed her handbag into her locker and pulled out her uniform. "Are you the only one in today?"

"Yup. Last service finished an hour ago, gonna have some lunch, finish off my paperwork and have me an early Friday."

"My work plan?"

"Already on the runner. You okay, lady? You look pastier than usual."

Daff mumbled something about a bad night's sleep and told Nancy to enjoy her early finish.

"Will do. I'll tell the cleaners to let you know when they're leaving. You got keys to lock-up after?"

Daff nodded and headed towards the bathroom to change. Her stomach had knotted itself into a ball of guilt. She took a few deep breaths, hoping it would unwind, but the action only reminded her of the meditation teacher's advice: breath into the areas of your body where you feel discomfort. The knot grew tighter. Despite the physical discomfort, Daff found a moment to appreciate the silence of the ladies' bathroom—no guests, no staff, no talking invisible men—while she slipped on the stiff and airless theatre gown and heavy boots. She exhaled the breath she'd been holding, only to take in the scent of hospital-grade disinfectant and lavender hand soap, smells that felt as familiar and comforting as blooming jasmine or loose-leaf tea, making her stomach relax a little.

In the morgue, Daff spotted her work plan dangling from the metal runner opposite her work bench and washing stations. Two names appeared on the sheet: Beth Dawson and Jake Reilly. If neither body had experienced much trauma, Daff calculated that she'd be finished by six.

She wondered what kind of trauma Liam may have experienced prior to his death. Melissa had mentioned his heart. Daff shook the thought away, slid open the coldroom door and stepped into a room that was the size of a double carport. There were two racks against the wall opposite her and one either side; all were full. Daff quickly checked the wrist bands on the female bodies. Eventually, she found the one she was looking for.

"Hi Beth, I'm Daff. Nice to meet you." It was a habit she'd picked up during her apprenticeship; most of the embalmers at Dean & Clayton's did it. Some might find this introduction silly, even morose, but Daff thought it was no sillier than talking to a pet; they can't understand you either.

It was clear that Beth Dawson had not died peacefully. The Y autopsy incision that crossed her torso was neatly stitched; the pathologist had done a good job. It was the short deep cut across Beth's throat that unsettled Daff as she reached up instinctively to check the condition of her own larynx. The cause of death was obvious, but Daff knew an autopsy was necessary regardless. It was standard procedure with a sudden, suspicious or unnatural death. For a moment, she wondered what the pathologist had found, then she wiped a hand over her brow and told herself to get her head back to work. She wasn't a pathologist or a cop; she was an embalmer and that's all she needed to worry about.

Dean & Clayton's Funeral Home was reasonably well equipped. Though Beth's frame was slight, Daff was thankful for both the 2.5 tonne forklift and the vertical hoist. She slid the forklift's arms beneath the body tray and gently escorted Beth back into the morgue before attaching the hoist around the tray and lowering Beth onto the wash bay.

Beneath the stark fluorescent lights, Daff could see the splotchy green bruises that covered Beth's neck and a large purple bruise blooming on the right side of her forehead—the kind you could get from hitting your head on a steering wheel. The kind of whack that took weeks to heal. Daff had experience with that. She checked Beth's age and swallowed hard: twenty-seven. The same age as herself. The young ones always got to her. She remembered how awful it had been to sit and listen to Tom's eulogy, not only because it was his, but because of the eulogy itself. It had been so impossibly short that she'd felt certain they'd left something out, which of course they had—the rest of his life.

Liam probably didn't have a funeral.

The knot returned as Daff wiped her eyes with the palms of her hands and resumed her work. She unravelled the wash hose while paying close attention to the minute muscular mechanics of her own body: the fattening of her thumb muscles as she gripped the hose, the pull of tendons in her legs as she circled the table, the tightening of her neck muscles as her head rotated. Once Beth was washed and dried, Daff wheeled out the embalming machine, and the formaldehyde sloshed around in the tall plastic cylinder. Mr Clayton had trained her, and she remembered how he'd always said that methanol smelt like pickles. Daff figured that Mr Clayton didn't care for pickles.

Daff had only just completed her Bachelor of Forensic Science, but it didn't matter. After Tom died, she had no interested in pursuing a career in toxicology anyway. It wasn't all wasted though; the three years of intense anatomic study allowed her to fast track her embalming apprenticeship.

It had been a year since her first practical training session and Daff's chest expanded as she thought about how far she'd come. The deceased on that first day hadn't been a young girl, but a fair-skinned woman in her late fifties. Mr Clayton stood on the opposite side of the table, his blue scrubs bright under the fluorescent lights. A man of few words, he'd encouraged Daff through the nod of his head or the quick point of an index finger. Back then she paid little attention to the deceased's name, preferring to know as little as possible. Clayton prepared the body: washed, dried and draped it with a clean cloth for modesty. Daff assumed the day would be non-contact; she was there simply to observe. Her hopes were extinguished when Mr Clayton leaned over the table, opened the palm of his hand and presented her with a scalpel.

He pointed towards the woman's clavicle. "Make the incision here, Daphne." He always called her that, despite her reminders that she preferred Daff. Up until now, she'd only seen embalming procedures on YouTube, or in the stilled frames of her course materials. Watching and reading were very different from doing.

Daff's hands shook in unison with her head, "I'm not ready."

She was surprised by her own rebuff. *Isn't this what you've been waiting for? Working towards?*

Mr Clayton remained patient. "You are."

He straightened, but kept his finger over the clavicle as if to say, *Go on.* She moved forward, the scalpel in hand, as she pressed its sharp edge into the woman's skin. It took more pressure than she'd expected to slit open the flesh beneath the collarbone and expose the carotid artery and internal jugular vein. Daff compared the opening before her to the images she had seen online and in books: they were similar, yet different. It was like comparing a photograph against one's reflection; all the elements are there, but something gets lost in the lens.

The incision didn't bleed—as Daff knew it wouldn't—but what she hadn't expected was the smell. If stillness had an odour, this was it. It smelt like bouquet water that hadn't been changed for weeks; the botanical material rotting in the liquid. She knew this particular scent was created by the build-up of interior gases, released into the room by the offending scalpel. Knowledge of the cause did little to dampen the effect and Daff supressed the urge to wrinkle her nose or peg it shut between thumb and forefinger. Instead, she breathed out through her mouth, hoping her revulsion wasn't too obvious.

Mr Clayton nodded towards the embalming machine, "You're ready to start draining now."

Daff's stomach clenched as she picked up the narrow black hose and slipped it neatly into the incision. She completed the procedure almost unaided—a comment here, a direction there; Clayton only stepped in when it was time to push the fluid through the body. The two professionals rubbed down the deceased, encouraging the veins that once housed oxygen, nitrogen and carbon dioxide to fill instead with petrifying formaldehyde. Daff wiped her forehead with the back of her sleeve, her underarms damp from perspiration.

Clayton held up a hand, his own forehead gleaming with effort. "Well done, Daphne. How do you feel?"

"Fine."

Daff blinked, breaking the trance, returning to the room and Beth Dawson. The machine was still running even though the cylinder was empty, and Daff switched it off. She glanced at the clock and was shocked to see it was nearly four-thirty. Quickly, she closed off the incision, gave Beth her final bath and dressed her.

She'd just removed her plastic gloves when she noticed a strand of ebony hair had come loose from its set and floated across Beth's face. Daff swiped the offending hair back into place and felt her throat tighten. Her head spun. She saw a flash of carpet and a heavy boot; her own face pushed into the ground by a meaty hand; a knee pressed between her shoulder blades; a hot unexpected slice across her throat. Daff snatched back her hand and the vision disappeared.

Sweat sprouted over her brow as she tried to catch her breath. She fingered her throat, but there was no pain. Slowly, she reached out a trembling hand and touched Beth's cheek. Nothing happened. Rushing towards the sink, Daff downed a glass of water and splashed her face. *That wasn't real. It was just another hallucination.* The thought wasn't very comforting. She dried her face with the last remaining clean towel and tossed it onto the counter where it landed, with a soft thud, on top of Beth's file.

Daff pushed the towel aside and flipped open the manila folder. It confirmed what she already knew. *Cause of Death: Violence.* Daff cut beneath the professional jargon: *she was murdered.*

Daff pushed opened the morgue's heavy doors and dashed towards the lockers in the tearoom. After the reading, Melissa Sweet had scribbled her number inside Daff's organiser, though Daff never expected she'd actually want it. With no other staff members on duty, the room was empty when she entered. Swinging open her locker, she hauled out her handbag and began searching for her organiser and phone. The door to the tearoom flew open and Daff dropped the bag with a smack.

"Oh, sorry to scare you, Miss Daphne."

"Daff, please. It's fine." She clutched her chest, feeling the clamminess of her skin beneath the scrubs.

"Right, Daff. Well, you have yourself a good weekend, Miss." The cleaner waved his heavy hand as he pushed the cart out onto the back lot.

Daff nodded, even though his back was towards her. Once the staff door closed, she grabbed her handbag off the floor and plonked it onto the small white table. She pulled out the organiser and thumbed through the pages until she found Melissa's loopy script. The psychic answered in three rings. Daff was quick to cut off any pleasantries.

"I'm at work," her voice unsteady, "I was preparing a body and I saw this weird vision."

"Tell me about it, hon." Melissa's voice was both warm and serious.

"It happened when I touched her, at least, it did the first time I touched her, but then nothing happened the second time—"

"Tell me about the vision."

Daff described the rough hand that held her down, the knee that pressed into her back and the knife that cut her throat open.

"This ever happened before?"

"What do you think?" Daff exhaled. "Sorry. No, it hasn't happened before."

"We best meet up again, tonight. I can talk you through some things. Were you wearing the watch when this happened?"

The watch. Daff adjusted the top of her scrubs even though the shirt was straight. She considered hitting the 'end call' button, but wondered what would happen when she returned to the morgue; if she looped the hoist around Beth's body, if she accidently touched the dead girl's sleeve, what vision would she see then?

"No, I wasn't wearing the watch. I … I got rid of it this morning. I sold it to a pawnshop in town."

There was a pause. "Okay, hon. That's fine, we can fix this. I'll come pick you up."

Daff glanced at the clock above the sink. "It's nearly five; the shop'll be closed."

"See ya in ten, hon." The phone went dead.

Melissa Sweet was true to her word, swinging her black Ford Focus into the funeral home's lot minutes after Daff had finished locking up. Daff opened the passenger door and took her seat. "Is this gonna take long? I still have one body to prep."

Melissa raised one perfect plucked brow. "You know hon, it's amazing what you can learn off YouTube."

Daff nodded in agreement, though she had no idea what the psychic was talking about.

For the second time that day, Daff found herself on Main Street. She expected Melissa to pull up onto one of the side streets, but instead, she turned down a narrow lane that led to a car park at the back of a row of shops. The slim lot housed nothing but a filthy dumpster and a pile of upended milk crates. Melissa parked beside a faded blue door, the back entrance to the pawn shop. The latch gleamed with the last rays of sun.

Daff suddenly realised why they were out the back of a closed shop, and she was surprised to find she didn't care. "You're not worried about someone seeing us?"

Melissa looked around the empty staff car park. "Not really."

Daff tapped her window and pointed up towards a black plastic dome secured beneath a short awning. "We should just come back in the morning—I don't want to get arrested and it's not like the watch is going anywhere."

"First of all, the camera is fake. You really think the owner of a pawn shop is going to go to the effort of installing a security camera? Uh-uh." The psychic waved a finger. "And secondly, we'll get the watch now. Ya can't leave your guy in there all night."

"He's not my guy."

The psychic popped open her door. "There's a black pouch inside the glove box, hon, can ya get that out for me?"

Daff opened the glove box and handed over the pouch. "You're not worried about this coming back on you, like, karmically?"

Melissa shook her head, reached into her pocket and brought out a small glass bottle the size of a sample perfume. Inside there was a delicate gold cross surrounded by floating red glitter. "I picked this up from a Filipino witch doctor for 2000 pesos. Karma can't touch me."

Daff wondered how often the psychic relied on that small bottle's false sense of protection, and for a moment she felt her respect for Melissa dim—until she remembered that it was her actions that had brought them here.

The two women approached the door and Melissa crouched down, unfolding the pouch across her knee. "This lock is a pin tumbler." Daff stared at her blankly. "The plain jane of locks?" Daff shrugged, showing no sign of recognition. "What I'm sayin' is that this should be easy."

The psychic withdrew two tools and mumbled their names; the pick rake looked like a nail file and the tension wrench was shaped like an L. She moved quickly then, slipping the wrench into the base of the key hole and lifting it before sliding the file on top. Her hand circulated the pick forward, around, back and down. She continued the scrubbing action until, at last, they heard the click of the dropped lock pins. The door opened and Melissa stepped back. "Go on hon, I'll wait."

Daff hesitated. This was basically a break and enter. *No, that's actually exactly what it is.* "Really, what harm would it do if Liam stays here the night? I can just come back in the morning and buy the watch back."

Melissa folded her arms across her chest. "I don't reckon Liam would agree with that."

"Right." Daff nodded, her face flushing. She turned and stepped into the small dark room, thankful that Melissa had opted to remain outside. The only thing more embarrassing than apologising to a ghost would be doing it in front of an audience. She patted the wall in search of a light switch before remembering that she was breaking into a premise; she'd have to wait until her eyes adjusted. Eventually, familiar shapes emerged from the darkness: a column of stacked boxes lined the wall to the right, a fold-out card table was plonked in the centre of the room, weighed down by a stack of newspapers, and the kitchenette was littered with plates, mugs and dirty glasses.

She moved towards the beaded curtain that separated the kitchenette from the shop front and jumped as a metallic crinkle sounded beneath her foot; an empty chip bag. With the windows and front door sealed, the stink of mouldy fabric was even stronger. The setting sun streamed through the shop window, casting enough light for Daff to manoeuvre around the stacked shelves and racks, heading towards the front counter. The watch was lying on the proprietor's ledger as if he'd forgotten about it the moment she'd left.

Daff picked it up and scanned the room, but there was nothing familiar amongst the gradients of shadows. "Liam?" She glared into the darkness, willing him to emerge.

"Hon!" The psychic voice called from the back. "We gotta move it!"

Daff looked down at the watch, her hand sweating in the tight grip as she pocketed it and headed back towards the kitchenette.

"You came back."

She jumped, but relief quickly followed. "I did." She turned, confronted his guarded face and was about to apologise before remembering they didn't have time. "I'll explain in the car." With the watch in her pocket, Daff exited the pawnshop, knowing Liam had no choice but to follow.

"You be sure to call me after knock off." Melissa's Ford Focus rumbled quietly in the back lot of Dean & Clayton's Funeral Home. When Daff didn't immediately agree, the psychic pressed further. "I don't go pickin' locks for just anyone, so don't be givin' me that silent treatment, hon."

"I'm going to be a couple of hours; it'll be late when I finish." The car's digital display showed that it was nearing seven.

"Do I look like an early riser?"

With her heavy eyeliner and black Motorhead t-shirt, it seemed likely that Melissa had probably watched most of her sunrises from the wrong end of the day.

"I'll call you."

"Good."

Daff got out of the car and waited until the psychic pulled out onto Bulcock Street before she unlocked the staff door. Liam, who hadn't spoken since they'd left the pawn shop, stood with arms crossed and jaw hard.

"I'm sorry." Daff slid the key home and wondered how easily Melissa would be able to pick this lock. "I was upset and I didn't know what to do."

The tearoom was a sort of *déjà vu* as Daff, yet again, crammed her handbag into her locker and pulled out the scrubs she'd worn earlier. She tossed the watch, ergo Liam, into the hallway, before quickly dressing, re-collecting the timepiece and returning to the morgue. Liam remained silent—which was a waste, Daff thought, since she was the only staff worker on, so they could speak freely. Apparently, her apology had not been enough.

She pushed open the morgue doors and felt a momentary relief to see that everything was just as she left it. "I wanted things to return to normal, but clearly that's not going to happen now."

Liam's jaw clenched and he maintained his stoic stance.

"I don't know what you want me to say. I already said I was sorry." Without meeting his eyes, she returned to her work plan, searching for the next name on the list.

"That was a shit move." The words cut through his teeth. "You don't understand what this is like."

A pile of manila folders rested on a nearby desk. Thumbing through the stack she searched for the one corresponding to the deceased, afraid the knot would return to her stomach if she looked up at him. "What this is like? You think this has been easy for me?"

"I'm dead, you bloody princess; pretty sure I got the shitter end of the stick. Tied to a fucking watch and a selfish brat that can't get over the fact that her boyfriend died. You're choosing not to help me because you're too busy sticking your head in the sand."

Daff's jaw clenched as she thumbed through the folders, though she'd long forgotten the name she was looking for. "We'd been together three years; he wasn't just a *boyfriend.* I stuffed up with the watch yes, but I got it back and I've said sorry. So, you can continue to stand there being pissed at me or you can get over it."

"What happened?"

"Excuse me?"

"You came back for the watch. Why?"

Daff returned to the work plan, checked the name again, made it look like she was doing something official. "I'm not quite sure what happened. I saw … something." She turned and looked at him for the first time since she'd retrieved him. "I spoke with Melissa. She'll come over tonight when I finish here and we'll get this all straightened out."

Liam released his arms before scratching the back of his head. "So, this is your office?" He circled the room before stopping in front of a large sliding steel door. "Is this where you keep …"

Daff stepped forward and gripped the chrome handle. "The bodies? Yeah, it is. It's not unlike what you'd find in a commercial kitchen."

She slid the door open and stepped into the fridge. Beth Dawson lay on the rack closest to the door and Daff cautiously stepped past her. Shifting her focus towards the male bodies in the room, she checked each wrist band until she found the name that matched her work plan: *Jake Reilly*.

"Hi Jake, I'm Daff." She whispered. Starting up the forklift, she took a small pleasure in seeing Liam's eye widen as she neatly slipped the vehicle's arms beneath the tray and carried Jake out into the morgue. Once Jake was set up on his table, she retrieved the top file off her desk and checked the death certificate.

Liam leaned over the young man as though he were only asleep. "Never trust a man with two first names."

"Traditionally speaking, Reilly *is* a last name. Now, stop distracting me, else we'll be here all night." Daff waved him away and searched the certificate for an age: Twenty-one.

There was a deep gash on his forehead and bruising around the neck. The cut would require adhesive, but the bruising could be hidden with cosmetics and a high collar. The cause of death was listed as a motorcycle accident. He looked like the type too. His shaved head gave the sharp angles of his face a mean quality. Rough tattoos dotted his arms, chest and stomach. Spider webs were etched into each elbow, a hula girl danced over his heart and a blotchy Southern Cross covered the back of his right hand. There were swallows, a reaper, a pirate ship and an anchor. The strangest, though, was a simple circle on the top of his arm, slashed by a slanted line.

"And I thought you were chatty at home."

Daff looked up and realised she'd been staring. She coughed dryly, snapping the folder shut. "I could have left the watch in the tearoom you know." Liam's jaw clenched and she instantly regretted the threat.

Returning to the task at hand, she unravelled the hose from the bench behind her and turned the tap. The water ran over the steel table in ripples, reminding Daff of the watering hole she'd played in as a child, only this water was clean and cool instead of thick and muddy. The Beerwah Waterhole—called the Boiler by the locals—was a good hour's drive from their home, so Daff was surprised when her old man came home early, on a blisteringly hot day, and suggested that they head up there for a swim. Jon Lawrence wasn't a playful man. For him, police work had always come first. On nights when he did come home early, he would shower, eat dinner and collapse on the couch. But that day at the Boiler was different; *he* was different. He laughed. He swam. He was *there*. Daff shook her head. She hadn't thought about that day with her father and the river in years.

Liam waved a hand in front of Daff's face. "Careful, love, I think you're in danger of drooling."

"What?" Daff patted her face and realised she'd been staring again.

"Now that you've finished checking out this stiff, how's about we nut out some kind of a plan?"

She could have corrected him, but that would only lead to more questions and she didn't feel like talking about her dad. "We will." Daff shut off the valve, grabbed a towel and started to pat down the body, wishing Liam could give her a hand. "I've three days off starting tomorrow. That will give us some time to work out … whatever this is."

The file lay open, displaying a photograph of a younger Jake, pre-tattoos. He looked about fifteen, his cheeks were flushed and face damp from perspiration. He wore a blue cap backwards. Daff wondered what sport he'd been playing that day as she pulled out the dyes needed to recreate his colouring. His cheeks had sunk and hands withered too; both would need plumping up. *Humectant will help with that.* She opened a drawer and drew out the syringe needed for the restorative fluid.

"You would have said something, right? If you'd seen me … in here." Liam stood back, crossing his arms over his chest.

Daff's mental work plan vanished in an instant. "Of course, but that would be impossible. Funeral homes don't take John Does."

"You think I'm a John Doe?"

She nodded. Between Peta's theory of unfinished business, Melissa Sweet's psychic reading and Liam's amnesia, it was the best hypothesis Daff could come up with. If Liam had died peacefully, surrounded by family and friends, then why couldn't he remember them? Funerals are for the living, but they must serve some purpose for the dead. If his body had been properly prepared, buried or cremated, then why had he come back?

Melissa said there was a connection between Liam's death and a sharp chest pain. She couldn't rule out foul play, but he looked *so* damn normal: attractive, tall, white, middle-class, ordinary. He could have had a heart attack in a remote location, his body never found. If he had been discovered (even without a wallet), it wouldn't take long for coroners to ID the body. Of course, neither of them knew how long Liam had been dead. She'd found Liam's watch at Golden Beach, a highly populated slim strip of sand with little vegetation. If he'd died there, his body would have been quickly discovered.

Drowning was a possibility, though unlikely. The Pumicestone Passage that carved the eastern boundary of Golden Beach was a flat channel with a reasonable pull, but the water was clear and rarely deeper than two metres. She doubted that its currents would have the strength to overpower Liam's lengthy and lightly muscled frame. Plus, if he *had* drowned, someone would have seen. Daff could go back and look for more clues, but she doubted there'd be anything to find. She couldn't question the staff at the lifesaving club, coffee shops or other facilities because there were none—the closest were at Bulcock Beach, four kilometres away. Someone may have seen Liam if he'd strolled the popular walkway that connected the two beaches, but how would Daff even broach that subject? *Hey! So, I was wondering … about five days ago did you see a tall, pale man with brown hair walk by?*

Liam stepped forward, breaking Daff from her reverie. "A John Doe, eh? So, you think that if I do have family, they may not even know that I'm gone?"

"I'm sure someone knows. We just need to find them."

Daff snapped on her latex gloves and poured the two-to-one ratio of preserving fluid and water conditioner into the embalming cylinder. The scalpel felt cold as she leaned over to make the small incision above the clavicle to expose the carotid artery. Her left hand pressed lightly into Jake's shoulder and she felt her head spin. Her knees weakened beneath her, she reached out to grip the steel table for support—but it wasn't there.

Daff blinked against the sudden light. The sun was so bright on the water, but she was standing in the shade. She looked around. She knew this place. That water was the Mooloolah River, and above her was the short bridge that connected the Brisbane Road to Kawana. She was standing beneath it on a narrow concrete walkway. She could hear the traffic travelling along Nicklin Way, heading north towards the beach and south towards the shopping centre. Daff pushed back the hood of her jacket and ran a hand over her cleanly shaved scalp, though she hadn't consciously decided to do either. Her hands were bigger now, broader across the back with long fingers and short nails. A Southern Cross was inked into the back of her right hand. Her mind swirled. *What's happening? Why can't I stop this?*

Daff was wearing a leather jacket and she could feel herself sweating inside it. She wanted to unzip it, but her hands slipped into the pocket of her jeans instead. There was something in the right one, a roll secured with a rubber band. *Cash.*

"Jake, you're early."

Daff swivelled and nodded involuntarily. A tall man in jeans, biker boots and a bandanna was walking towards her. "How did those lads go?"

She pulled out the wad of cash and dropped it into the tall guy's hand. "All good, bro. Where's Henry at?"

The tall man slipped the roll into the front pocket of his jeans while glancing left and right. "Not your fucking problem mate. We'll be back in a month. Meet me back here. Same time."

"Wait, Henry's gonna patch 'em, right? The boys aren't gonna keep doing all this for nothin'. Ya gotta make 'em members."

The tall bloke sneered, hawked and spat at Jake's feet. "What the fuck did you just say? You tellin' me how it is, eh? Them fucking pups got their cut. I don't need any shithead new members, what I need is dealers. You got a problem with that?"

Daff shook her head.

"Fucking right." The man turned and strode off the way he'd come.

Daff turned and went in the opposite direction. Boiling rage coursed through her veins. *Fuckin' dirt-bag talk to me like that. I'm the one out there risking everythin'. Go sell your own fuckin' coke … mate!* Jake ranted and raved, though Daff longed for him to stop, for fifteen minutes until they reached Jessica Park. There was a silver Kawasaki Ninja parked beneath the shade of a banyan tree. She grabbed the open-face helmet off the hand grip and shoved it on, swung a leg over the seat, turned the key, flicked the ignition switch and pulled out onto Nicklin Way. Daff heard the screech of tyres. Her body flung forward—

"Daff! Daff! Jesus, get up! Wake up!"

Daff tried to cover her eyes against the stinging fluoro light; a web of pain spread across the back of her head. "What the hell happened?"

"You're asking me?" Liam cried. "Christ, I don't know! You were about to cut up old mate and then *boom*—you collapsed. I thought you'd carked it the way your head smacked the floor."

She sat up cautiously, using the cabinets for support. She'd kill for a glass of water, but right now standing felt like an impossibility. "I think I was just in Jake's body." The statement sounded even more idiotic out loud. The vision she'd experienced when touching Beth had been a single moment. She'd felt Beth's fear and the tight grip around her neck, but the memory had been fleeting. "The death certificate said he died in a motorcycle accident."

"Okay?" Liam stared at her, baffled.

"He pulled out without giving way." Daff's head spun as she pieced together the vision with the facts. "Jesus, that was Jake's last memory. I just relived Jake's final moments."

"You can do that?" Liam dropped down beside her, his face momentarily blank. She was about to answer, but he cut her off, his features returning to their usual brightness. "Do you know what this means? Shit! If we can find my body, then you'll know what happened to me."

Daff held back a dry laugh. If finding Liam's body was so damn easy she would have done it by now. "Hold on. I have no idea what just happened and I definitely don't know if it's going to happen again. Just shut up for a minute."

Liam looked like that was the last thing he wanted to do, but instead of arguing he slid into position beside her. Daff pressed the back of her head against the cupboard, relieved that she was once again in control of her actions. Her heart was racing as the memory replayed again and again, though she wanted it to stop. She pushed up the sleeves of her undershirt and tugged at the collar as she broke into a sudden sweat. Her body was going into shock. *Why the hell didn't he look?* There was no way to be certain that the memory was authentic, but Daff couldn't ignore the violent reaction of her body. "You said I fell; did you see anything else?"

Liam shook his head. "You looked like you were in a trance and then you just collapsed."

Daff palmed the cabinets as she rose to her full height. She took a deep breath and the air burned against her dry throat, making her eyes water. She didn't know if it was the shock of the accident that forced her from the memory or whether it had been her body instinctively protecting itself. Either way, she didn't want to think about what may have happened if she'd stayed in Jake's body during those final critical moments.

She glanced at Liam, his eyes as big as saucers. Filled with concern. And hope. She looked away and tried to swallow, but the action failed to relieve her sore throat. Conversations with dead people was something that only happened on sentimental television shows and psychic radio programs. This doesn't happen to sensible people. Sensible people understand grief; death. They know that there is no life beyond life. That when someone dies, they are gone.

"This is bullshit."

"What?"

She looked at him again. Willed his brown eyes to turn blue, his skin to darken, his hair to shorten, the features of his face to shift into something familiar: the face of a beloved. "Nothing."

It took longer than normal to finish preparing Jake's body; Daff's hands shook badly and she found herself dropping instruments as she picked them up. Jake Reilly hadn't been a good man, but as she rolled him back into his cold chamber and closed the door, Daff thought it strange that for once she had an answer to the question: *Who were you?*

CHAPTER 10

Detective Lawrence

Friday July 1, 2016

McPhee and Lawrence spent two hours gathering statements from every member of the Jackals, and they were all sticking to the same story: they were at the clubhouse from eight on Wednesday night, through until early Thursday morning. Apparently, Wednesday night was poker night. Whether or not any poker got played was another matter. Lawrence was determined to crack the nineteen-year-old nom, Blake, but the whippersnapper gave nothing away. He knew *something*; they all did, but it wasn't the seventies any more. Lawrence couldn't beat it out of them.

When they arrived back at the station, Lawrence collapsed into his desk chair and cracked open the plastic container that separated him from his egg and lettuce sanga. He'd grabbed a coffee too, his third that day, even though the convenience store attendant always burned it. He bit into the fluffy white bread while trying to convince himself that its few flimsy green leaves counted as a salad. Though the Jackals' statements needed to be typed up, Lawrence wanted to switch tasks for a bit. Thinking that the images from the Sundowner scene would be up on the photo log by now, he took another bite of his sandwich and logged onto his computer.

Lawrence skipped over the images of Beth's and Sarah's bodies, not because he had a weak stomach, but because he was more interested in the photos of the room. His face hovered inches from the monitor as he zoomed in on the messed-up bed, the stained carpet, the bathroom vanity. He didn't stop until he reached the series of photographs of the blood-smeared mirror.

A mouthful of egg and bread lodged in his throat. The images were all distorted. Every single one of them. *Shit.* Of course, the photographer botched up those photos, Lawrence thought. The only damn photos that contained any evidence. Pushing back the papers on his desk, the detective made a note on his dated desk calendar to send Officer Gibbs back over to the motel. Maybe he'd take a decent photo this time. Lawrence took a swig of his coffee, hoping it would help the sandwich down, and noticed the red light on his desk phone was blinking. Pen still in hand, he picked up the receiver and hit the message button.

"Detective Lawrence, hello, it's Heather Miller. I found something that you might find interesting. Call me back."

Lawrence scribbled down the number, though he needn't have worried since he planned on calling her back right away.

McPhee walked in and pulled up a chair as Heather answered the phone. "Hello?"

"Hi—yes—it's Detective Lawrence returning your call."

There was a brief pause, as though Heather had somehow forgotten why the detective would be ringing her. "You said you found something?"

"Oh yes, that's right. I'd prefer to discuss this in person, you never know who is listening."

Lawrence dropped his pen into his front pocket. "My partner and I can meet you in thirty minutes. Are you home?"

"No, not here at the house."

"Has something happened?"

McPhee raised an eyebrow and Lawrence shook his head.

"No, no, nothing's happened. Not like that. Thank you for the extra security too."

Lawrence appreciated the thanks; house security was expensive and he'd had a hell of a time getting that detail approved. "Where can I meet you?"

"Santini's. It's an Italian restaurant in the city. It's popular, so you can google the address, you know."

Lawrence placed a hand over the mouth piece and told McPhee to go make a start on typing up the club's statement. The detective barely concealed his eye roll as he left Lawrence's cubical and headed towards his own.

"Heather, I'm a simple fella, but it almost sounds like you're asking me out on a date."

"We'll you mustn't be too simple, because I am."

Lawrence cleared his throat and adjusted his collar. "That wouldn't be appropriate."

"It's just dinner, Detective, I'm not asking you to take your shoes off. Would you like the information or not?"

Lawrence cleared the desk with his forearm, exposing a blank square on his old desk calendar. "I'm not so good with computers, can you give me the address?"

McPhee reappeared cradling his laptop to his chest. "Found something."

The detective held up an index finger to indicate he needed another moment; he noted down the restaurant's address, told Heather he'd meet her there and hung up.

McPhee eyed the cradled phone and scrawled address. "We doing another interview?"

"Nah, it's personal, I mean it's not *personal* but it's not … I don't know. You said you got something?" Lawrence nodded at the laptop and pushed a pile of scrap paper aside.

McPhee returned to his seat and flipped open the laptop. Clicking on his browser, he pulled up a website whose existence continued to baffle Lawrence; though he had to admit that it was occasionally useful. Strange how folks can be more honest online than they can be with a cop.

"If you're here to show me your updated profile photo, I've got better things to do." The detective didn't know much of the lingo, but he enjoyed tossing it about whenever he could: show them pipsqueaks that he wasn't such a crusty old dinosaur after all.

"Why waste time showing you my profile pic when I've already set it as your lockscreen?" McPhee grinned as Lawrence pulled out his phone and then sighed with relief when he saw that McPhee was pulling his leg.

"So, I was checking out old mate's profile—" McPhee began.

"Who's *old mate*?"

"Our buddy Blake." McPhee typed the nom's full name into the Facebook search bar and clicked on the third profile on the list of results, then on the *about* tab, then on another that said *work and education*. "Blake's nineteen yeah? And look, he went to Kelvin Grove."

Lawrence leaned closer to the computer. According to the profile, Blake had attended the prestigious state college, but what the page didn't tell him was why that was important. "And?"

McPhee's grin broadened. Returning to the search bar, he typed in Beth Dawson and clicked on the right face. The first post on her page was a series of hearts and crying emojis followed by the brief message:

WTF?! I can't believe this is happening! I MISS YOU!!!!!!!!

Lawrence's stomach hardened. Instead of scrolling down the page to read similar messages of grief and sympathy, McPhee followed the same series of links he'd clicked on before and arrived at the same result. He ran his index finger beneath the school name. "Kelvin Grove State College."

"They knew each other."

"Want to find out how well?"

McPhee pulled up Blake's profile, picked the phone up from the cradle, and was dialling the nom's number before Lawrence had a chance to answer.

***

Blake Kingstone took his seat opposite the detectives. He wore the same faded shirt and unconvincing expression of malice that he'd had on a few hours earlier. It was obvious that he'd never been interviewed at a police station before. The small windowless office contained one table and four chairs, yet his eager eyes were hungry to take in every inch of the unremarkable room.

"Good of you to come in so quickly." McPhee had taken the seat closest to the laptop and microphone. Lawrence gave him the nod and the detective set the laptop up to record.

The senior detective told the wannabe-biker that he had the right to remain silent, pointless given that Blake had agreed to the interview. Still, rules are rules. "Please state your name and address."

"Blake Lewis Kingstone. One hundred and sixty-three Gordon Street, Paddington."

Lawrence suppressed a grin. He knew the lofty suburb of Paddington well. He also knew that a nineteen-year-old couldn't afford that kind of rent and he made a mental note to give the kid's parents a bell after the interview—see if they're aware of their son's entrepreneurial activities. "How well did you know Beth Dawson?"

"Like I said before, I don't know her."

McPhee pulled a photo out of the manila folder that lay in front of him and slid it across the table. "Maybe this will help."

Blake glanced at Beth's smiling face, her cap, her gown, and shook his head. "Nope. Sorry."

"Do you know where this picture was taken?" Lawrence tapped the glossy image.

The nom shrugged and glared at the wall behind his interrogators.

"Kelvin Grove's graduation ceremony, 2014. The same ceremony you would have attended if you'd stayed in school. Still, you were a student there for two years before you dropped out, plenty of time for you to become familiar with your class mates. Remember, Mr Kingstone, that concealing information from an investigating officer is a punishable offence. So, I'll ask you again, did you know Beth Dawson?"

Blake's eyes darted from the picture to Lawrence to McPhee to the picture. "There's not a lot to say."

Bull's-eye. The detective steepled his fingers and rested them against his lips, waiting.

"We went to school together, yeah but, I didn't like *know* her. Just saw her around."

McPhee picked up the photograph and tucked it back inside its folder. "Why didn't you tell us this before?"

"I dunno. It didn't seem important."

"Did you ever see Beth around after you finished school?"

Blake hesitated. Eyeing first the manila folder and then the oversized microphone beside it. After what felt like an eternity, the kid nodded. "Yeah, once."

"When?" Lawrence relaxed his hands, realised how tightly he'd been squeezing them.

"Last weekend. Saw her having drinks out in the Valley."

"Who was she with?"

Blake screwed his face up with obvious annoyance, whether it was at the question or his answer, Lawrence couldn't tell. "She was with some of the Dogs, alright? Before the tussle, I saw her hanging about with some of their crew and their girls."

"Did you recognise any of the members?"

Blake nodded, lips pursed together like maybe he could stop himself from talking. It didn't work. He rattled off half a dozen names; Lawrence wasn't surprised to hear that Henry was among them.

After the interview was wrapped up and Blake was back out on the street, Lawrence and McPhee huddled around the senior detective's desk. "Whatcha wanna do, Hitch? Track down Henry and hear his take on last weekend's punch up, or re-interview Jim's crew?"

Lawrence checked his wrist watch, he still had a couple of hours until his shift ended. "Don't worry about the whole crew, not yet anyway, but we should talk to Jim. See if he's more willing to have a chat now that the nom has cracked." He grabbed his keys and manoeuvred around the desk as his partner fell into step beside him.

McPhee pushed open the glass door that led out into the parking lot. "What do you reckon they'll do to the kid when they realise he's talked?"

"They won't give him a patch, that's for sure. Maybe knock him about a bit, tell him to bugger off. He's a kid and a nothing member, so the retaliation will be pretty minor, I imagine." At least, he hoped it would be.

Thirty minutes later, they pulled up in front of the Jackals' clubhouse. The three bikes that had occupied the curb earlier were gone, but the front door behind the flyscreen was open. The two officers swung their car doors open and crossed the front lawn, the winter-dead grass crunching beneath their feet. Lawrence was about to announce himself when a guttural voice cut in from beside him.

"What are you doin' back here?" Jim came around from the corner of the house, a rag in one hand and a half-emptied tallie in the other. "Change of heart on those possession charges, huh?"

"No," McPhee raised his chin. "We need a bit more information about what happened last Saturday night."

"I gave my statement on Saturdee and I don't have nothin' to add to it."

"You working out back?" Lawrence nodded towards the rag and beer bottle. "Don't let us hold you up, we can talk while you play shop."

"*Play.*" Jim shook his head and disappeared back the way he'd come.

McPhee looked up at his superior, who shrugged. The two followed the bikie president's lead.

The back of the clubhouse was as unimpressive as the front. A concrete slab served as both workshop and bar: a motorcycle had been rolled beneath the awning and a plastic fold-out table covered in bottles, parts and cleaning products squatted alongside it. The scent of bike polish and freshly wetted concrete filled the air. Jim took a swig from his bottle, resumed his position on an upended crate and returned to the task at hand: buffing out his fuel tank.

"Who was there on Saturday night?" Lawrence began without preamble.

Jim snorted. "If you'd read my statement, you'd know."

"Was Sarah Miller there that night?"

The biker shrugged. "Maybe. Can't remember."

McPhee pulled out his phone, tapped the screen a few times and held up the image of Beth Dawson. "Do you recognise this girl?"

Jim's hand paused briefly. "Why?"

"This is Beth Dawson. Her remains were found with Sarah Miller's." Lawrence stepped closer, was about to rest his hand on the tail guard and then thought better of it. "We need to know if Sarah and Beth were there on Saturday night, before the fight."

"'Cos you think I got one of my boys to kill them?" Jim snorted again. He was good at that. "I don't kill sluts. Even ones that lie with Dogs."

McPhee slipped the phone back into his pocket. "Timing's kinda crazy though. Henry and your clubs going at it on Saturday night, then a few days later two women associated with the Dogs are killed …"

"It doesn't look good." Lawrence added.

Jim put his bottle down with more force than was necessary and rose to his full height. "I didn't kill no girls."

"There was some suspicious evidence at the scene—"

"Then why are you standing there watchin' me polish my ride? You got nothin' on me. I don't like Henry, but I ain't gonna kill his missus 'cos of it and that's all you got to know."

"Can you tell us who Beth was with that night?"

"Couldn't tell ya, *mate*."

Lawrence cut a look towards McPhee, who replied with a reluctant nod. "Alright then. We'll be in touch."

"I hope not." Jim muttered under his breath as he turned his back on the coppers and returned to his bike maintenance.

Back in the car, Lawrence buckled his seatbelt and pushed down the window, but he didn't start the ignition. Bikers are professional liars. They have to be. That's how they survive. He hadn't expected a confession and he didn't get one; yet the venomous tone of Jim's response had convinced him, mostly, that the Jackals were innocent—of this homicide anyway.

***

Later that night, Lawrence slipped a notebook and pen into the back of his jeans. Heather may think their meeting was some sort of date, but the detective was determined to treat it as a casual interview. The fact that he had showered and splashed on some aftershave was beside the point. That was simply called being polite.

Heather had arrived early and reserved a table for them. "We didn't make a booking, so I thought this the best solution." She was wearing a white flimsy blouse and her wispy blonde hair had been pinned in a loose bun at the back of her head. When Lawrence had seen her from across the room, he'd done a double take. From that angle, in that light and with the menu opened in front of her, Heather looked just like Ruth. He felt awkward enough without adding marital guilt to the mix. When the hipster waiter appeared at their table, Lawrence ordered an *Old Fashioned*: straight whiskey over ice with a twist of orange peel. It was a cocktail that had been around forever, but the waiter's approval would make you believe it was the latest trend. Time was circular like that, the old coming back disguised as something new.

"Shall we have entrees?" Heather peered over the menu. "Or save room for dessert?"

"Heather, why did you ask me here?"

"I recommend the scampi linguini if you're having trouble deciding. You're not allergic to shellfish, are you? That would be a shame."

"Did Henry Ernst put you up to this?"

Heather lowered her menu. "I haven't spoken to the man since … well … you know. And why on earth would he want me to ask you to dinner?"

"It was just a thought. So, you wanted to meet me here?"

"Yes. Now, pick up your menu."

Lawrence pulled the notebook and pen out of his pocket and laid them beside his knife and fork. She had clarified her intentions; so should he. In the end, they split a garlic bread and ordered mains only. He emptied his tumbler after finishing their starter and declined a second. Heather wanted an update on the investigation before revealing her own discovery and Lawrence told her enough to make her happy without really telling her anything.

He waited until she'd finished her second wine before returning to his original line of questioning. "You said you found out something interesting?"

She nodded, and waved to the waiter for another carafe of water. "Yes. Scandalous really. I had planned to go through Sarah's things today, though there wasn't much, I just couldn't bring myself to do it any sooner." She spoke as though her sister had been dead for years, not days.

Lawrence knew widows who kept their late husbands' wardrobes intact for years, parents who left their children's rooms like time capsules, nephews who garaged their favourite uncles' cars while their latest model Prados sat on the lawn.

"Anyway, I logged on to her computer to check a few things—"

"What things were you checking?" Lawrence flipped open the notebook and regretted it; Heather shrunk back into her seat.

"Nothing sinister. My sister ran a small part-time business online, jewellery making mostly. She'd hoped it would take off enough that she could quit nursing. Anyway, I wanted to notify any new clients that the business had become defunct and that their money would be returned."

"Did you think that was something you had to do today?"

"Yes." Heather thanked the waiter as he set down a fresh chilled bottle of table water. "We're getting off topic. What I wanted to tell you is that I found an email from an editor at a boutique publishing house. Apparently, Sarah had sent them a proposal for a tell-all memoir. The title was *Sleeping with Dogs.*"

Lawrence stopped mid-scribble. "Your sister was writing a book?"

"Who knew? I'd never even seen her read before."

The email had arrived in Sarah's inbox a week ago. The editor had been looking for a new true crime pitch in preparation for the following year's winter selection. He'd liked Sarah's proposal, but he'd requested a copy of the first three chapters.

"Did you find any documents on the computer? A manuscript?"

Heather shook her head. "No, she wasn't very good at finishing things. But still, you can see why I wanted to tell you." He could.

If Henry had known his wife was writing a tell-all, that would be motive enough for murder. "Heather, I'm going to have to take your sister's computer as evidence."

The blonde nodded before downing an entire glass of water. "I expected as much. You can come and collect it tomorrow. I could give it to you tonight, but that wouldn't be appropriate."

CHAPTER 11

Daff

Friday July 1, 2016

It was an hour past Daff's usual bedtime when she at last sat down at the dining table and handed Melissa a cup of peppermint tea. The psychic listened as Daff described the quick vision of Beth's strangulation and the longer vision of Jake Reilly's final moments: the bridge, the cash, the biker and the accident.

"That's … quite a lot," Melissa's eyes widened as she took in the story. "So, you believe this deal with the bandanna biker happened under Nicklin Way? If Jake died after failing to give way, there may be a report on it. It shouldn't be too hard to verify."

"You think the vision is real, then? Have you ever known someone with this … ability?"

"Sounds real to me, hon. I've never meet anyone with this gift before, but I heard some old duck talking about it at a convention once. She said people with those kinds of gifts were called *death walkers*."

Liam, who was sprawled across the couch, let out a dry bark. "Makes you sound like a *Star Wars* extra."

"You don't remember your own name but you remember *Star Wars*?"

"Excuse me?" The psychic raised her eyebrows.

"Nothing. Sorry. Melissa, go on."

"Given your job and Liam's sudden appearance in your life, it's not all that surprising. A *death walker* is a psychic who can speak to the dead. Some connect with spirits, the way I do, through mediumship. Others read objects. You seem to experience full-blown visions. Anyway, a death walker's mission is to assist spirits through the death process."

Daff didn't think she'd helped Jake through anything. She was inside his mind, his memory, but as far as she could tell he'd had no awareness of her presence at all. She'd merely been a witness to his death. She told Melissa as much.

"You don't know what his soul needed in order to crossover. He may have just wanted someone to know what happened. Maybe he felt regret over his lifestyle? Whatever the reason, hon, your abilities are expanding—rapidly."

Daff wasn't so sure; all she knew was that she never wanted to experience that again. Being inside Jake's head was a crossover between a dream and a virtual experience, only she'd had no control over her own actions. It was frightening to be inside a body that refused to submit to her will. She'd been unable to walk away from the conversation beneath the bridge, unable to stop Jake from swinging a leg over his bike, unable to glance back over his shoulder to check if the road was clear and unable to snap herself awake before their body was thrown forward and—*This is insane*. It is scientifically impossible for a person to enter the conscious mind of another person—especially if that person is dead. *I am insane.*

Yet Daff's body told a different story. It felt the thrust of their airborne body, heard the grating of their helmet dragged across bitumen, the piercing screech of tyres, horns, crushed metal, the taste of liquid iron in their mouth. Of course, she'd experienced some of these sensations before, from the confines of her own body, in the dark of night, on a quiet highway lined with pine trees, a loss so horrific that her broken soul was now descending into madness.

Daff sipped her tea. Hoped it would wash away the memory of warm blood. This couldn't go on. The visions had occurred when she'd touched Beth's hair and, Jake's shoulder. That had to be the catalyst: physical touch. "How do I block the visions? I have to be able to do my job."

Melissa slipped her fingers through the handle of her mug and drummed them on its side. "You can try to block it out, but why would you? Darl, do you seriously think your decision to become an embalmer, your ability to re-experience a person's final memory and see ghosts—"

"Ghost." Daff held up one finger.

"Whatever, my point is, this shit ain't a coincidence. And I think you'd be making one helluva mistake if you blocked out these visions. If you want to uncover Liam's identity, you're gonna have to rely on a search engine bigger than Google. You're gonna need some cosmic juju on your side. In fact, I think it's about time we did a *vision quest*."

Daff had no idea what a *vision quest* was, but she was pretty sure she didn't want to do it. "Right, and I suppose you're wanting to do this now?"

"The only time *is* now." Melissa stood up and headed towards the door.

Daff looked at Liam, then back towards the departing psychic. "Am I supposed to be following you?"

"Oh no, no, no." The psychic waved her hand. "I just need to get the ceremonial stones out of my car."

"I've got some ceremonial stones you can use." Liam's voice was as dry as toast.

Supressing a smile, Daff ignored his comment and reluctantly pulled herself up out of her seat, too exhausted to query the psychic about her magical rocks. "Do you need a hand?"

Ten minutes later, Daff was sitting cross-legged on her lounge room floor while Melissa carefully placed nine white rocks the size of apples around her. The psychic mumbled a quiet incantation before setting each stone in position, answering Daff's questions in between chants. She explained that *vision quests* were a type of guided meditation used to gain divine insight into complicated situations or spiritual crises.

"And, hon, you're experiencing both of these." Lighting a wad of dried sage leaves, the psychic circled the room, spreading the sweet earthy smoke. "Are you ready, Daff?"

She nodded as Liam crossed the primitive circle and crouched down beside her. "Your living room looks like a poor imitation of *The Craft*."

Before Daff could laugh, Melissa instructed her to take off the watch. "Our hands are incredibly sensitive—you'll pick up more messages if you hold it. Now, close your eyes and concentrate on your breath. Very slowly, I want you to expand your awareness outwards. Listen to the sounds in this room, then stretch to the room beyond this one, stretch further, to the outside of this house, to the street, on and on as far as you can reach."

Daff heard the strike of a match, then the sharp crackle of the candle flames, the clink of Melissa's many silver bangles, the creaks and pops as the walls of her home shrunk in the cool evening air; beyond that was the low tones of crickets, and then the infinite space of a street asleep, a town now still, a region gone quiet, and the distant wailing of a siren moving closer and closer. She could see a flicker of circling lights above her: red, white and blue. It was night-time here too, only the sky was blanketed out by those bright, bright lights.

She stood up. There was a woman crying, but all Daff could see were men dressed in forest-green suits crowded around a car, folded around a tree.

"Is this really the memory you want to go back to?"

Daff turned to see Tom standing beside her. She smiled for a moment before doubt started to creep in. "Are you actually here?" *Or are you just my subconscious?*

An unexpected primal hunger clawed through her veins. She needed to feel the warmth of his skin beneath her fingertips, but she didn't reach for him; couldn't bear to see her hand pass through him the way it did with Liam.

Tom didn't answer. Instead, he took her by the arm, and Daff melted into him as they turned away from the crumpled car and the busy paramedics. He was *here*. She could feel the heat radiating from him, warming her right-side while her left remained cool. She could see the fine hairs on his arm, the constellation of freckles on his neck, smell pepper on his skin. These small, often ignored, physical traits now became vital. He was here. She could see him. Finally. They walked the length of the highway until the night became stars again.

"Where are we going?" Daff stepped off the road, following Tom as he entered some suburb she didn't recognise. She'd only lived on the coast for the last eighteen months, but she'd been coming here for holidays her entire life and she knew damn well there was no suburb here. This field was filled with pine trees, not homes. Picket Crescent, Olive Court, Bembooka Street—she'd never heard of them. "What is this, where are we, what are we doing?"

Tom stopped and pointed towards a small demountable at the end of the street. "We're looking for clues." Daff didn't understand how a crappy house in a suburb she didn't know, in a vision that probably wasn't even real, was going to solve anything.

"The sooner you accept that not everything can be explained, Daff, the sooner you can get on with things."

"How did you do that?"

"One of the perks, Miss Daphne." Tom winked and squeezed her arm.

She relished the warmth of his touch, but her interior sceptic told her to be careful: *don't get your hopes up. A vision quest is just a mystical version of a dream.* The argumentative side of her brain quickly countered: *Yes, but you can still feel in dreams.*

"It also helps that your face gives away your every thought," he added.

Eighteen months ago, Daff would have pulled her arm away and called him a jerk. Now, she clasped her hand over his. "I've accepted that Liam is a ghost and that it's my bizarre 'universal duty' to find out who he is."

Tom nodded and patted her hand before continuing towards the house. A swirl of questions filled her mind: *Where have you been? Why do I see Liam and not you? Is there a Heaven? Is that what you call it? Do you know what's happened since you've been gone? Do you forgive me?*

"Tom, are you okay?"

They stopped in front of the demountable's low brick fence. The letterbox's gold plate announced that it was number forty-eight.

"That's the only question that matters. And yes, I'm okay."

He unlatched the little metal gate that was wrapped in chicken wire and made towards the house's small porch. Daff followed, but the two giant frangipanis that stood sentry over the night garden cast dark shadows on the stone path, and she stumbled often. Tom stood in front of the door, but made no attempt to open it.

"Are we going inside?"

"It's your call, Daff."

She glanced back towards the shadowy shrubbery of this unfamiliar street in this suburb that didn't exist. "Will you come with me?"

"I'll wait."

She nodded, reaching out for the door. "Will you be here when I come out?"

He took a deep breath, but said nothing.

He always went quiet when he felt vulnerable. Or hopeless.

"I wish things were different. I wish I could stay." But she couldn't.

"I know you do." His hand graced her shoulder, leaving a trail of fire as he moved off the porch. "Do you remember the street names, Daff?"

She nodded, smothered her internal flames, twisted the doorknob and woke up.

The light was too bright and Daff squinted against burning candles, her eyes watering.

"Did you see anything?" Liam crouched in front of her.

She nodded, her throat too thick for speech.

"I'll get you some water." Melissa disappeared into the kitchen, returning a moment later with a tall, full glass.

Daff wanted to gulp it down, but then she'd have to talk, and she needed a minute to catch her breath, to unwind her chest. When Tom died, she'd accepted that she would never hear him say her name again. She'd never touch his arm or walk beside him. She thought those simple gifts were gone, but in the space of one minute, they'd all come back.

Melissa stretched out a hand, helping Daff to her feet. "What did you see?"

"A house." Daff decided to stick to the facts. "But I didn't recognise the address: Forty-eight Bembooka Street. I don't think it's here on the coast."

"Maybe it's my place? What did it look like?" Liam leaned in so close she could smell him, or she could've if he had a smell.

Daff described the house and the surrounding streets, but none of it sounded familiar to him.

The psychic had listened intently while gathering up the stones and returning them to their bag. "You got the number and the street name, hon. Five minutes on the web and you'll have a city too, but right now, you should probably get some sleep."

"Wait, Melissa, there's one more thing." The vision with Tom had given Daff an idea. "I can't go on looking like a nutter every time I need to talk to Liam in public. Is there a way we could talk, like, telepathically?"

"With the way your abilities are increasing, I reckon it's worth a try, hon. It's sort of similar to how I receive messages."

A needling pain spread through Daff's head, but she encouraged the psychic to go on. "How do I do it?"

"Come on, Daff, we don't need to do this now. Melissa looks just as stuffed as you." Liam went to brush her arm, then remembering he couldn't, dropped it lamely by his side.

"No. The only time is now, right, Melissa? So how do we do it?"

The psychic dropped the heavy bag with a thud and resumed her seat. "It's pretty straightforward, really. Clear your mind with a few deep breaths, like we did just now for the vision quest, and then concentrate on Liam. Think the thought or message you want to send and then push it out, directing it at him, like you're leaning forward. It'll take some practice—he probably won't hear you straight away and you may have to imagine that you're shouting—but you'll get there. Come on, give it a whirl."

Daff turned towards Liam—who seemed determined to look at her left ear rather than her eyes—took a deep breath and imagined her message cutting through the air between them. *Your shoe is untied.*

His face shifted. "Have you done it yet?"

Daff winced against the prickling headache. "Hold on, let's do it again." She took a deep breath and refocussed. This time, she pushed the message forward as if she were throwing a ball.

Liam glanced down at his feet. "Did you just say *shoe*?"

Daff smiled, but her grin faded quickly. "Wait, if Liam and I start communicating telepathically, how do I stop him from reading my mind?"

Liam scoffed as if he were above such things, though they both knew that he wasn't.

"He can't hear anything you don't want him to hear, hon. And vice versa. No one can read your mind unless you let 'em." Melissa stood, grabbing her weighty bag, and gave Daff a quick hug. "Now, I've got to get me some sleep. If you need anything—call."

Daff thanked Melissa and promised to keep her updated. She closed the door behind the departing psychic, feeling both exhausted and wired. She could try to sleep, but she'd probably just wind up tossing and turning, replaying the day's events. Still, Melissa was right, she needed some rest. Daff switched off the overhead light and switched on the yellow beaded lamps that sat either side of the couch. She collapsed into the sofa and flicked the throw rug across her knees.

"Wanna check the address from your vision?"

If he'd asked her a minute ago she would have said yes, but with the lights lowered and a warm blanket over her, moving felt like an impossibility. "Later."

She closed her eyes, feeling how easily she could sink into sleep. The house sighed around her, encouraged by the evening wind. Now that it was quiet, she could hear the buzzing in her ears. Ten percent of the population suffer from tinnitus: a high-pitched ringing that is usually drowned out by other noises in the environment. Most sufferers don't even notice it until they try to sleep at night or find themselves in a silent room. Tinnitus, Daff knew, resulted from a damaged auditory nerve. The part of the brain responsible for processing sound, the temporal cortex, spontaneously fires off in the absence of sound. It's amazing what people can get used to, and what they can't.

Daff had just fallen into sleep when Liam spoke again. "There was more."

"Hmmmmm?" She lifted one eye and saw Liam sitting on the opposite end of the couch. "What?"

"There was more to the vision than just the demountable."

Had she been more prepared, Daff would have brushed off the comment. Unfortunately, it takes a few minutes for sleep inertia to wear off and cognitive skills—like lying—to kick in. "The rest was private." She straightened in an attempt to clear the fog. "I told you what you needed to know."

"I think we're a little past *private,* don't you? Back when you first met Melissa, she said that you can see me for a reason, that we're supposed to be helping each other out or whatever, so …"

"So, you want to know what else I saw?"

"Maybe it'll help." He shrugged. "I've got as good an idea as you about how this stuff works."

The line was far from inspiring, but she was tired, and he might be right. "Tom was there."

"Your dead boyfriend?"

She made a face and he quickly apologised. Relenting, she snuggled further into the couch. "There *really* wasn't that much to it. It was the night of the accident—"

"Accident?"

"Yes, about eighteen months ago on New Year's Eve, I ran off the motorway and hit a tree. That's how Tom died." Daff was amazed how succinctly that moment could be described. "We talked a bit, nothing significant, I just wanted to know if he was okay."

"I'd say that's pretty significant."

The corner of her mouth lifted briefly. "Then we walked down the highway until we arrived at the demountable."

"The demountable that's not technically there."

Daff nodded: there was definitely no suburb hidden amongst the pines. She considered getting up and typing the address into Google, but the couch was too comfortable and she was too exhausted to move. "Can I ask you a few questions?"

"I don't remember anything. And believe me, I've tried."

She shook her head. "No, I was going to ask how it is you can walk through walls and sit on my couch?"

He glanced at his legs that were looped over the seat and looked pleased. "Pretty nifty, eh? It took me a little while to get the hang of it. It's pretty simple, actually, if I think about walking through the wall then I can, same goes with the couch."

"So, if you concentrate on an action, then you can do it? Have you tried to *will* your memories back or break that twenty-metre radius thing?"

"Yup and yup, but no dice. Go figure." He shrugged. "I've been giving it a crack at night while you're sleeping. Been trying to move things too, I thought I'd gotten a leaf going one night in the yard, but I'm pretty sure it was just the wind moving it. Point is, I won't be floating a penny into Demi Moore's hand any time soon."

Daff rolled her eyes. "The ghost of movies past; you sure you didn't die in the nineties?" A thought struck her, "Wait, have you seen other ghosts?"

"No." He shuffled, though the couch didn't move in response, and Daff wondered whether spirits could feel uncomfortable.

Daff couldn't understand why Liam was the only ghost she could see. Though she'd supposedly tapped into Beth and Jake's final memories and spoken with Tom, all those interactions had occurred as living daydreams, visions, images in her mind's eye; Liam was the only one to crash on her couch—so *why*? He came into her life after she'd discovered the watch and brought it home, but she couldn't brush off what had happened before that: the sudden ball of light, the shadowy figure with its outstretched hand.

Maybe Melissa was right, maybe that figure was her mother. If that was the case, why couldn't she see her now? The only thing Daff knew for sure was that everything had changed after that night. She felt her head swirl; this pondering was like a mystical version of which came first, the chicken or the egg? Only in her case, it was what broke my sanity first, the vision or the watch?

"Me neither, not really. Unless you count seeing Tom in the vision." She hesitated for a moment. "My mum's passed too, but I haven't seen her."

There was a part of Daff that would like to see Ruth again, but the other part worried over what something like that would do to her. After her parents had split, Daff had asked her mother why she continued to see Lawrence every week; Ruth had shrugged and said sometimes it was hard to let go of a person you'd known for so long. She'd been gone for four years, but the memory of Ruth's pale and failing body could still draw Daff's breath short, and she knew she couldn't say goodbye a second time.

Daff tried to brush the thought aside and focus instead on the ghost in front of her, but the memory of that ball of light had got her thinking. "You said you can't remember anything before the beach, so what exactly happened?"

He shrugged, again. "I was just there, like a movie switching scenes, only I couldn't remember what had come before."

"So, no white light, chorus of angels or bearded men?"

"There were a few bearded men, but they were all walking their dogs."

She laughed, covering her mouth.

"You look nice when you smile."

"I look *nice*?" Daff raised an eyebrow.

"Yeah."

He replied with his own grin, which she had to admit, was quite nice itself. "How long before you realised?"

"That I was dead?" The edges of his lips softened, trembled. "Well, I'm still getting used to that part. Didn't take that long really; no one could see me or hear me. For a minute, I'd thought I'd gone crazy. It wasn't until this chick jogged right through me that I realised things were a bit more complicated than that."

Looking at him now, Daff found it hard to believe that she was the only one who *could* see him. He looked as real and solid as her outstretched hand. She could see every strand of hair that graced his shoulders, the folds of fabric in his black shirt. Without her conscious decision to do so, her arm extended forward, reaching for the edge of his lintcovered sleeve. But her hand moved through Liam's arm and he shuddered. They looked like the world's strangest case of conjoined twins. She withdrew her arm, the skin prickling slightly, and looked up at Liam's amused face.

"Looks like I'm still dead then."

"Just checking."

They fell silent and for a moment Daff thought the conversation was over.

"Why did you become an embalmer?"

She'd been answering different variation of this same question for the past year or more. It hadn't taken her long to realise that *I'm a waitress* provoked fewer follow-up questions. "I was good at biology, so why not?"

"How long have you been doing it?"

"My apprenticeship was about a year; I've been qualified for the past few months." She could see him comparing the short timeframe against the invasive procedures she'd completed on Jake Reilly only a few hours before.

His eyes narrowed. "Seems like a tight turnaround."

"It's not usually that fast, but I'd just finished my science degree so I already had a solid understanding of anatomy. The apprenticeships are flexible, and I opted to fast track mine."

"You weren't ever grossed out by it? It was pretty full on in there today."

She was in her first year of high school when she made the correlation between botanical and anatomical matter. Her class had been instructed to dissect a grasshopper, and with scalpel in hand, Daff had seen no difference between the critters' fibrous legs and the stems of the gerberas in her mother's garden.

Daff pointed at the small barrel cactus plant on the coffee table in front of her. The terracotta pot was painted white with red and yellow squares, the brim dotted with blue wishing stones. Daff didn't like the pot or the plant, but she kept it because Ruth had bought it for her on a whim during a market trip, back before things had turned bad.

"You see that cactus plant?" Her throat thickened; Liam nodded. "The molecules and soft tissues that make it need air, nutrient, water and sunlight in order to survive. Sound familiar?"

"So, you drain the blood out of corpses because you think people are really plants?"

Daff massaged the space between her brows. There was nothing gory about the release of bodily fluids, the shaking out of rigor mortis or the injection of formaldehyde; and logically she knew that people were different from plants, but the moment her young mind balanced the two as equals, the belief had become deep-seated. It was a certainty that no training, text book or teacher could dismantle. "It doesn't affect me is what I'm saying."

Liam pushed further. "But you never found it creepy? Working with dead people I mean."

Daff sighed, exhaustion funnelling into her bones. "Look, I get that most people would find it creepy, but there's nothing creepy about working in a morgue. Death isn't scary, it's unavoidable. People shouldn't be afraid of their loved ones."

She'd seen the slow way funeral attendees approached the casket, not with reverence but caution. As though Aunty Betty might reach up, grasp them by the collar and pull them down for one final cold kiss.

Feeling her eyelids growing heavier, Daff took advantage of Liam's momentary silence to flick off the lamp nearest her. "No offence, but I really need to get some sleep." She was about to get up to switch off the other light when Liam stopped her. "Can you leave it on?"

"Why?"

"I'd … rather not be in the dark."

"Okay." She pulled up the blanket and closed her eyes and wondered if Liam would stay with her or resume his tests with the leaves in the garden. The couch didn't move.

When she woke, half a day later, her living room was filled with bright sunlight. She rubbed the sleep out of her eyes and checked the watch; it was two in the afternoon. She shot up, suddenly alarmed by how long she'd slept. Liam cleared his throat.

He was standing beside the single-seat recliner, a smug look plastered across his face. "Morning, gorgeous, or should I say, afternoon?"

Daff kicked off the throw rug and tried to smooth down her hair.

Her laptop was balanced on the recliner's arm; Liam's gaze peeled from her to it. "The only time is now, right, hon?"

Daff had to admit, he'd nailed the impersonation of Melissa perfectly.

***

Daff's arms were covered in goosebumps. There it was. Forty-eight Bembooka Street, Redcliffe. The shabby demountable home with its low brick fence and frangipani trees filled her computer screen. On a good weekday run, a drive to Redcliffe would take an hour, but at three on a Saturday afternoon, weekend traffic could make it longer. Daff snapped the laptop shut and snatched her keys off the kitchen counter. Her whole body hummed as she stepped out onto the front verandah.

"Feel like checking out your old stomping grounds?" She asked, even though the watch was firmly secured around her wrist.

"Nah, think I'll just kick back here."

Daff rolled her eyes as she locked the front door. A moment later, Liam walked through it.

They sat in comfortable silence during the hour-long drive to Redcliffe. The buzz of the previous night's insights had faded, and Daff let out a giant yawn as she pulled off onto Anzac Parade. Traffic around North Lakes Shopping centre was solid with weekend shoppers, adding an additional fifteen minutes. Eventually she hit the Esplanade. She needed to take the next left, and then the first two rights.

Now that they were closer, Daff could feel her heartbeat quicken. Neither of them knew what to expect. In the flurry of discovering their first real clue, Daff hadn't stopped to come up with a plan. If she knocked on the door and no one answered, then this whole expedition was for nothing. Of course, the alternative was worse. *Christ, what if he was married?* Daff didn't know Liam's real name or how long he'd been dead—if the cops were investigating him, her sudden appearance would seem very suspicious.

"Daff, Daff! Brake, brake! Daff, brake!"

Daff slammed her foot onto the brake pedal and the VW screeched to a halt. An elderly woman stepped onto the pedestrian crossing, flipped Daff the bird and mouthed something offensive.

"I'd offer to take over but …"

"Sorry." Daff shook her head as the GPS instructed her to turn left in three hundred metres. "If this is your house, Liam, you may not be the only one who lives there."

He nodded, as though he'd been thinking the same thing. "We don't have much choice, though, Daff. And, look, if it starts to go south then you just have to bail." He paused, looking around the busy little shopping precinct.

"You recognise anyone or anything?" She asked.

Liam shook his head. "I'll go into the house first, check that it's empty."

A few minutes later, the GPS announced that they'd reached their destination. The street looked quiet as they pulled up in front of number forty-eight. Liam scoped out the house and returned a moment later. "Empty as a church on Monday."

The letterbox's narrow slot was overloaded with junk mail and letters. Daff pulled out the bundle and flipped through it until she found three envelopes; two were addressed to a Mr H. Jones and one to an M. Harrison. She returned the junk to the letterbox and stuffed the envelopes into the back of her jeans. Daff opened the short chicken wire fence for the second time, only now it was real. With the sun floating high above her, she could make out the uneven path easily. At the front door, there was more mail. A couple of boxes, a bundle of envelopes and the latest print-run of the Brisbane phonebook. Daff tried the door knob, but it was locked.

"Maybe there's a spare key?" Liam looked around the slim porch, but there were no pot plants to hide a key beneath.

Daff looked up at the lipped edge of the eaves. There was a rusty aluminium garden chair pushed into the corner of the verandah; using it as a step ladder, she ran her hand over the ledge until she heard the familiar grating sound of metal on metal. She laughed, stepping down with the key in hand.

Liam looked at her, dumbfounded. "What made you look there?"

"My dad used to hide his in the same place." The comment fell out like it was no big deal, but a shadow fell over Daff's face as she remembered her own childhood verandah and how, when she was old enough, Lawrence had shown her the secret hiding space. He was so tall he could just reach up into the eave and grab it; a feat that astounded her pre-teen self. Daff pushed away the chair—and the unwelcomed memory—and slid the key into the lock as Liam walked through the wall.

Daff stepped into what was obviously meant to be the lounge room, only there was no couch or TV. No rugs, photos, lamps or books. Nothing except cheap curtains, all of which were drawn.

"Cosy." Daff closed the door behind her and flicked on a switch. At least there was power. "Does any of this seem familiar?"

"None of it."

"Maybe it's a mate's house or your girlfriend's place?"

"You know any girls who live like this?"

She didn't.

Across the room was an open doorway. Daff stepped through it and flicked on the light, revealing the kitchen. The wood-panelled cupboards were empty, the fridge was near bare, and the dishrack contained only two plates, some cutlery and a single glass. Daff didn't know anyone—man or woman—who lived like this.

Liam's brown eyes were flat as they moved around the impersonal pokey kitchen. "I guess I was a minimalist?"

Back in the living room, Daff headed down the corridor, the floorboards creaking the whole way. There were three closed doors—one, Daff hoped, would be a bedroom containing something useful.

When she pushed back the left-side door, all she found was a mattress dressed in dark blue sheets and thinning pillows. In the corner of the room was a shoebox, a duffle bag filled with clothes and an empty water bottle. The air was still, as if the room had been locked up for days. She unzipped the duffle and pulled out its contents: black shirts, jeans, socks, undies, and finally a leather jacket. She rifled through every pocket, but they were all empty. No wallet.

Daff flopped onto the edge of the bed. "You didn't live here."

"Maybe I was a druggie?"

"There aren't any drugs here and you don't have track marks. Druggies don't live like this either. The place is empty, but it's clean. Maybe you were hiding or something?"

"Maybe I was. Shit. Daff, I've got about as good an idea as you. Maybe something will turn up out of that mail you got. We can search the names, see if any of them are me."

Daff didn't feel like pointing out the flaw in Liam's logic. Whoever lived here didn't want to be found. This mail wasn't for him. She stuffed the clothes back into the bag and dropped it onto the floor with a metallic thud. "What was that?" Daff looked to Liam who shrugged. She lifted the bag, but all she saw was floorboards.

"Maybe it was something in the shoebox?" He offered.

Daff knelt down beside the brown box and flipped the lid open. Inside there was a rolled shirt; maybe there were drugs here after all. She lifted out the shirt, surprised by its weight, and carefully unwrapped the bundled fabric.

Lawrence had shown her his gun a few times, but she'd never been allowed to hold it. This gun was heavy and long, longer than her hand: a 2.45-calibre revolver. Lawrence had one just like it. Someone had hidden it here, along with a handful of loose bullets.

Liam's face went slack with shock. "I reckon we better go, Daff."

She shook her head. *No backing out now.* She scooped up the bullets and placed them on the bed. The gun looked as open and threatening as a bear trap. Acting on impulse, Daff slipped her index through the trigger guard and curling her hand around the grip frame.

The room turned white. Daff felt like she was spinning, folding in on herself. Her stomach cramped and temples pulsed until suddenly everything stopped.

She was standing on the slick concrete floor of a warehouse. Behind her was a makeshift bar, a few cars and motorbikes; above her, a corrugated iron roof; and, all around, the thick scent of petroleum and shaved metal. People were talking. Men. They were standing in a circle, three of them: a medium-sized bloke with a long wiry beard, a tall man with his head wrapped in a bandanna, and Liam.

Daff's chest collapsed. *It can't be* …. Relieved to find that her consciousness had remained in her own body, rather than transferring to the gun, she shuffled forward until she could see the men more clearly. It was him, alright: the guy Jake Reilly had spoken to minutes before his own death. Her breath went shallow and her heart rate increased. *How do you know Liam?* She approached the party of men cautiously, until she was certain they couldn't see her.

"It's your fuck-up mate, so you're the one that's gotta clean it up." The shorter man stabbed the air with his finger, glaring at Liam.

"Come on, Henry," Liam said. "Ben fucked up. I get it. He shouldn't have said anything to that apprentice, but I've talked to the young'un and he knows what'll happen if he squeals. I'll have a word to Nicko on Tuesday, see if we can move him outta imports. Trust me, Ben won't be blabbing to anyone else."

The tall man stepped in. "Do you know what will happen to *you* if he does? You gotta end it, brother, now."

Liam's face hardened and he nodded. "That's how it is, eh?" He looked at the two men. Neither of them spoke. "Alright, then." He turned and walked over to the southern end of the warehouse, pulling the revolver out of a concealed pocket in his vest.

The tall one hung back a moment. "You reckon he'll do it?"

"Fuckin' better."

Daff followed the men as they followed Liam to the end of the warehouse, where a scruffy-looking guy in a loose black t-shirt and tradie pants sat tied to a chair.

"I'm sorry Mike, really," the scruffy guy pleaded to Liam. "I wasn't thinking, you know. It was the first time I'd opened a crate and my apprentice was with me and I just got caught up in it all? You understand, right?" The fluorescent lights made his skin gleam, shiny as plastic. "Kenny won't say nothin', I swear."

"Kenny says you showed him how to pull apart the lawnmowers, says you got him to help you re-pack the coke into crates," said Liam. "Shit, Ben. You got a non-member to help you? What the fuck were you thinking?"

"I know, I know. But I'll fix it, I will. Kenny knows not to say anything."

"He's a fuckin' eighteen-year-old kid! You gonna make me kill a kid?"

Ben's face was slick with sweat, his shirt sticking to him unflatteringly. He looked towards the bearded guy and the tall bandanna man. "Henry, please. You don't have to kill anyone, just make the kid a member. Make it worth his while to stay quiet."

The shorter man, Henry, stepped forward. "That's not how this works, Ben, and you know it. Normally, I'd take care of you myself. But since Mike here—" Henry pointed to Liam "—is the one who vouched for you, it's up to him to clean up your mess. We know you've made some kinda deal with the cops too, or maybe you *are* a cop. Mikey here saw you just last week, getting into the back of a cop car. No cuffs. Are you a pig-cunt, Ben?"

"What? I ain't no fuckin' cop! What is this shit? I ain't a fuckin' rat. Henry! I'm a Road Dog for life. I'd never sell out the club."

"You already did." Henry turned from him and gave Liam a nod.

"Mike. Brother. Don't do this." Ben's voice thickened and Daff could see he was struggling to keep it together.

"Sorry, buddy, just can't trust you." Liam raised the gun and released two shots.

Daff dropped the revolver. The warehouse and the men disappeared. She stood up too quickly, tripped on the corner of the mattress and clutched the wall to right herself.

Liam stared at the gun on the hardwood floor. "What the fuck was that?"

Daff turned and bolted for the door. Her hands fumbled over the watch's straps until they came loose; the timepiece clattered onto the floor. Her ears thumped in time with her steps as she ran out the front door, down the garden path and into the golden afternoon light.

CHAPTER 12

Detective Lawrence

Saturday July 2, 2016

Lawrence called McPhee on his way home from the restaurant.

Though the dinner with Heather had been useful, providing a motive for their prime suspect, he continued to be baffled by Ms Miller's motives. The photograph in Heather's home suggested that the sisters were close, and when Sarah had planned on leaving the city, she'd invited her sister to come with her; yet Heather appeared in control, calm and even mildly flirtatious. She kissed his cheeks before they'd parted to their separate vehicles; Lawrence's stomach warmed at the recollection of her touch. He was jolted from the memory of Heather's embrace by McPhee's answer.

"Dead body?" McPhee said.

"Not yet, but it's only nine-thirty."

"Nine-thirty on my night off."

The heat travel from Lawrence's belly to his neck. "I'm aware. I also know that tomorrow is your day off, but I'm going to pick Henry Ernst up for questioning in the morning and I thought you'd like to be there."

"What have you got on him?"

"Enough."

Lawrence hit the 'end call' and allowed his thoughts to return to Ms Miller. She may be peculiar, but he saw no harm in enjoying her attention.

The next morning, Lawrence met McPhee at the station before making the drive out to the Road Dogs' clubhouse. He explained the emails and the tell-all book contract to his partner while leaving out the split entrée, squid linguini and company.

They crossed the Ted Smout Memorial Bridge in record time. As it was a Saturday morning, traffic was flowing in the opposite direction as Redcliffe residents headed into the city for their overpriced weekend breakfasts. Lawrence hit the Esplanade as the sun broke through the morning cloud, its rays fanning in piercing beams as good as any biblical painting.

He took a left turn off the Esplanade and a right after that. It wasn't until he hit the dirt road that led to the club's shed that he wondered if anyone would even be there. The club's auto repair business ran out of a backstreet garage that was a strict weekday affair. The business was obviously intended for money laundering, and with the VLAD laws tightening up tattoo parlour licences, opening up a mechanic workshop must have been the next best thing. They'd gone through the books of Beachside Motors and all was in order; Lawrence figured one of the members was simply stuffing mattresses or keeping a second set of ledgers, at least until the crack down on motorcycle gangs ended. The workshop had quickly become the Road Dogs' clubhouse, the long driveway and shrubbery buffering any noise made at club barbecues and piss-ups.

Lawrence hoped he was about to pull up on the remnants of such a gathering. Not only would it mean that Henry was on site, but a biker sporting a hangover would be easier to manage. He came around an outcrop of wild bush and was rewarded with the sight of empty beer bottles, glasses and half-finished bottles of bourbon. Though the small concrete verandah and upturned cable drums were littered with evidence, the place was empty. Lawrence swung himself out of the car and edged around the side of the building towards the rear. Three bikes were lined up by the back sliding door. They could belong to customers, but even Henry would have enough sense to lock-up another man's bike. Lawrence was heading back towards the main door when he heard the shriek and shudder of the sliding corrugated door.

McPhee was leaning against the car. At the sight of the opening door, he slid aside and unlocked the rear passenger door. Lawrence stepped around the previous night's rubbish; Henry Ernst walked over the top of it. "Morning, Henry."

"Whacha want?" The old biker leaned against a cable drum, his eyes squinting against the morning light.

"There's been some developments in your wife's case. You'll need to come into the station with us."

"We can talk here."

Lawrence crossed the verandah, mindfully stepping over the half-eaten sausage someone had dropped on the cement. Beside it was a roach. The detective bent over, tried to hide his wheezing, and picked up the joint. "I'd rather talk at the station."

"That ain't mine." He straightened, levelling his eyes to the detective's.

"Maybe not, but it's enough to justify a search warrant. So, are you going to come peacefully, or do I need to handcuff you?"

Henry's mouth curved, displaying the gold cap that was now his canine. "I wouldn't give you the pleasure."

Once Henry had slid into the back of the unmarked Holden Commodore, Lawrence tossed McPhee the keys. The younger detective's mouth fell open. "You want me to drive?"

"Yup." Lawrence slid into the back seat opposite the old biker and buckled his seatbelt. There'd been a lot of empty beer bottles on that verandah, and Henry wasn't looking so good. His jaw hung like a slack hammock, the bags beneath his eyes had increased, and when Henry closed his peepers, Lawrence wondered if the dirt-bag was psyching himself up for a vomit. McPhee had already given up a day off, he probably wouldn't appreciate the task of hosing out the vehicle's back seat.

They were halfway down the Esplanade when Lawrence spotted a familiar looking VW Beetle, powder blue, coming off Anzac Ave. His throat tightened as he peered through the windshield, trying to catch a glimpse of the driver, but the reflection of the morning sun obscured them.

"Never pegged you for a cradle-snatcher, Lawrence." Henry's eyes were open and he flashed the detective a quick smile.

Lawrence leaned back into his seat, but he cast a quick glance as the Beetle turned right onto Redcliffe Parade. A pale brunette was driving; her face turned away as she rounded the corner, hand flung in the air as though she were talking to someone, although the passenger seat was empty. His throat tightened again.

They pulled up at Fortitude Valley Station fifty-minutes later, and Ernst had the good sense to stay quiet for the entire drive. Lawrence told McPhee to take Henry into the back holding cell while he fixed them both a cuppa. He could feel a caffeine withdrawal headache coming on, and he wasn't going to stuff up this interview because of a lack of coffee. The station was buzzing when he entered. It always was on a Saturday morning; the holding cells usually filled with drunks: guys picked up for disorderly conduct or fisticuffs, while women filled up the pen with statements about drink spiking. Lawrence was surprised then to find the kitchenette empty, though he was glad. He needed a minute to prepare for this; his heart was already skipping before he had his first sip. He was too eager; he wanted to nail Henry too badly.

McPhee walked in and nodded towards the full mug that rested on the kitchenette counter. "That one for me?"

"Yup. You got him in there no worries?"

McPhee nodded. "Ready when you are."

Lawrence threw back the last of his coffee and headed towards the door. The fluorescent light in the corridor flickered as he entered, and he hoped it wasn't an omen. The interview room was at the end of the hallway. With his hand on the knob, he looked up at his partner. "It'll be better if I speak with him alone."

"Roger," McPhee nodded and stepped aside. "I'll keep tabs from the other side."

Henry Ernst was seated in the chair opposite the two-way glass. You could attribute the decision to a lifetime of midday movies and television shows, but Lawrence knew that for Henry, it all came down to experience. He offered his suspect a glass of water, which was promptly declined. "I need to call my lawyer."

A microphone and a small recording device sat towards the end of the table. Anyone who found themselves in this room had good reason to be nervous. Instead of reaching over to hit that small red record button, Lawrence pushed the device aside, pulled out his chair and took a seat.

"How about I save you a grand by keeping this off the record?" *At least, for now.*

Henry flicked his hand as if he was swatting a fly, but said nothing. It was as close to an acceptance as Lawrence was likely to get.

"Where were you on Wednesday night through to Thursday morning?"

"Like I said before, Tramp and I were at the shop, working till late."

"You mean, Paul Sinclair, who is the number two of your club, Road Dogs?"

Even though it was off the record, Lawrence found himself dropping into the familiar protocol.

Henry smirked and made a show of snorting some phlegm. "It's not *my* club. Road Dogs is a social group. We drink together and we ride together, but never at the same time, officer." The old biker leaned forward. "You know, I just realised we got something in common."

"I don't think so, mate." Lawrence replied, acutely aware of McPhee's presence on the opposite side of the glass.

"Sure we do: both our missuses are dead. You lost Ruth to the cancer, that right? Wait, weren't you two separated when she carked it? That's too bad, *Jono*."

Lawrence curled his hands into fists, though he kept them hidden beneath the table. He knew this trick: Henry was trying to unsettle him, catch him off guard, show that he knew all the intimate details of Lawrence's life. Still, he was ready to give the outlaw pres a good thumping, but McPhee was watching and they were in a station full of cops. There was nothing Lawrence could do and Henry knew it.

"You and Sarah had separated?" He asked the question even though he already knew the answer.

"Yup. Guess we're just two peas in a pod, *officer*."

"Our department has been going through your late wife's laptop and we came across an interesting email."

It was close enough to the truth. The fact that the department had not yet legally seized the computer and Lawrence had only received a forwarded copy of the email from Heather earlier that morning was beside the point. Henry didn't need to know that.

The biker leaned back in his chair, lifting his chin like he was preparing for a blow. "So what?"

"You and Sarah separated two weeks ago. After she caught you with another woman at a club barbecue."

"Like I said, brother, two peas, one pod."

The air rushed from Lawrence's lungs, yet his face remained calm and neutral. *He knows about that?* The vision of Ruth sitting at the kitchen table rose before him. Her eyes were watery, brow creased and lips downturned as she listened to her husband of twenty-seven years tell her what she already knew. He'd been having an affair. It'd been four years since then, though Lawrence could recall that moment perfectly. They handled their divorce discreetly and the only people who knew the cause of their separation were Ruth, Daff and his accomplice: a woman from Gaming and Vice who left the city soon after.

Major outlaw clubs had their ways of uncovering information, but Lawrence didn't think the Road Dogs had those kinds of connections or capabilities. More importantly, why was the club digging into his past?

A small shudder rippled across the detective's back, but he continued as though Henry hadn't spoken. "After the barbecue, she went to live with her sister, Heather. The only thing is, I think Sarah had been planning to leave you long before Saturday a fortnight ago. On Monday, your late wife received an email from a major publishing house that was interested in buying a tell-all book about what it's like to be the wife of an outlaw motorcycle club president."

Henry's face lost its hard edge for a moment. True shock only lasts for two or three seconds. You gasp. Your mind goes blank. After that your cognitive ability and processing faculties kick back in. Lawrence knew genuine shock when he saw it, and he felt his own stomach drop. Either Henry really didn't know about the book deal or he was a damn good liar.

The biker's eyes shifted towards the table. "She wrote a book?"

From what Heather said, it didn't sound like it, but Henry didn't need to know that either. "We're still going through the content on the laptop." He pushed back his chair and made to leave. "We're done here. My partner will show you to your cell and arrange that phone call to your lawyer."

"You're keeping me?"

"For the next eight hours. I'd offer you a Panadol, but it's against policy."

Lawrence smiled at the small lie.

Lawrence called Heather and told her that he was sending a constable around to collect Sarah's laptop. She was disappointed that the detective would not be collecting the item himself and hinted at a second dinner date. Ignoring the small thrill sparked by her suggestion, Lawrence replied with a noncommittal noise and ended the call promptly.

He was halfway through typing up the notes from his non-date with Heather when McPhee pulled up a chair and dropped a cuppa onto the Laminex desk.

"A sergeant from the Goldie is waiting on you."

Lawrence glanced down at his desk calendar, but couldn't see any notes about a meeting with a Gold Coast officer. He glanced around the bullpen and out towards the reception, but could see no unfamiliar faces. "Well, where is he?"

"He wants to speak in private, says your cubical isn't going to cut it."

Lawrence rolled his eyes, took a sip of his coffee and stood. "Right-o. Did he give you the coordinates for his location?"

"The interview room was still empty, so he's in there."

The detective was halfway around his desk when he stopped and pointed towards the recorder. "You're good with a keyboard, aren't you? Why don't you type up those Jackals interviews from yesterday?"

Lawrence gave the sergeant a once-over as he entered the interview room he'd left only moments before. The man certainly looked like a Goldie regular. Though he was pushing forty, he was cut into the coast's classic triangle shape with a barrel chest and narrow hips. He hadn't taken a seat; instead he stood behind the chair, gripping its back with broad, flat hands.

He looked up as the detective entered. "Lawrence? Senior Sergeant O'Neil."

"Have we spoken over the phone? I don't recall making an appointment." Lawrence shook O'Neil's outstretched hand and wondered how many coppers came from Irish descent.

"We didn't. I was told you were the man I should speak to."

Lawrence's knees were aching, but he didn't want to pull up stumps just so this bugger could loom over him. He stood instead and waited for the sergeant to begin his yarn.

"I understand you have a history with the Road Dogs?"

Lawrence's brow shot up and he involuntarily resumed his seat. *Should've brought the cuppa with me.*

"Two years ago, we stationed an undercover officer here in the Valley. He became a nom and, not long after, a patch member. He's supposed to check in at the start of every shift, but we haven't heard from him."

That still didn't explain why O'Neil wanted to see Lawrence. If this sergeant's UC hadn't made contact, his department should have dismantled the investigation immediately. "Why are you here, O'Neil?"

The sergeant pulled out a chair and took a seat. "Our UC said he'd be out of touch for a few days." He shook his head like he still couldn't believe he'd agreed. "A couple of the members were going on a run up the coast and he doubted he'd be able to get away and check in with us without being noticed. He needed three days—it's been four. You know these guys, know what they're capable of …"

Lawrence wouldn't have agreed to those terms; anything could happen in three days. If a handler believed his UC's identity had been jeopardised, it was his responsibility to dismantle the case, to get his guy out of there. Lawrence wouldn't have wasted time chatting to an old cop about the likelihood of 'something' happening. At least he hoped he wouldn't. The sergeant looked as though he hadn't had a good camp in days; his tanned face was deeply creased and his eyes puffy. Lawrence knew how much time went into the logistics of an undercover investigation. The sergeant didn't want to expose his UC unless he had to.

"Your guy was due back today?"

"Yup."

"Did he say whether or not the pres was going on the run?"

The sergeant nodded.

"I have Henry in custody right now. Either he didn't go or the club is back from their run, in which case, your guy should have checked in. If I were you, I'd pull the plug. You want to question him now?"

The sergeant nodded, clearly relieved to have been given direction. Lawrence stood and headed towards the door. "Take a seat, I'll get him."

"What were you questioning Ernst about?"

He paused with his hand on the door. "A double homicide at the Sundowner Motel. Ernst's wife was one of the victims."

"No men at the scene?"

Lawrence told him no, went to apologise but thought better of it. If the Road Dogs had found out the UC's real identity, the retaliation would be brutal. A quickie motel murder would be too kind. "You mind if I stick around?"

"Sure." The man's voice sounded strained. "You been trying to get these guys for a while?"

"Yup, and I got close once. But Henry, well, he interfered with my personal life."

The words fell out before Lawrence could stop them, much to his horror. He'd never been one to bring his personal problems to work, but Henry's insinuations had brought all those memories to the surface. When the Road Dogs failed to show at the set-up two years ago, Lawrence thought that was it. Then he got a knock on the door. Henry showed up at Lawrence's unit and told the detective to back off or he'd regret it. It wasn't the first threat Lawrence had ever received—far from it—but most were hollow, and there was no reason to think that one was any different.

Then Henry said something that chilled him to the bone. "If I can find your address, pig, then I can find your daughter's, no worries. Fancy that, a dead wife and a dead kid."

The comment unsettled Lawrence enough for him to back off, but that was it. Then Tom died and Lawrence wasn't willing to take any more chances; life was just too fragile. He'd given Daff enough cash to move and set herself up; he told her it was time to start somewhere else. He made the suggestion sound like a solution for grief, when really he was just trying to keep her alive. But to say nothing about Henry's threat would be irresponsible. So he told her about the unnerving message with the strict instruction to call him if anything out of the ordinary happened. She left for the Sunny Coast soon after, and he hadn't heard from her since.

Lawrence pulled the door open and let the sergeant go first. "I hope you get more out of Henry than I did."

CHAPTER 13

Daff

Saturday July 2, 2016

Daff only made it two blocks before pulling over. Her hands shook as she fumbled over her phone's six-digit lock screen; the mobile vibrating violently with each failed attempt. She knew she should keep moving—the more distance between her and the watch the better—but she couldn't. She needed to talk to someone; to put that experience into words, to distil the chaos and confusion into something measurable and precise. The double crack of Liam's gun was on a permanent loop, and her hands hummed with the warmth of those fatal shots. She had thought that being with Beth and Jake in their final moments was bad, but the memory she'd tapped into when she touched the gun was something else—something fatal—because this time she *knew* him; knew the person who pulled the trigger. Her phone opened to reveal a photograph of last winter's blooming hydrangeas, her background; she clicked on her contacts app and hit the first name listed below *recent.*

Peta answered on the second ring. "Heya."

The hand that had been clenching Daff's stomach loosened at the sound of her friend's voice. "Something's happened and I don't know what to do." Explaining the vision of the demountable and her spontaneous trip to Redcliffe as quickly as she could, Daff delved into the brutal memory she'd experienced only moments before. "What if Liam's not a good guy, what the heck am I supposed to do now?"

Peta's voice was steady, but quickened with her own curiosity. "Why was Tom in your vision quest? Why did you go back to the memory of the accident?"

Tom's reappearance had torn Daff's heart apart and sewn it back together all in the space of a few seconds. His presence was a gift she had longed for since the moment of his death and she had no interest in ruining their private, brief and treasured reunion with analysis. However, the vision that was attached to the gun was another story.

Ignoring her friend's contemplations, Daff continued. "I've left the watch behind, Peta. Liam was a member of that bikie gang that Lawrence was investigating before …" *Tom died.* Before the accident, Lawrence had told her to be careful; that this gang was determined and gutsy. He'd told her to be cautious and not take any unnecessary risks. She'd ignored him, of course. Her father was always being threatened. It was part of the job. It wasn't the first time he'd warned her either. She'd been the recipient of many a lengthy lecture: always lock the car doors as soon as you sit behind the wheel, never walk home alone at night, don't wrestle a bag-snatcher—just give him the damn purse! "I don't see why I should risk my life so some drug dealer can be sent to eternal rest."

"Maybe he made a mistake? We *all* make mistakes."

"Are you saying I should keep trying? Peta, these guys are drug dealers and killers."

"Yes, but you found the watch." Peta sighed. "Look, I don't know what's going on here any better than you, but I think you need to ask yourself a few questions."

"Like what?" Daff's face flushed as numbed shock gave way to anger.

"Has Liam ever given you a creepy vibe? Have you ever felt like he wasn't being totally honest with you? Maybe his bad-boy personality got washed out with the rest of his memories. Maybe he was a good guy that just wound up in the wrong place. Either way, Liam is attached to that watch—a watch that *you* found. He's *your* responsibility, Daff."

"He killed someone, Peta, and those guys in that warehouse were pressuring him to do it. I don't want to get messed up in their stuff."

"Maybe you should go see your dad?"

Daff's head flew back against the seat. "What?"

"He's a cop, and he's dealt with these guys before. He can help you in a way no one else can. Your psychic visions have taken you this far, but maybe it's time you started looking for a little outside help."

Her throat had thickened, and though Peta couldn't see her, Daff nodded. Her friend was right, but that didn't mean Daff was happy about it. There'd been four years of unanswered phone calls, four years of silent resentment, unspoken truths and blame. She'd buttoned up those feelings for so long that she didn't know what would happen when she did see him again. "I can't see him. Christ, how would I explain Liam?"

"No easy segue into *that* conversation .... You'll just have to go with the truth and see how it lands."

It must be the day for lousy plans, Daff thought. The knot in her stomach returned as she said goodbye to her friend and hung up. Switching on the ignition, she swung the Beetle around and heading back the way she had come.

A minute later, the demountable was once again in view. The gate was open. The door too. She'd been gone less than twenty minutes, but in that time the sun had set and evening shadows had settled over the garden. The darkness resembled her vision so closely that she took a cautious glance to her left and right, half expecting Tom to appear amongst the silhouettes.

Her skin prickled with fear as she stepped into the hollow lounge room. The large open space had become unwelcoming now that it was dark, and Daff felt vulnerable as she fumbled for the light switch by the door. There was a sharp click and the overhead light lit the wide empty room immediately.

The floor was bare.

She'd dropped the watch here; she was sure of it. It had cluttered against the timber when she'd launched herself out the door. She circled the bare room unnecessarily, checking behind the door and then the kitchen too.

"Liam?"

The floorboards creaked again as she made her way down the corridor towards the humble bedroom. The bed was still flat on the floor, but it had been stripped of its blue covers. The duffle was gone; the shoe box and its incriminating evidence too. Her heart kicked double time. Click, crack, boom. Click, crack, boom. In the short time she'd been gone, someone had been here.

Aware that her back was to the door, she spun around and tried to quieten her breath. *They could still be here.* Daff edged out of the room, treading lightly in the hopes the floorboards wouldn't creak and give her away. The door to the bathroom was closed; had she done that when she walked through it the first time? Her hand trembled as she reached for the handle, twisting it slowly and then shoving it with such force that the door ricocheted off the wall. Slapping it back, she held it in place and flicked on the light. The bathroom was empty. The air rushed from her lungs in relief.

"Liam?" She called his name again even though she knew there would be no answer. "Shit."

The engine idled for five minutes in front of the demountable before Daff finally made up her mind and pushed the gear stick into drive. The sun had set by the time she hit the M7 that spat her out into Fortitude Valley. She hadn't crossed Brunswick Street for eighteen months, and though the odd business had changed, the place looked entirely the same. At least there was some comfort in that. She parked a few blocks back, both because it was the only option and because she needed the extra time to prepare. Even though she was Lawrence's daughter, there was no guarantee that he'd want to speak to her. He had hurt her and their family, but she had also hurt him.

One of the last times Daff saw Lawrence was at her childhood home. At that point, Lawrence had moved out and Daff was living on campus while finishing her degree; despite being alone, Ruth had decided to stay in the home she'd known for so long. Between classes and study, Daff had managed to squeeze in one or two weeknight visits and spend most of her weekends there.

It was after lunch one Saturday that Lawrence knocked on the door and Daff answered. The stifling heat of February came in with him. It'd been two months since they'd last spoken, though he called Ruth every day to see how she was doing and paid her a visit once a week. Lawrence wanted to be there for her, and Ruth had the good grace to let him. Their tenderness for each other remained somehow, despite the affair and the cancer.

"Daphne." He stood stiff and awkward in the entryway—a guest in his own home.

"Mum's asleep. You should come back later."

"It's been a while."

Daff bit her tongue; was about to say that he had her number, that he could call anytime … then she remembered that he *had* called. A lot. She was the one who refused to pick up the phone. "I suppose."

"How are you?"

She couldn't do it. She couldn't stand in her childhood home making small talk with her deceitful father at the front door as her mother died by inches in the bedroom behind them. Daff grabbed the second set of spares that dangled by the door. "I'm going out for a walk, stay as long as you like, just lock-up afterwards." She left the door open and was careful when she passed him. Their shoulders would not touch. His hand would not find her arm. She crossed the overgrown lawn where she'd once learnt to cartwheel, the footpath where she'd ridden her bike for the first time. He called out her name, once, and for a moment, she couldn't tell whether the sound was real or a memory.

Travelling down Hynes Street, Daff rounded the corner on to Brookes towards a heritage-listed, red-brick building. This was the police station, massive and intimidating. Daff crossed the street, mounted the stairs and went in search of her father.

CHAPTER 14

Detective Lawrence

Saturday July 2, 2017

Detective Lawrence went back to his desk with his palms sweating; he could feel the regret of his impromptu confession to Sergeant O'Neil warming his face. He never talked about the affair, the divorce or Ruth's death to *anyone* at work and now he was blabbing those private regrets to a total stranger—one that had come to him for help!

McPhee was still sitting at the detective's desk, though Henry's statement remained untouched on the top of the case file. Lawrence was about to give his partner what for, when a movement in his peripheral vision caught his attention. A young woman, with dark wavy hair, straightened her back against the uncomfortable fold-out chairs that filled the bullpen. The recognition was instant, but the shock of her appearance; here in his station; here at his desk; here in front of him, was so unexpected that his mind was wiped blank. The dumb surprise showed on his face, and hers hardened in response.

"You have a visitor." McPhee had abandoned his task and leaned back against the chair to absorb the real-time family drama.

"I can see that." Lawrence felt his chest tighten as he gave Daff a nod, a helpless smile tugging at his lips. This was it. The moment he'd been waiting four years for. The moment when he would apologise, she'd apologise and they'd both shake their heads at what numbskulls they had been and how much time they had wasted—or at least that's what he'd hoped for a thousand times. He'd tell her about all the times he'd reached for the phone before talking himself out of it, and the times when he had hit call, but then hung up before the connection was even made. He hoped she would have similar stories. Maybe now she'd be his daughter again, and he'd be her father. Hope was a terrible thing. So was fear. Why was she here now, today of all days, when Henry Ernst was still in the building?

"Daphne." His mouth stumbled over the name.

"Lawrence."

McPhee shifted his gaze, suddenly uncomfortable at what was clearly a private moment, scooped himself out of Lawrence's chair and slipped back towards his own desk at the other end of the room. Lawrence became aware that he was standing in the very open, very public office of the

Fortitude Valley Police Station. *As if these yappin' coppers don't have enough to gossip about*, he thought.

"There's a room out the back, we can talk there." Lawrence took a step back and hesitated before turning, fearing that she would vanish as soon as his eyes were off her. As if she could read his thoughts, his daughter rose from her own seat. "Alright, after you."

Lawrence guided her towards the interview room that he appeared to be spending his entire shift in. He held the door open as she entered. She looked almost the same as the last time he'd seen her at her home; only now her dark hair was longer and—although she hadn't grown a millimetre since the age of sixteen—she seemed taller. Glancing down at her feet, Lawrence noted that she was wearing low boot heels and his breath shortened. Had she always been into that style of shoe? He could only remember her wearing flats. Sitting down opposite her, he searched her face for any signs of aging. There were none. He supposed there really wasn't *that* much difference between twenty-five and twenty-seven.

"How are you?" He cringed at the routine question, but figured he had to start somewhere.

"I'm …" Her gaze flicked around the room as though looking for a prompt. "Not sure where to start."

"I haven't seen you since …"

"You gave me the money. I remember."

He tried to pick one of a million questions, knowing that the wrong one would send her packing. He wanted to know how she was doing—really doing. What her life looked like in the absence of Ruth, Tom, himself; but that was the wrong question. "Are you still up on the Sunny Coast?"

She nodded, pulling a disposable water bottle from her handbag and cracking the top. He noticed her hands were shaking slightly. "I'm working at a funeral home there."

That took him by surprise. "So, you didn't follow through with a career in toxicology?"

"No," her voice came out with an edge. "I'm an embalmer."

"Good pay?" The question fell out as he tried to imagine his little girl dressing corpses, and he instantly regretted it.

Daff smacked the top of her chest as she choked on a mouthful of water, "Jesus! You're already asking about my salary?"

"What's wrong with that? I just want to know that you're okay."

"I'm fine." She wiped her mouth, looked up at him and waited.

"Sorry. Seems I'm bit out of practice huh? It's just so good to see you, Daphne, but I don't really know what to say. These last few years have been hard. Too hard."

It was true, but he hoped the comment didn't come out sounding like an attempt at parental guilt; though that technique had never worked on her anyway. She pushed back her sleeve like she was checking the time, but Lawrence notice that she wasn't wearing a watch. *Maybe she forgot to put it on.*

"Is there somewhere you're supposed to be?"

"No," she drew the sleeve down, but continued to look restless. "I'm sure things have been *difficult* for you, but I didn't come because ... the thing is ... Look, something has happened and I need your help."

He saw a bloody circle slashed by a line and his own fatherly voice telling his daughter to call him if anything ever happened. He cast the memories aside. Maybe it was the room, or the badge that pressed into his hip; either way, Lawrence could feel his ingrained professional detachment rise up and take over the family reunion; through that weathered lens, he took in his daughter's appearance again.

Her eyes were clear, the whites were white, irises blue and pupils normal. She sat square in the chair, shoulders back and hands folded on the table in front of her; though they'd shaken earlier, now they looked stable; no visible scabs or scratches. That ruled out drug-related problems. The snug fit of her black turtleneck ruled out pregnancy. If it was money she was after, he'd upend his wallet in a minute. Looking closer, he could see a light shadow beneath her eyes. Whatever had prompted this visit had also affected her sleep. Forty years of law enforcement and twenty-seven years of paternal experience had taught him one thing: you can't push anyone who won't talk. You have to wait them out. You have to be ready to listen.

"You remember the Road Dogs?"

"Yes." His chest jolted.

"I've been seeing someone and—"

"Christ, you *are* pregnant."

"What?" Daff's face screwed up in disgust. "I'm not pregnant! I came here because *I think* the Road Dogs killed someone and if they did then there's a very good chance they're about to get away with it!"

"How do you know about the Sundowner murders?"

Daff raked a hand through her hair. "*Murders*? As in more than one? Wait, what are we talking about here?"

Lawrence sat back in his chair, told himself to zip it. He couldn't talk about an active case to anyone outside the investigation, but in the presence of his daughter, he could feel that commitment soften. He had to look away. The only homicide currently linked to the Road Dogs was the case he was working on, yet Daff appeared to know nothing about it. "Why are you here, Daphne?"

The question was meant inquisitively, but it came out harder than intended and Daff pushed back her seat. "This is a waste of time; I knew I shouldn't have come."

He stood too, grabbing her loosely by the shoulder. "I haven't caught a glimpse of you since Tom died, and you show up here at the station late at night talking about them scumbag Road Dogs and the fact that they may have killed someone, so I'm sorry, but I need to know what's going on. If you need help you have to give it to me like it is."

She'd recoiled at the mention of Tom's name, but he could see the edge of her eyes soften. "I don't think you'll believe me."

"I've heard it all."

Daff gave a hard, dry laugh. "You want to know? Fine. I can see a ghost. The ghost of a man who I believe was murdered by a member of the Road Dogs."

Lawrence stepped back, his hand falling free of her shoulder. "I don't understand … ghosts … what?"

"He showed up a few days ago and I am the only one who can see him. I know he was a member of the Road

Dogs before he died, but I'm not sure when exactly that happened because he has no memory of who he was or how he died."

Lawrence wanted to ask how she could possibly know that the Road Dogs were responsible for the death of a man suffering from amnesia, when he realised the question itself was illogical. She was holding his gaze; she'd spoken firmly, not hysterically, and yet how could he entertain her story? It was obviously some kind of psychosis. He was afraid something like this would happen. "Daphne, I know what the date is. Is that why you're here?"

Daff's breath deepened, the sureness of her face crumbling. "I know damn well what the date is! This isn't about Tom. I came here because I thought you could help me, but clearly that was a mistake." She turned then, flung open the door and disappeared out into the corridor. By the time Lawrence rounded the corner and stepped out into the fluorescent lights she was already gone.

CHAPTER 15

Daff

Saturday July 2, 2016

Daff knew it wouldn't take long for Lawrence to return to his desk, so she'd have to be quick. It was getting closer to nine and the bullpen was nearly empty as the bulk of on-duty officers hit the pavement in anticipation of a busy Saturday night. The tall redhead who had been sitting at her father's desk when she came in was lost in a landscape of paperwork on the other side of the office. Lawrence hated how paper-heavy the job had become, Daff could remember him complaining all the time about how "back in the day" it was about getting out there, making shit happen (or not happen), interrogations, arrests, stake-outs, a bit of biff-o. He said that eighty percent of the job these days was paperwork. Right now, it was those meticulously kept reports that Daff was after.

Lawrence's desk was covered in paperwork, but one file was open, displaying a photograph of a familiar face. The beard was long, the eyes wide and hooded. There was no forgetting the man from her vision, the one who had clearly been the leader, who had forced Liam to pull the trigger. *No one can force you to pull a trigger*, she thought, hearing glimpses of her father within herself.

She noted the man's name: Henry Ernst. Henry, that's what they had called him. She could hear the rumble of her father talking out in the corridor, and her heart picked up speed. Flicking through the fat report, Daff scanned the pages, taking in scraps of information while looking for any mention of the Road Dogs' clubhouse and a possible address. Lawrence's voice was coming closer; he was talking and walking at the same time. She willed him to walk past the door to the bullpen, to continue down the hall towards the kitchenette, towards coffee. She turned a few more pages, worrying whether the sharp snap of the paper was as loud to others in the room as it was to her, when she finally spotted it. The clubhouse was three blocks away from the demountable Liam had been living out of. She snapped the file closed and looked up just in time to see Lawrence cross the threshold. "Daff, what are you doing?"

Before he could reach her, she bolted back across the room and cut through the glass door that divided the station from reception.

CHAPTER 16

Detective Lawrence

Saturday July 2, 2016

"You want me to go after her?" McPhee stood beside the detective, his eyes running across the barely disturbed surface of his superior's desk.

"No, no. I just wish I knew what she was looking for. I'll give her some time to settle down then I'll give her a call, check that everything's alright." Lawrence thumbed through the file on Henry Ernst, the file he thought Daff had been looking at. Nothing was missing, and she'd closed the file before leaving. What would she have been looking for? The quick sting of regret was masked by the scent of roasted coffee.

"Drink up, Hitch." McPhee placed a full mug onto Lawrence's paperwork.

The sergeant from the Gold Coast was patiently waiting for Lawrence, whose family dramas had occupied the interview room, and now the officer was keen to get started on his interview with Henry Ernst. But he'd have to wait a little longer, for Daff's sudden appearance had stirred up all the memories, regrets and apprehensions that Lawrence preferred to stew over in his private time. He had prided himself on never bringing his personal issues to work, and now that Daff had stormed out, he'd have to somehow get his head back in the game.

"Did you get that laptop off Heather?"

McPhee nodded. "Yup, and we've found zip. The only thing on that laptop is pictures and pirated movies. There were a few Word files: resumes, cover letters, and a brief book proposal—the one she must have sent to the publisher."

"But no book?"

McPhee shook his head. "There isn't any writing on the computer. Maybe she kept the file on an external hard drive or a USB, but so far we got zilch."

"Was there anything interesting in the book proposal? Scandalous material or any info that could get her killed?"

"Nah, nothing like that. She hints at the club's business, the drugs, drinking and partying, but she doesn't say anything specific. I know this chick, a freelance writer, so I gave her a call."

Lawrence stopped himself from rolling his eyes. "And?"

"She said with non-fiction you usually pitch an idea to a publishing company; if they like it, they buy it. They might even throw a book advance your way."

"So, the book doesn't have to be written first?"

McPhee once again shook his head. "Nope. There's no way to verify yet, but I'd say old tricksy-licks was just trying to make a fast buck. Her sister said she was going to leave town, maybe she needed a bit of extra cash to make that happen."

"Your freelance *friend*, did she give you any idea of how much a book advance might be?"

"It varies," the detective took a sip from his own mug, "it can be as low as nothing and as high as ten."

It wasn't enough to retire on, but a low-end offer might be enough to cover a cheap relocation. Lawrence was about to ask McPhee to ask the publishing house how much they would have been willing to pay Heather when Sergeant O'Neil appeared. The officer stood in front of Lawrence's desk with his hands on his hips and a look that told the detective that his patience had run out. "You good to go?"

Lawrence nodded and followed the sergeant back down the corridor towards the interview room.

This time, it was Lawrence's turn to stand on the other side of the two-way mirror.

Henry Ernst sat facing the interview room's mirror, facing Lawrence as if he knew that he was there watching. The detective could feel his knee whining as he stood, firm footed, his arms crossed over his chest. He knew he should take a seat; this interview would likely go for a while but between Daff's appearance, the coffee and the chance that

Ernst might get nailed, Lawrence felt too wired for sitting. Despite the circumstances, Henry looked smug, even calm, as O'Neil—following Lawrence's advice—pushed the recording device aside and introduced himself. The interview room's door swung open with a bang as McPhee and a tall, thin man in a grey suit stepped through it.

"Hey, Graham." Henry's gold tooth shone.

"What time was my client detained?"

O'Neil pushed back his seat and stood up. "At ten this morning."

The lawyer made a show of checking his watch. "That was eleven hours ago, which means you've been holding my client illegally for the last three hours."

"We have reason to believe that Henry Ernst is responsible for the disappearance of my undercover agent and a double homicide here in the city."

"What evidence do you have?"

"My UC hasn't checked in for four days and he's been uncontactable." The sergeant turned towards McPhee, looking for backup, but the officer simply shook his head. He had nothing on Henry.

"I'm sorry about your UC officer, but if you don't have any solid evidence to link my client with the disappearance of your agent, then you're going to have to let him go."

The sergeant turned towards the mirror and Lawrence dropped his gaze. He knew the other officer couldn't see him through the reflective glass, but he *could* see O'Neil's scowl—it was crystal clear. Lawrence had stuffed up. Had Daff not shown up when she did, the interview would be over by now. Her timing couldn't have been worse. The detective pulled a seat over from behind him and flopped down beneath the weight of the evening's many disappointments.

CHAPTER 17

Daff

Sunday July 3, 2016

Rage licked Daff's insides, made her skin pucker against its invisible heat. She scrubbed her eyes with the back of her hand, telling herself that her frustration was merely the result of her amygdala reacting to a perceived threat. Reducing her feelings to physiology.

It had rained while she was inside the station, lowering the temperature of the city's already chilly night air. She buried her bare hands into the pockets of her jacket and scuttled the two blocks back to her car. The purple and green oil stains that rested on top of the bitumen shimmered beneath the street lights. She crossed the street cautiously. Slipping into the even frostier cab of her Beetle, she cursed her lack of heating and sensible gloves that might have made the hour-long drive back to the Sunshine Coast more pleasant. Before she had the chance to wallow in self-pity, Daff pulled out onto the motorway and attempted to ignore her numbing fingers.

It had been a mistake to see Lawrence.

She should have known better.

After all, it had taken days for *her* to believe that Liam was real—and *she* could see him. Why did she think it would be any different for Lawrence? She wiped a chilled hand across her clammy, puffed cheeks—her frustrated tears. From the vision, she knew that Liam's real name was Mike, but she still had no evidence that the Road Dogs were responsible for his murder. She had rounded the corner of Hynes and come up onto the M7, Wickham Street, when she swung into the gutter and left the car idling for a moment, her indicator blinking. Lawrence had mentioned the Sundowner Motel.

Daff knew of the motel, or at least its reputation, having heard her father's frequent recounts of the call-outs and busts that helped establish its seedy status. When she'd mentioned the Road Dogs, Lawrence had let slip that the gang was involved with a recent homicide at the motel. The Sundowner was five minutes away. Daff flicked on her right indicator and turned on to Wickham, heading in the opposite direction to Liam and the watch.

The Sundowner car park was rough. The bitumen stones were loose, crunching beneath the Beetle's tyres, and the many gaping potholes had been half-heartedly filled in and smoothed over. The digital clock's green glow told her it was approaching ten, and the idea of a hot shower and toilet break sounded too good to pass up.

Daff popped open the car door and was hit with the Valley's signature traits: drunks screeching and the wafting smell of oily Chinese take-out. The motel was two storeys: five rooms on the bottom and five on the top. Just like a cold chamber, Daff thought, only one of the doors on the second floor was hashed with yellow police tape.

She reconsidered, her hand lingering on the car's door handle, but the promise of hot water and the potential discovery of more clues trumped her hesitation at entering the grisly crime scene. She slammed the door and looked up at the motel's back-lit flickering sign that advertised the low rate of eighty dollars a night. For access to a shower, Daff would have paid double that—and then some.

Despite the late hour, the office light was still on and the front desk occupied by a bored-looking teenage girl. The spark of irritation she felt at the sight of the irresponsible staffing choice disappeared as soon as Daff opened the sliding door and leaned against the counter; the emotional exhaustion of her encounter with Lawrence combined with her late night, and she felt as wrung out as a rag. The girl's head was down and, thinking that she was involved in some administrative task, Daff waited to be acknowledged. It took her a few moments to realise that the receptionist was wearing headphones, and that her eyes were on the scrolling screen of her smartphone. Daff coughed loudly and the young girl slowly looked up, removing her earbuds. "What size?"

"Excuse me?"

"What size room do you need?" The girl, unfazed at being caught with her phone in hand, ran her eyes up and down Daff's modest figure. "I'm guessing a single."

Though the assumption was correct, the girl's tactless delivery threatened to crack what little cordiality Daff had left. "I'll take a double."

The teenager rolled her eyes as though she could see through Daff's attempt at assertiveness. "One-twenty a night. Cash or card?"

"Your sign says eighty."

"It's an old sign."

Daff pushed out a breath as she passed over her key card; the girl returned it a moment later, accompanied by a large plastic room key.

"We hope you enjoy your stay at the Sundowner Motel." The teenager picked up her phone and returned to whatever it was she'd been doing prior to the interruption.

"What happened upstairs? I see there is a door covered in police tape."

The girl looked up at Daff and shrugged. "Something bad, I guess."

Daff glanced up towards the second storey as she passed the stairs and headed towards her room on the lower level. She doubted the teenager was watching, but having blatantly asked about the crime scene, Daff figured she probably shouldn't go straight to room eight.

She slid the key home into room three—which looked exactly as Daff had expected: dim and dated—and headed towards the bathroom. At least the towels were clean, even if they were as rough and thin as sand paper. She flicked the shower on, carefully folded her clothes (she'd have to put them back on again) and stepped into the welcoming warmth. Thankfully, the shower pressure was decent, and she could feel the tight knots of her shoulders release beneath the flowing water. Aware that she was in the room directly beneath the crime scene, Daff closed her eyes and tried to stretch her awareness out and up into the empty crime scene. All she could feel though was the hot water turning tepid, and she flicked off the tap before it had the chance to turn cold.

She quickly dried herself and re-dressed. She was halfway towards the door when her stomach gave a familiar flip. Her hand instinctively clasped her mouth and she ran back to the bathroom and flipped up the toilet lid. It wasn't the illegal entry of a crime scene that made her sick. It was the knowledge that the *Road Dogs* were the primary suspects; that *they* were capable of committing a double homicide; that they had the watch and Liam; that Liam had been one of them, that he too had been capable of murder; and *she* knew all of this: she, who was not a trained professional, a cop or investigator, she who was without resources, she who couldn't convince the professionals *with* resources to help her, and yet *she* was the one lumped with responsibility to resolve it.

If she wanted the watch back, she was going to have to get it herself. She was going to have to go to the Road Dogs clubhouse and find it. Unaided. Alone.

She wiped her mouth with the thin motel toilet paper and waited for her stomach to settle. There was a bang above her. Daff stared at the ceiling as a pair of heavy footsteps crossed overhead. There was a muffling of voices. She stepped back into the shower and pushed the window ajar, but all she could hear was the distant doff-doff of nightclub music and thinning traffic.

On impulse, she crossed the small room and headed out onto the motel landing. From the stairs that led to the second storey, Daff could hear the voices more clearly, though she could only catch the odd word: *blood, here, careful.* She reached the top storey and quickly scanned left and right; not a single light was on, except in room eight. The voices were still mumbling behind the door sealed off with police tape.

Daff slid towards the window and, seeing the sliver of an opening in the curtain, she peered into the room. The two men were of medium height and build, both dressed in their high-vis traffic control jackets. One had a camera looped around his neck; he raised the SLR to his eye-level as he stepped into the bathroom. There was a snap and bright flash. The second officer, who had been crouching and examining a blood stain on the carpet, looked up. "You all done, Gibbs?"

A second flash. "No good, mate. The light's too shit in here. Without the flash, you can barely see the mark; with the flash the reflection is blown out. Sorry, Jimbo, but we're gonna have to come back in the morning."

"Lawrence needed the extra pictures tonight."

Daff felt her throat tighten.

"Tough titties. It ain't my fuck-up. If Lawrence wants a clear picture, then he'll have to wait 'til morning."

"Bags you telling him."

Gibbs emerged from the bathroom and made for the door. "Come on then, there's a joint around the corner where we can pick up a couple of coffees. That'll soften the blow." Daff slipped from her peeping Tom position and pressed beside the thick decorative pier that separated room eight from room nine. The two officers stepped out onto the landing. Gibbs moved towards the stairs as the one dubbed Jimbo fumbled for the light switch.

"You right there?" Gibbs palmed the railing, looking back over his shoulder towards Daff.

She jolted, her breath trapped in her throat.

The landing plummeted into darkness. "Yeah, mate. Got it."

Daff held her position until she heard the sharp snap of two car doors. Finally releasing her breath, she pushed away from the wall and risked looking out over the car park. The police-issue Holden flicked on its headlights and pulled out onto the street.

Though Jimbo had switched off the light, Daff hadn't heard the door lock click. Turning, she reached for room eight's doorknob, briefly remembering how easy it had been for Melissa to pick the lock at the pawn shop and wondering, if the door were locked, whether she would be able to recreate the technique with a bobby pin from her hair. Thankfully, she needn't find out; the door opened easily.

Daff ducked beneath the tape and quietly closed the door. She considered turning the light on, but decided against it. The receptionist, had she bothered to look up from her phone, might have seen the officers leave. If she were to look up towards room eight and see a light on, Daff would be hard pressed to come up with a reasonable explanation for why she wasn't downstairs in her own overpriced room.

Daff pulled out her phone and found the torchlight app. The room was identical to the one downstairs. Only the bed in this room was unmade, the covers flipped back, and there was a dark stain in front of the wardrobe, in the centre of the floor. Tip-toeing around the bloody patch (Lawrence had referred to it as *the Sundowner murders,* so it didn't take a genius to work out what the mark was from), Daff crossed into the bathroom and closed the door before switching the light on.

At first, she couldn't see what it was the officer had been trying to photograph, but as she turned towards the vanity, her own reflection was interrupted by an angry smear. The crimson symbol was crudely drawn, looking like a ghoulish child's finger painting. A circle slashed with a diagonal line. She'd seen this before. It was the same simple image that Jake Reilly had tattooed on his biceps. She stepped forward and gingerly pressed her fingers onto the glass. The blood that had been used to draw the picture was dry and lightly flaking. Pushing aside any thoughts of disturbing trace evidence, Daff spread her fingers wide and covered the symbol with her hand. Her stomach tightened as the room began to spin; she locked her legs and pushed her feet hard into the floor, focussing on the symbol, as its memory took over.

There were voices coming from outside the room. Two men were talking quickly, impatiently. For a moment, Daff thought Gibbs and Jimbo had seen the light on and come rushing back, but when she looked back towards the mirror, she saw not her own face but Melissa Sweet's hazel eyes and corkscrew hair. Daff's head spun as her mind raced from blank to a hundred questions. She lifted her shaking hand—Melissa's hand—and saw that the pads of her fingers were wet and red.

She looked up at the mirror and its freshly painted symbol. "That's the best that I can do." She whispered to her own reflection. Feeling suddenly lightheaded, she pressed the back of her hand against her forehead, mindful of her bloody fingers. "Better than nothing." Snapping on the tap, she scrubbed her hand in the vanity sink.

Daff pushed against the boundaries of her friend's mind, trying to catch a thought, a reason for why she was here, *how* she was here, why she was drawing a symbol on a mirror at a crime scene. But Melissa's mind was focussed elsewhere: *He's gotta believe that I won't squeal. I drew the symbol; I've got as much to lose as he does. Well, maybe not quite as much—shit—I'll never be able to leave Tramp now.* Melissa's stomach coiled in a knot. *I'm not dying in this fucking motel room.* The thought was fierce as the psychic quickly composed her features. She pulled off her black shirt, the chains around her neck jiggling, and wiped down the taps and door handle. Her palms still damp, she slipped the top back on, straightening, and re-entered the motel room.

"You finished, babe?" A tall man wearing a bandanna stood in the open doorway. *What's he doing here?* Daff thought as the memories of Jake Reilly's drug deal and Liam pulling the trigger merged with the shocking knowledge: *Melissa knew this man too.*

"Close the damn door!" Melissa's voice came as a harsh whisper and Daff felt a swirl of conflicting emotions: Melissa was relieved not to be alone any more, but she was also nervous about what was coming next.

Tramp stepped into the room, half closing the door behind him, eyebrows raised.

"Yes, I'm finished." The psychic tried to swallow despite the thickness in her throat. Her fingertips buzzed. *I touched her blood. We're connected.* "Where did Henry go?"

"He's waitin' downstairs. We'd better get going." The bandanna man, Tramp, pushed the door open and stepped out onto the landing. She could hear the quiet thump of his footsteps leading away from her. *He won't go far; just in case I do something stupid.*

The psychic started to follow, but then paused, glancing over her shoulder towards the corner of the room. She'd told herself not to look, but now that's all she wanted to do. It was worse than she thought. The body of Sarah Miller sat propped in a chair, her mouth open and drooping. Melissa had never liked Sarah, but that didn't mean she wanted her dead. The psychic's eyes shifted towards the second body dumped on the floor. Beth had been young, sweet, naïve;

given more time, the girl may have had enough sense to wake up, see through the false glamour of this life and build something real.

Daff felt as if she'd been punched in the stomach. Beth Dawson. The memories of Beth's final moment—her head pushed in the carpet, a knife dragged over her throat—overlapped this memory like the psychic version of a before-and-after shot.

She could feel Melissa's heart starting to gallop as the gravity of the scene sunk in. Her breath was quickening, sweat glands opening. *Stop it, calm down. Keep your shit together, girl. They can't see you freak out.*

"Come on, love." Tramp reappeared in the doorway; his voice was gruff and impatient. Melissa turned, bile filling her throat as she stepped across the barrier that separated the criminal from the psychic.

Daff's hand dropped from the mirror. She remembered again that her presence there could mess up the trace evidence, but when she rubbed the tips of her fingers together, she found them soft and powdery. The place had already been dusted. She flicked off the bathroom light and stepped back into the motel bedroom. A moment ago this same small room had been filled with light and panic and people: two alive and two dead. Now, it was just Daff and the darkness.

Melissa Sweet was with the Road Dogs.

She was with Tramp, though she'd looked at him more with fear than affection. Daff's knees wobbled and she reluctantly sat down on the corner of the unmade bed. Tramp knew Liam. If Melissa was with Tramp, did that mean she knew Liam too? The psychic had described Liam physical appearance: tall, pale, dark eyes and hair, yet, she had genuinely appeared not to recognise him.

Lawrence's words echoed in her ears, *Bikies live off lies. They have to be good at spinning shit, because if they're not it could be the end of a club.* In the memory, Melissa had been nervous, she'd thought she could be next. Remorse for the lost lives had been there too, but she'd chosen Henry, Tramp and herself over them. If she recognised Liam in her vision, would she have kept that information to herself?

Daff felt her stomach go cold: *does she know that I'm Lawrence's daughter?* She had to get out of this room; the musty air was suddenly suffocating. Crossing the room with three wide steps, she threw the door open without caution. There was no breeze outside on the narrow landing, but the night's air was a vast improvement, and Daff ran a hand over her clammy face.

"What are you doing?"

The air rushed from her lungs as she turned to face the receptionist leaning against the railing, a cigarette dangling from her fingers. Her panic eased for a moment—it was only the girl—then she remembered that the door to room eight stood open behind them.

"Those things will kill you." She nodded towards the girl's hand.

The teenager flicked her eyes towards the open door. "Ah-huh."

Daff absently checked her wrist, then remember that the watch was gone. She didn't have time for small talk or the energy to create a diversion. "Are you going to call the cops?"

The receptionist blew out a mouthful of smoke and stubbed the cigarette out. "Only if there's another body in there."

Daff shook her head and said that there wasn't, that she'd only wanted to look. "Never seen a crime scene before," she lied. Whether the teenager believed her or not, no cops showed. Daff pulled out of the Sundowner Motel ten minutes later; the only sirens she heard were inside her head.

Daff didn't need a GPS this time; she drove north on the Deagon Deviation and crossed the Ted Smout Memorial Bridge. The clubhouse was a few streets back from the end of the Esplanade. When she realised she was ten minutes from her destination, her heart quickened. There was no plan, only two simple steps: find Liam, get the watch back. There was no guarantee that the Road Dogs had the watch, but it was the only lead she had.

It was after midnight when Daff's Beetle hit the Esplanade, and the waning moon lit a strip of glitter across the water's surface. She took a left turn, disappearing into the empty backstreets of Redcliffe.

Lawrence's report had said the clubhouse was number seven, but the aged letterbox plates were nearly impossible to read. The left-hand side of the street was filled with poorly cared-for beach shacks, and the right was a hodge-podge of light commercial buildings, mostly empty—some had faded *For Lease* signs displayed in the window. Between a flaking butcher's shop, number five, and a dilapidated Queenslander, number nine, there was a wide dirt road. Banyans stood either side of the driveway. Beyond that first line of trees, Daff could see nothing.

Her hands were clammy on the wheel as she swung the VW onto the shoulder of the road. She would have preferred to keep the car close, but there was no knowing how long the driveway was and she didn't exactly want to announce her arrival. She opened the car door, slipped out and headed towards the shadowy drive. The thick canopy blocked out both the street lights and the stars, and after just a few steps, Daff had to stop until her eyes adjusted to the dark.

The dirt road was smooth and flat. Probably been recently graded, she thought. The only sound that travelled down it was the crash of nearby waves and the padding of her own feet, but she found some comfort in the closeness of the trees, and her hammering heart began to settle. The road was shorter than she had expected, ending at a small clearing that must have served as a car park during the day. It was empty, though there were two Harleys parked alongside the building. The shed was large and dotted with windows, and in front of the corrugated iron door was a concrete slab.

She stepped onto the makeshift entertainment area and carefully rounded the upturned cable drums littered with beer bottles. The shed's main entrance, a large sliding door, had been left open and Daff was suddenly thankful that she had parked out on the street. There was a dim light coming from within and when Daff stepped inside, she could see a few small lamps dotted around a pieced-together bar. Behind the L-shaped counter were two wooden cupboards, their doors pulled off and their shelves filled with bottles of spirits, glasses and stubbies. Past the bar, three sedans were parked in the corner and a few bikes lay in scattered pieces across the concrete floor. The place smelt like any workshop, a combination of oil, ethanol and metal. Her chest sunk as her eyes fell onto a black metal-framed chair. She recognised it immediately as the chair Ben had been sitting in when Liam shot him.

Daff! The hairs on the back of her neck stood up as she spun around. A rickety staircase connected the workshop to a second-floor office, and at the base of the staircase stood Liam. She released the breath she'd been holding and smiled uncertainly as the horrific memory of Ben's ricocheting body mixed with the relief that she'd been right: the watch was here. Liam's own face relaxed and Daff moved towards him, pushing the memory of the murder aside; she raised her arm, illogically, to embrace him before remembering that she couldn't. She stopped in front of him, her arms falling awkwardly by her side. "Are you okay?"

He laughed and Daff felt the tips of her ears redden at the idiocy of the question.

"Yeah, I'm fine, but don't talk out loud. Two of the fellas are here." Seeing the alarm on Daff's face he hastily added, "They're asleep."

I'm sorry I left the watch behind. When I picked up that gun, I had another vision.

"I know, Daff, I saw it too. I gotta say, I didn't think I'd be seeing you again."

You saw the vision?

He nodded. "Yeah I did, so I get why you split." There was a note of disappointment in his tone, but she wasn't sure whether it was directed at her or himself. Daff raked a hand through her hair and looked around; wherever the men were sleeping, she couldn't see them. Though she was relieved to have found Liam, she knew now wasn't the time for a D&M.

Where's the watch?

"Henry threw it in a drawer upstairs. Be careful though, the stairs squeak like all get-out." He turned and soundlessly mounted the stairs, leading the way. Unlike Liam, Daff had to grip the handrail in attempt to distribute her body weight as she gingerly ascended the stairs.

Have you found anything out?

"Nah. After you left, Henry and Tramp—the guys from your vision—came into the house and picked up the watch. They brought my stuff back here, for now anyway, then the police came and took Henry away for questioning. He got back about an hour ago, had some beers with Tramp and crashed out."

After you left. Three small words that renewed her shame. *After I abandoned you.* They reached the top of the stairs and, though it was dark, Daff could see that the narrow landing was made from sheets of sturdy metallic grids; opposite the stairs was a donga with a single door and window.

"It's not locked." Liam pointed at the closed door before walking through it.

He was right. Daff twisted the knob, opening the door by inches, thankful that it was quieter than the staircase. Inside, the modestly sized office was divided in two by a six-foot long counter; to the left was a kitchenette and to the right a desk, covered in grubby ledgers, ripped envelopes and loose papers.

"It's in the top drawer." Liam stepped towards the desk that housed three drawers on its right-hand side.

Daff slipped her fingers into the lip of the drawer and pulled gently at the chipped pine. Inside was more paperwork, opened mail and loose receipts, but on top of the scattered papers lay the watch. She felt her relief renewed as she scooped it up, looped the straps over her wrist and pulled them tight.

A heavy thud echoed from the staircase, followed by Tramp's coarse voice. "No, mate, I'm telling ya, I saw you drop your keys on the desk."

Daff's eyes flicked over the chaotic mass of paperwork spread across the desk until she spotted the dull glimmer of a key and its attached leather chain.

"Hide." Liam pointed at the kitchen. "The other side of the bench. Crouch down there. Now!"

Daff rounded the slim breakfast bar that separated the kitchenette from the small office, wedging herself into the corner where the counter top butted against the fibro wall. Thankfully, she hadn't turned on a light, but it was the second time that night she'd been caught out because she'd left a door open; hopefully Henry and Tramp weren't that observant. Her heart thumped in her ears, yet she could still hear the rasp of her breath. Daff clamped a hand over her mouth and nose in an attempt to stifle the sound. She tried to recall Melissa's breathing exercises, but the memory of Melissa's bloody fingers only caused Daff more panic.

Liam stepped around the counter and crouched beside her. "They're coming. Be quiet." Daff had no intention of doing anything else.

There was a click as the overhead fluorescent lights flickered to life. Daff's breath hitched as she instinctively shielded her eyes. The floor vibrated as the two men thumped into the office.

"Told ya, mate." There was a crisp shuffling of paperwork. "Think fast."

A metallic clink sounded as the owner of the keys caught the projectile. Daff pressed herself further into the corner, knowing that if either man stepped over the plastic edging that segregated the shitty carpet from the shittier vinyl, she'd have nowhere to go.

She glanced at Liam. *Why aren't they leaving? Get up, tell me what they're doing.*

He whispered a half-apology. Then he stood and his jaw dropped. "We left the drawer open."

"Where's the watch?" Henry's voice came over the sound of shuffling papers, the snapping of each drawer as it was yanked opened and then slammed shut.

The drumming of Daff's heart was so loud she was certain they could hear it. She had to get out of here. There were two exit points: the window and the door. The latter was closer, but it was on the other side of the bench, beside Henry and Tramp. She scanned the counter tops for anything that could be used as a weapon; there was nothing except a couple of unwashed mugs.

"I threw it in the top drawer, can't ya see it?" Tramp's voice came from the other side of the counter, so close it felt as though the tall biker were standing over her.

"It's not fuckin' there, mate. You were muckin' around over there before, check the counters."

Daff's eyes met Liam's. *Shit.*

The office shook as Tramp's heavy footfall crossed the thin floor. Daff could feel her mind shifting, focussing. She knew what was happening and she tried to calm herself by concentrating on the physiology: her amygdala had released a dose of catecholamine, a neurotransmitter chemical that would boost her energy supplies and help her outrun this immediate threat. Hopefully. Daff curled up onto the balls of her feet, bracing one arm on the cupboard beside her and the other against the wall.

Liam couldn't help her, and the pain of that knowledge was plastered across his face. "Fuck, fuck, fuck."

The footsteps came close and Daff braced herself as she saw one leather boot hit the linoleum, then the other. Everything slowed down. Each second stretched out, just as it had on the night of the accident. She'd been aware of every moment: the car in front of her, the instinctive response to swerve, the arc of the headlights across the pines and their thick unforgiving trunks. It hadn't happened quickly. It was slow, and still she'd not be able to act, to correct the car, to save Tom's life. Click, crack, boom.

Tramp stepped into the kitchenette. His wallet chain clinked against his hip as he scanned the far counter, his meaty hands opened the cupboard drawers, idly scanning their contents. A cramp rippled up Daff's right calf and she bit down on the inside of her lip.

"Get ready." Liam's hands curled into useless fists beside him.

Tramp straightened and turned towards the centre counter, his eyes briefly locking with Daff's.

"What the—"

Daff sprung from the corner and skimmed across the dividing bench as she felt Tramp swipe at the back of her shirt. "Henry! Get her!"

Daff bolted for the door as Henry scrambled after her. The stairs were steep, and she gripped the railing to stop herself from toppling down, but as her foot hit the first step she felt an arm tuck around her waist and pull her back. Henry locked her to him, clasping his left hand over her mouth. She reached up and grasped his hand, trying to pull it off, to scream, but he was stronger than her. She could have kicked off the ground, forcing the full weight of her body back onto him, but she knew he was too solid for that trick.

"Tramp! Give me a fuckin' hand." The stink of tobacco blew onto Daff's face.

The landing shook as Tramp stomped up behind them, stepping into view. He pushed back her hair before his wide mouth pulled up into a half-smile. "Fuck me."

"What?" Henry tightened his arms around her.

"It's the fuckin' detective's daughter." Tramp pulled at the hand that was still clasped over Henry's and held up her wrist. "Found the watch."

"Daff, don't say anything." Liam stepped in beside Tramp. "Try and stay calm." Daff wanted to argue that that was the exact opposite of what she needed to do. She knew he was right though; if she panicked, she could miss her opportunity to escape.

"Take her. Bitch is stronger than she looks."

Henry released his grip and pushed her towards his number two. Tramp wrapped his meaty hands over her shoulders and shoved her forward, away from the stairs and back into the office. Crammed between the desk and the dividing counter, Daff felt as if the room was closing in on her.

"Close the door." Henry looked towards Tramp, who released Daff and did as he was told.

She swivelled and stepped to the side, determined to keep her eyes on both of them. Tramp locked the flimsy door before leaning back against it, crossing his arms over his chest. Her adrenaline had started to fade, and with the door blocked off, the unwelcomed thought arose: *I'm not leaving this room.*

"Yes you are." Liam came in close beside her, though they both knew the protective stance was futile.

"It's been a while, kiddo. You know, I can't actually remember your name—was it Danni? Debbie?" Henry's eye ran over her and she shuddered. When she didn't answer, he continued. "Why are here? And why the fuck are you wearing my watch?"

"Say you were at a party, that you were playing a drinking game and someone dared you to bust into the clubhouse and steal something." Liam moved forward, stepping between herself and Henry.

Daff had never been a good liar, but the truth wasn't an option either. "I was at a party. The guys dared me to break in here and steal something."

"Fuck off. Lawrence sent you, didn't he? Couldn't be bothered gettin' a warrant so he sent you to find some kinda evidence." He straightened and looped his thumps through the top of his jeans. "Nah, that can't be it. Your dad wouldn't have the balls to do something like that." He looked down at the watch that was still strapped to her wrist. "You went to the Sunny Coast." It wasn't a question. Daff's eyes shot up and Henry's smile broadened to reveal his gold-capped canine. "You haven't seen your old man for near on eighteen months. So, why the fuck are you here?"

"How do you know that?" Daff's vision began to blur and she wiped at her eyes with the back of her hand.

Henry laughed. "I keep tabs on pig-cunts. Why are you here?" Before Daff had the chance to respond, Henry stepped through Liam and crossed the space between them. "Tell me." Daff stared at the biker, lips pressed, rising to her full height. The old biker snorted before swiftly pulling a blade from the back of his jeans and slipping it against her throat. "Tell me!"

Remembering the clean burn of Beth's slit throat, Daff struggled to push the word out. "Mike."

Henry lowered the knife. "What about him?"

"What are you doing? Daff, shut up." Liam's face looked horrified as his glance moved from Henry to Tramp.

"I was seeing him."

Henry dropped his hand. Daff coughed while also trying to take in as much air as possible.

"You were fuckin' Mike? You gotta be kidding me." Henry's brows shot up towards his hairline. "You just can't seem to stay away from us, huh darlin'?" The biker's eyes narrowed as his hands moved towards his belt, freeing the strap from its buckle. "Like a bit of biker dick, eh? Tell ya what, love, if you're any good at head, I'll let you walk out of here with all your teeth." He undid the top button and let the jeans fall unto the floor.

Daff looked towards Liam; his brows knitted together and he shook his head.

"Nowhere to go, darlin'." Henry's hand tugged at his flaccid penis, encouraging it into life.

"Henry," Tramp stepped forward and grabbed the bikie president by the arm. "Her dad's a fuckin' cop. You really want to do this?"

Henry pulled his arm free and shoved the bandanna man back. "Stay in front of the door, she's not goin' anywhere."

There was no sense of time warping or slowing down. Instead, Daff felt her mind empty, her senses becoming numb.

Liam moved towards her. "Daff, do as he says."

"What?" She spat the question at the invisible man, no longer caring if she looked insane.

"Trust me, I got this."

"You *got this*?"

Henry looked over his shoulder towards his sergeant-in-arms. "Ice Queen?"

Tramp's eyes narrowed and he shook his head. "Don't reckon—too coordinated, and her pupils look normal."

Henry shrugged, his eyes meeting Daff's before nodding towards the floor. "I like the crazy ones betta anyhow."

"Trust me." Liam's face hardened as he stared down the old biker. "Please."

This better be a fucking good plan. Daff felt her entire body harden as she sunk to her knees. She looked directly at Tramp, her face wrinkled with disgust, and the tall biker shifted against the door before turning his attention to the kitchenette.

"Now or never, darlin'." Henry's hand clasped the back of her head.

Liam suddenly crouched down beside her, his arms wide. For a moment, Daff illogically thought he was trying to hug her, then his voice cut through her mind urgently. *Don't fight me; let go!* Daff shuddered as a cool tingling spread over her skin then abruptly burrowed inward. Suddenly, her whole body felt tight, as though her organs had swelled to twice their size. *Daff, relax!* She blew out a breath of air as her right hand shot up and punched the biker in the balls.

Henry released her head, sinking to his knees as he cupped the space between his legs and groaned.

Let go! Liam's voice echoed inside her head, and Daff reluctantly released her control. Involuntarily, she felt herself curl around the biker's crumbling frame and snatch the hunting knife from its sheath. She could feel Liam's thoughts pushing and pulling her limbs as though they were on strings; her arm lifted swiftly before being forced back down, her elbow smacking into Henry's temple. The biker howled again as Daff leapt over him and made for the door. Tramp lunged forward, his arm swinging wide, but Daff ducked beneath the blow as she drove the blade upwards, slicing the biker's ribs. The cut was shallow, but the shock of the assault caused the biker to drop to the floor and he landed on all fours. His mouth fell open as he pressed a hand to his side and Daff brought her leg down on the back of his neck. Her lungs burned, but she couldn't catch her breath; her chest was too full, too tight. She could feel her brain firing, trying to push Liam out, trying to reassert its control.

Daff, stop! Not yet. Let me get us out of here.

Daff forced the instinct down as she sprang forward, flung open the door and bolted for the staircase. Angry shouts bit at the air behind her as she hit the concrete of the floor below and sprinted out the warehouse door. Blinded by the sudden darkness, Daff felt, rather than saw, her feet hit the dirt driveway as Liam pushed her body down the narrow track and out onto the street. She squinted beneath the street lights as she bolted around her car. Fumbling with the VW's door, she realised she was still holding Henry's blade. Slipping it under her arm, she popped the door open, flung the knife onto the passenger's side floor and jammed the key into the ignition. It wasn't until she'd crossed the Ted Smout Memorial Bridge that she felt Liam's influence slip from her limbs.

After Daff passed the Deagon Wetlands, she pulled the car over; her hands no longer able to grip the wheel. The VW's digital clock told her it was approaching two in the morning. She pressed her head back into the car seat as her muscles hummed with an ache that drove to the bone.

"How did you do that? What *was* that? Possession?"

He didn't answer at first, not until she shifted her gaze towards the passenger seat.

"You know how I've been trying to move objects?"

Daff nodded, the action igniting a fresh cramp across her shoulders and making her wince.

"It never worked. No matter how hard I tried or how light the object. There was this one night though, I was kicking about in the yard, and I could hear your neighbour's dog whining."

"You mean Molly?" The image of her neighbour's cocker spaniel rose in her mind.

He grinned. "Yeah, Molly, and I thought, maybe she could sense me, you know? Like she did that morning you went over to feed her. So, I stepped through the fence and right into her. There was this sinking feeling, like our energies were mixing. It only lasted for a second, 'cos the next thing I know, Molly's bolted back up the stairs to her bed on the verandah, and I was myself again. I didn't know if it would work tonight, but thought it might."

Daff felt a flicker of rage spark as she realised how easily Liam's plan could have failed, but the exhaustion that plagued her limbs stopped any impending argument. Besides, she thought, the plan *had* worked. "Thank you."

He snorted. "You're welcome. You feeling alright?"

"Yeah." She shifted in her seat, rubbing her side. "I mean, everything hurts, but otherwise yeah, I'm fine."

"We should probably keep moving. I don't know if those guys are gonna follow us, but if they do, I don't have the energy to do any more body jumping."

Daff tried to steady her hands as she started the ignition and pulled out onto the street, but they shook anyway. She'd never punched anyone before, and though she was used to slicing open bodies, they hadn't been breathing. "You're a good fighter. I couldn't have done what you did," she said.

Though her eyes were on the road, she could tell from his voice that Liam was smiling. "Lucky you lift corpses for a living, if you were a paper pusher, the *possession* wouldn't have made a difference." Despite his modesty, she could hear a glimmer of pride; it must have felt good to finally have been able to *do* something.

Keeping her eyes on the road, Daff held out her hand as if she were holding an invisible tray. "See if you can touch my hand."

"What?" Liam shrunk away from her extended hand. "I can *walk* through you. It won't work."

"That was *before*; what's the harm? Just give it a go."

From the corner of her eyes she saw Liam slowly raise his hand and lay it over the top of hers. A cool prickling sensation plucked at her palm—a subtler form of pins and needles.

"That's how it feels for me too."

Daff raised her eyebrows.

"Sometimes I can hear your thoughts, even when you're not directly talking to me."

"Great," Daff added dryly.

Liam released his hand and sunk back into his chair. "Before I jumped into you tonight," he paused, as if considering whether that was the best way to describe what had happened, "I hadn't felt anything … well … ever, I guess. I can't even remember what it felt like to hold a cup, let alone—"

"Another man's balls?" Daff laughed, thinking she must be beyond exhausted to be making jokes about Henry's attempted assault.

"I was gonna say 'knock someone out', but sure, what you said works too. Anyway, where are we going?"

Daff had been wondering that herself. Though she'd paid for the night at the Sundowner, the idea of returning there wasn't appealing. It's not like she'd actually be able to fall asleep in that room, having seen the bloodstained carpet in the room above her. Plus, she was a little worried that receptionist might change her mind and call the cops after all. She could go to the station, but a second round with Lawrence was even less appealing. Driving home was an impossibility too; no way could she make the hour-long trip back to the Sunny Coast.

"Peta." She felt the dull spark of inspiration. "Her flat is over in Clayfield, just fifteen minutes from here." Daff had never been so thankful for her hippie friend; she could feel the adrenaline leaving her system and her eyelids beginning to droop. Now that they'd settled on a destination, she could feel herself settling into the drive as she followed the curve of the road, turning out onto Sandgate.

"You reckon we ever would have met?"

Her breath hitched and she risked a tired glance towards her passenger. "When you were alive, you mean? I guess it's possible, but it wouldn't have been on good terms. You were a member of the outlaw club that my father was trying to shut down."

"Yeah, I guess you're right." Though he sounded unconvinced. "But why *you*?"

"What do you mean?" Daff's brow scrunched, the tiredness she'd felt only a moment ago beginning to dissipate.

"Why can *you* see me? Why did *you* find the watch?"

Daff shrugged, recalling the many metaphysical arguments she'd had with Peta over the years. "It's not just elderly people that I embalm, you know."

"What does that—"

"You saw me embalm that girl and that guy who were in their twenties, right?"

"Yeah?"

"They're not the youngest." Daff stared out into the empty street as she passed through a succession of green lights. "I've embalmed a kid before, he was only six, died of leukaemia. What reason could there possibly be for that? Not everything happens for a reason. Maybe some stuff is just random."

She crossed the intersection at Junction Road and the small cluster of shops beyond that and pulled over in front of Peta's small apartment block. "I'm sorry—look, maybe there is a reason, maybe there's not. Either way, I'm glad I know you now."

Liam nodded, but said nothing.

Daff pulled the phone out of her jeans pocket—miraculously still there—before deciding to pocket it again; there didn't seem much point in calling Peta now that she was outside her building. She leaned across the centre console, and Liam jumped.

Daff looked up at him, eyebrows raised. "I was just reaching for the knife." As she picked the blade up from the passenger side floor, she felt her stomach clench and her head swirl. She hadn't been prepared. Though she couldn't remember when she'd last eaten, the slim contents of her stomach threatened to come up.

The back of Daff's head hit the soft cushioning of the car seat. Though the vehicle was stationary, it took a moment for her churning belly to settle. She glanced out the rear passenger window and gasped.

The gum trees that surrounded the car were smooth and almost glossy, the way they always were this time of year. In summer, though, when Ruth used to bring her here for afternoon swims, the trees were shedding; their bark dipping into the water in long strips and flaking curls. She couldn't see the river from here, but she knew it was there; the tall eucalyptus trees gathered around the channel like sentries, looking out across the multiple dirt tracks that led into the area. For a moment, she felt the ghost of her mother's hand touch her own, but when she looked down her grasp was empty.

She hadn't moved, and yet she felt the cushioning beneath her shift, and she turned. She found herself in the back seat, and Liam was sitting beside her. His hands cupped in prayer, forced together by the zip tie that bound his wrists. If it wasn't for the tightness around his eyes, he would have looked calm. She followed his gaze. Henry Ernst sat in the passenger seat in front of her, though he was looking over his shoulder towards Liam. Tramp sat snugly behind the wheel, tossing the car keys between his hands.

"Who you working for?" Henry's golden tooth shone between each word.

Liam said nothing, his eyes shifting back and forth between Henry and Tramp.

"Is it that bastard Lawrence or Sergeant O'Neil?"

Tramp stopped fiddling with the keys and shot Henry a look as he reached for the car door handle. The president shook his head, turning his attention back to Liam.

"You haven't squealed, have ya? You been handling the crates at the port for nine months, which makes me think you've kept your mouth shut, 'cos if you hadn't, Tramp and I would be in handcuffs."

Liam opened his mouth, but all that came out was a ragged breath; he shifted away from the old biker and looked out into the depths of the Beerwah Waterhole. The Boiler.

Tramp had parked on the right-hand side, parallel to the narrow river. It was always shady here thanks to the established gums and dense grass that took root either side of the bank; their density cast a dappled light so that even in summer the temperature stayed cool. Daff remembered how she'd once slipped on the bank's smooth stone while crossing the short waterfall that spilled into the pool, and twisted her ankle.

"What do they know, *Mike?* You know, a member on the inside would be pretty fuckin' handy. I don't have to kill you."

Liam snorted and raised his chin towards the water. "Then why did you bring me here?"

"I said I don't *have* to kill you, not that I *won't.*"

"It doesn't matter what you do to me now. You're fucked, mate. No way are you getting off a double homicide."

Tramp opened his door and stepped to Liam's side in a single stride. He flung open the back door, grabbed Liam by the throat of his shirt and hauled him backwards onto the hard, compacted soil. Henry got out of the car, strolling around the front. Daff's heart thumped as she slipped over the seat and out the still-open door.

She needed to do something. She needed to stop this. Tramp tossed Liam on the ground, dragged him by his linked hands closer to the water and stopped, raising his fist. Instinctively, she reached out to grab his swinging arm, but his meaty hands went through her own unhindered. The fleshy smack as knuckle met eye socket made her wince. Liam groaned.

"Take it easy, Tramp. Kid's still gotta talk." Henry grabbed Liam by his shoulders and lifted him onto his feet. "You betta tell me, boy. What do the cops know?"

"Nothing." Liam spat out a mouthful of blood, scarcely missing Tramp's boot. "I haven't reported shit, alright? They know nothing about the port. But it doesn't matter 'cos Tramp's goddamn girlfriend drew the fuckin' club logo on the bathroom mirror."

"It's not enough for a conviction."

"No, but it's enough to spark Lawrence's attention again. You think he ain't comin' after you? The scene was a mess anyhow, you would have left something behind, a fingerprint, hair. They'll find it and then you're done. It's over. Road Dogs are dead."

Henry whipped the blade from its side sheaf and held it against Liam's throat.

"It's one thing to kill your wife, mate. It's another to kill a cop," Liam hissed. His gaze was steady, but Daff could hear the waver in his voice.

Tramp must have heard it too. "Well, if we're so fucked, *Mike*, or whatever the fuck your name is, what's one more body to the count?"

Henry stepped back as Tramp gripped Liam's throat with one hand and hooked the other around his shoulders to steady him, his biceps pulsing. "Go old school, straight in the heart." The bandanna man's voice was gruff with the effort of holding up Liam's six-foot frame.

Daff knew how much force it took to drive a knife into a grown man's chest cavity.

Henry took his stance. The tendons of his sinewy arms were taut. "Why didn't you rat on us?"

Locked in a death grip, Liam's answer came as a strangled whisper. "If I had, Beth wouldn't be dead. Fuck you Henry, I don't owe you shit."

Henry smirked, raised the knife and lunged forward. Daff reached out, but as she grasped the knife, Henry's blade cut through her and plunged into Liam's heart.

She hadn't been prepared for the blood.

Henry withdrew his blade, stepped back and gave Tramp one quick nod. Tramp released his grip and Liam landed with a thud, his hands instinctively clutching the wound. It wouldn't be long now; death following a stab to the heart is almost instant as the vital organ fails to maintain its normal pressure, causing a stop to the cerebral blood flow. Daff knew all this, but it didn't help.

Daff knelt beside Liam, determined to stay with him during those last few moments of life. His head was turned towards the sky, the brilliant light of morning caught in his brown eyes, bringing out hues of chestnut and gold. Her outstretched hand hovered over the wound, and she cursed its uselessness; now *she* was the ghost. The scene was too familiar; she'd been here before. She'd replayed a moment just like this a thousand times, a constant loop on nights when she couldn't sleep.

He always died. Not once could she save *him.*

Now, Liam would be added to that miserable feedback loop. "I'm sorry."

Liam's head shifted, his gaze crossed hers. He couldn't see her—she knew that—but maybe he could hear her. Daff allowed her eyes to soften as she willed a message forward. *You are not alone.* Her vision blurred, but she caught a twitch at the corner of Liam's mouth before it relaxed completely. His heart accepted its fate.

"Can't move him, there's too much blood. It'll get through the boot and then the pigs'll have a field day." Tramp marched back towards the car, popped open the car boot and pulled out sheets of hessian. "Wrap him in this. It'll be less noticeable. I haven't got a shovel."

"Don't bother, lad, throw him in the river." Henry waved a hand at the still water.

Tramp shook his head. "Nah, mate, too risky. The body'll float or some kid will swing off that rope and land on him. We don't have time to weigh him down proper and I got to meet up with Jake soon. We'll come back and get him after. Blood would've dried by then."

Tramp grabbed Henry's knife, cut off the zip tie and held up Liam's limp left arm, examining the watch.

Henry collapsed with a thud, his face drained of colour. "Whatcha doin'?"

"I don't want this watch winding up on some pig's desk." Tramp tossed the knife at its owner, freeing his hands so he could slip the watch off Liam's wrist and into his pocket.

"Right-o, right-o." Henry panted. The exertion had tired him and he was showing his age. "We'll get one of the noms to take him out on the next shipment. He'll be floating in the Tasman Sea before long."

Daff watched numbly as the two aging bikers rolled Liam's limp body in the fibrous material and tossed the bundle into a dense crop of bush away from the water. Daff watched as Henry gingerly washed the blade in the river and slipped it back into its sheath as though he'd just sliced an apple.

She could feel the pull. Her stomach tightened, but this time she was ready for it. When her consciousness returned to her body, she was startled by the sudden presence of urban buildings and darkened sky. The breath she'd been holding escaped as she caught sight of Liam, his face loose with amazement.

"You saw that then?"

He nodded. Though his gaze was distant and internal.

"You were a cop."

The hunt for Liam's identity had been a beacon, something to steer towards, but it didn't feel like they'd arrived at a lighthouse so much as uncovered the ashy remains of a campfire.

It would have been easier if he'd been an outlaw. Her grief would have been conflicted, but at least Liam would've died on his own terms: in pursuit of whatever freedom life on the fringe could offer. He wasn't an outlaw, not really. He'd been a boy in blue like her father—like Tom. He hadn't been chasing an anarchical existence, he'd been chasing a pay slip. He'd died doing his job, honouring his oath to serve and maintain Her Majesty's peace in accordance with the law. To act without favour or affection, malice or ill-will until legally discharged.

And he was discharged, only Daff wasn't so sure that he had maintained his oath. In the memory attached to the knife, Liam confessed he hadn't reported the details of the Road Dogs' operation, even though he could have. Perhaps his time in Henry's pack had kindled new loyalties or blurred old ones. Whatever the case, the fact remained that Liam really was dead … and Daff was the only witness to his murder.

"Daff, please shut up. I can hear everything you're thinking." She looked up and saw that Liam's face was drawn with exhaustion.

"You can hear me?" She felt her cheeks warm despite her own exhaustion.

He nodded. "Yup, clear as a bell, love. Saw the vision too. I'm dead 'cos I fucked up. Christ, I didn't even try to talk Henry out of it, if anything I only egged him on. I didn't even put up a fight. I just … let him do it."

"Your hands were bound and there were two of them, Liam. Odds weren't exactly in your favour and I think you knew that."

"I told them they were fucked. Why did I do that? I could have been their *inside man*, or at least I could have lied and said that I would."

Daff shook her head. She knew why Liam hadn't made that offer. It wouldn't take long for his handler to discover that Liam had more than enough intel on the Road Dogs to smother their business and lock-up its members. He'd be dishonourably discharged, charged for withholding information and receive an unwelcomed sentence of his own—and they both knew what happened to cops in prison.

"Daff, stop, please."

"Sorry."

She looked up towards the windows of Peta's apartment. It was well after three and the lights were, unsurprisingly, off. Daff opened her door and headed towards the open brick fence that surrounded the four-storey building.

"Where are you going?" Liam fell into step beside her.

"I've got a vital piece of evidence and I'm the only witness to your murder. If something happens to me, then that's it; your body may never be found, your family will never be notified, and Henry gets away with murder. I need to tell someone what happened."

"And what, your detective father isn't good enough?"

"I need to tell someone who will believe me."

CHAPTER 18

Detective Lawrence

Sunday July 3, 2016

Lawrence had heard the other coppers describe the smell of blood as metallic or like iron. From his experience, it took a lot of blood to make that smell. Standing outside the closed door of room eight, he could smell the crime scene's multiple blood stains and knew something wasn't right.

Wait, was it multiple blood stains or just the one? Regardless, the Sundowner Motel murder happened five days ago; the blood should be dry, the smell shouldn't be this bad. Good luck to the bio tech responsible for cleaning this up. Maybe he should pop down to reception and speak to the manager, tell her it'll be easier if she just changes the carpet.

The sun had broken up the previous night's storm clouds and the detective could feel his back warming in the morning light. He paused for a moment, enjoying the heat while looking over the motel's second storey balcony. The car park was empty; the reception sign was flipped to 'closed' and there were no maids or cleaning trolleys in sight. His nose suddenly became itchy and as he lifted a hand to scratch it, he was hit in the face with the motel's plastic custom key ring. When had he gotten the key? Turning back towards the room, he slipped room eight's key into the lock and pushed back the door. The room was pitch black. Lawrence glanced over his shoulder and out onto the sunny car park. The stench of blood was stronger now, drawing his attention back to the darkened room. He crossed the threshold and flicked on the light.

Sarah Miller's blonde hair shone beneath the florescent bulb, the thick strands covering her limp face. Lawrence stepped forward when he heard a squish and looked down. The pool of blood was bigger than he remembered. Another step and he would have trodden on Beth Dawson's back; no way would the lads at forensics let him forget a mistake like that. Where was forensics? He was sure the coroners had already come to collect the bodies; he could remember seeing the release forms for Beth's body.

He crouched down, his knees screaming in protest. Something was wrong. The blood splatter was different, pooling beneath Beth's chest rather than her throat, like she'd been stabbed in the heart. Her long black hair was loose, the strands wet and steeped in her own blood. Lawrence padded his pockets, but they were empty. How had he forgotten to bring gloves? He shrugged and put it down to old age. Maybe he'd gotten the cause of death wrong too. Reaching forward, Lawrence carefully pushed back the victim's sopping hair to reveal Daphne's lifeless face. The detective fell back, his shoulder slamming into the soaked carpet as his daughter's dull eyes burrowed into his.

"Oi, Lawrence, wake up."

Lawrence's eyes snapped open and he slapped away the hands that had been shaking his shoulders. "What?" He looked around at his paper-littered desk and the embarrassingly full bullpen of the Fortitude Valley Station.

"You fell asleep." McPhee's mouth twitched, but he managed to supress the smile.

Lawrence rubbed a rough hand over his crooked neck and looked up at the station's clock. It was coming up to three o'clock. "How long was I …"

"Maybe a half an hour, not that long. I would have let you sleep, but you were starting to mumble."

Lawrence raised his eyebrows. "What was I saying?"

"I don't bloody know." The younger detective shook his head and went back to his desk.

Lawrence stood up, grabbed his chipped mug and smartphone and headed for the tearoom. He opened and closed the phone three times as he listened to the kettle boil. He knew that dreams were simply your mind's way of processing a day's events, but the look on his daughter's lifeless face—imaginary or not—was enough to unsettle any father.

Ruth had always been into dreams; she'd even owned one of those dream dictionaries. It took everything Lawrence had not to roll his eyes as his wife recounted the previous night's dreams while checking that damn book for definitions. A spider meant abundance, a snake rebirth; the idea that these images meant something—that they meant the same thing to everyone, like a shared subconsciousness—was more than Lawrence could handle. It was as far-fetched as star signs.

Lawrence's thumb hovered over Daphne's number; he didn't want that blasted dream to be his last memory of her face. The kettle binged and he closed his phone. He'd give her a bell to check that she was alright once the sun was up.

CHAPTER 19

Daff

Sunday July 3, 2016

It took three rounds of knocking before Peta opened the door. Despite the odd hour, she greeted Daff with her usual warmth and immediately set about brewing a pot of tea. Daff sank into her friend's couch and dropped Henry's knife onto the coffee table. Amongst the crystals and tarot decks, the blade looked startlingly out of place. While the tea steeped, Daff recounted the night's events, from Melissa's betrayal to the clubhouse and the memory of Liam's death.

"Do you think Melissa's been lying to *us*? Do you think she's known this entire time who Liam is?" Peta wanted to know.

Daff shrugged; it was hard to say. She knew Melissa was the real deal when it came to psychic readings, but other than that, she knew very little about the woman. "I don't know. When I go back into people's memories, I can only hear their thoughts when they're thinking them. It sounded like she wanted to leave Tramp—the guy with the bandanna—but then she drew the symbol on the mirror."

Daff grabbed a pen and pad from the end of the coffee table and drew a circle slashed through by a line. "It's the Road Dogs' club symbol, I recognised it as the tattoo Jake Reilly had on his arm." Daff shivered. The sound of screeching tyres and crushed metal that signalled Jake's final moments filled her ears, but she had to stay focussed. "I think she drew it as a kind of misdirection—after all, why would the Road Dogs leave their own mark at their own crime scene?"

"You think she was trying to make it look like they'd been framed?"

"Yup, or at least cast some doubt. She was acting tough on the outside, but in her head, she was terrified. She was convinced they were going to kill *her* next." When Daff had flicked through the paperwork on Lawrence's desk, she'd seen that the Sundowner murders had occurred on Wednesday night. She hadn't met Melissa until the following afternoon. "I think her meeting us was a coincidence. After all, *you* called *her*," Daff raised her eyebrows and Peta looked slightly ill. "But it's impossible to know if she put two and two together, if she realised that my ghost is also hers."

"You have to go to the police." Peta filled their cups, though neither of them reached for the tea.

"I already did, and Lawrence didn't believe me. I need more. I need to know what happened in that motel room."

"You know what happened. Henry killed those women and then Liam. You'll explain it to your dad and he can take it or leave it." She stood up swiftly and snatched her car keys off the table. "I'll go with you."

"No. Even if Lawrence does believe me—and it's a long shot—then that's it. I can't go back to the motel room or look for further clues. They'll find Liam's body, notify his parents and he'll get buried a dishonourable cop; a UC that sympathised with outlaws and was willing to kill for them. There'll be speculations on what happened, but no one will know for sure—and I need to know." She flicked her eyes towards Liam, who had been quiet since they got there. "*Liam* needs to know what happened."

He'd been sitting in the chair opposite her, and at the mention of his name looked up. "You don't have to be the one to do it. What happened tonight … I don't need you to get hurt looking for answers. I'm already dead. Nothing can change that. We know who I am now, it won't take much for the cops to fill in the gaps."

"No." She held up her hand like a stop sign. "It's not good enough, I need to know."

"Well I don't. I don't need you to redeem me. We've found out who I was, that's all we needed to do, that's all I asked. There was no clause about proving I was a good guy."

Ignoring him, Daff pulled a couple of tissues out of her pocket and wrapped them around the knife's handle and blade. It seemed a shallow gesture—her fingerprints were all over it already—but she needed to preserve whatever trace evidence remained.

"There's something that I need to do, and I want to make sure the knife is safe. It's the only solid piece of evidence that links Henry to Liam's murder." She held the knife out like an offering. "If something happens, you need to take this to Lawrence and tell him that there's a body out at the Boiler in Beerwah. He knows where it is."

Peta's face hardened as she took the blade carefully in her hands and marched towards the kitchen. She opened what Daff assumed was the cutlery drawer and dropped the knife with a metallic clatter.

Coming back into the room, she dropped back into the couch and gave Daff a look that felt like a punch in the gut. "I think you're being a fucking idiot." Peta's words came through cut teeth. "If I don't hear from you by eight, then I'm going down to the Valley Station; I'm going to find your dad and I'm going tell him everything."

Daff had hoped for more time, but figured it was the best offer she was going to get. She stood up quickly, before Peta could change her mind, and gave her friend a fierce hug.

"I'll see you soon."

Daff figured it sounded better than goodbye.

Out on the street, she caught a glimpse of a single blinking star; the rest of the night's sky was washed out by the city lights.

"Come on, *Columbo*, let's get this over with." Liam marched past her towards the Beetle and she fell in step behind him, feeling a twinge of regret as she abandoned that sole star. She opened her car door, started the ignition and did an illegal U-Turn. As she hit the M7, making her way into the Valley, she noticed the streets were empty.

Liam noticed too. "I don't like this."

Daff thought he'd already made that opinion pretty clear, and she didn't feel like rehashing her end of the conversation. He didn't want her to get hurt looking for answers—an intention she agreed with—but she couldn't believe that he didn't want to know, *for sure*, what had happened to him.

After what happened at the clubhouse, he would never ask her to keep looking, and now he wouldn't have to. Despite what Peta had said, it wasn't over. Daff had touched the knife and relived its final memory. She knew how Liam had died, she knew who killed him … and yet he was still here. Maybe he couldn't crossover until *he* remembered who he was? They'd both witnessed the memory attached to the gun, but Liam's own memories were yet to return. But even though his identity was still a mystery, they knew where his body was and they knew he was an undercover cop. Once Peta handed the knife over to Lawrence, it wouldn't be long until Liam's body was ID'd. Then Daff remembered that the whole "unfinished business" theory was a human idea about a metaphysical practice. Who's to say it was right?

"You're driving me mad." Liam moaned from the passenger seat. "If you can't stop thinking about me, could you at least think a little quieter?"

"How can you even hear what I'm thinking? I'm not intentionally sending you any messages!" Daff feigned annoyance while silently thanking whatever power was out there that she hadn't been thinking anything she didn't want him to hear. Feeling slightly exposed, she decided that fair's fair, she'd have a go at trying to read *his* mind. Concentrating, she imagined her mind as an outstretched hand; a hand that was reaching towards Liam, looking for a ledge. But the only thing she could hear was the light grind of the Beetle's four-cylinder engine. Apparently, *his* mind was his own.

"Maybe we're getting used to each other, or something changed when I jumped into your body? I don't know why you can't read my mind; maybe it has something to do with the amnesia?" He ran a hand through his floppy hair and sighed. "Anyway, that's the least of our problems. So, what's the plan? Go back into the motel room, touch the furniture and hope that you can get some glimmer into what the hell happened in that room?"

"Yup, that's pretty much it."

The street lights cut past overhead. Daff couldn't remember the last time she'd been awake this late. Probably the night Tom had died, she thought. Peta had made no mention of the anniversary but, given the late hour, the knife and Daff's peculiar request, it was understandable. She probably didn't even remember—but Lawrence *had.* Little wonder he didn't believe her, turning up at his office on the night of her and Tom's anniversary, claiming to be in communion with a homicide victim who was also the member of a notorious bikie gang.

"Tonight is your and Tom's anniversary?"

Liam's question jolted Daff from her reverie. "Yup."

There wasn't a lot to say and with the Sundowner Motel's backlit sign in sight, her attention needed to be here, not beneath the stars on an empty highway. She swung into one of the many open car parks in the lot.

"I'm sorry."

Daff waved the unnecessary apology away as her eyes ran over the motel for a second time. Under the moonlight, the peeling building looked still and shadowy. The five rooms that lined both storeys all had their curtains drawn. Daff quickly glanced to her right; there was no light on in the reception and the sign read 'closed'. She shouldered open the Beetle's door and stepped onto the eroding car park's bitumen. A few vehicles were parked up, all in various states of decay, like the motel itself, and Daff wondered if they were going out in sympathy.

Liam walked past her, heading for the stairs. "Come on then, it'll be light in another two hours."

Daff followed, slowly, careful to keep her footfall as quiet as possible as she ascended the stairs and crossed the top landing. Liam walked through the police tape and Daff stopped outside room eight, hoping the door was still unlocked. She twisted the knob and was relieved when it opened. It was cooler in the room than it was outside.

Despite the motel's lack of maintenance, at least the owners had the foresight to insulate the roof. She closed the door behind her, her hand hovering over the light switch. At this late hour, though, she figured the odds of attracting attention were small and she flicked the switch.

Liam stood in the centre of the room, his eyes gliding over the low breakfast bar and wooden cupboard on one side and the dishevelled bed on the other.

"I don't suppose any of this seems familiar?" Daff skirted around him as she pulled her dark hair up into a bun, securing it at the back of her head. She wasn't about to confuse the investigation by leaving a stray strand behind. Stopping by the bed, she put a hand on the crumpled duvet, hoping its last occupants had used it for sleeping and not sex. She tried to tune into the material, reaching for any memory that it had to offer, but there was nothing. Just cloth.

"Nope. None of the memories have come back. I saw the visions of me shooting Ben, and Henry killing me, but I can't remember anything for myself. It's just a void."

She moved to the nightstand, the drawer was open, revealing a Bible, the only object in the room still in good condition. There was little chance Henry had touched it, but you never know. Daff thumbed through the pages, feeling into them, and waited. A face flickered before her eyes, an older woman with a neck hanging loose and waxy beneath her chin. Her pupils were the size of five cent coins as she tore through the pages, reading sentences at random. Daff dropped the *Good News Bible* back into the drawer and reached for the lamp. Nope, nothing there either.

"If I knew how any of this worked, you would have been able to move on a long time ago."

"What do you think will happen? When this all ends."

Daff shrugged. Truthfully, she didn't want to think about it too much. It was all theory anyway, the only one who would come to know what will happened next was Liam. Her stomach twisted into an icy knot. Perhaps there'd be a big fluffy cloud, white robe and harpsichord waiting for him, maybe he'd be surrounded by loved ones or get reincarnated. Maybe he'd be nothing.

"I'm not religious or spiritual, so I don't really have any opinion. If you asked Peta, I'm sure she'd be happy to give you hers."

The ghost of a smile passed over his face. "Yeah, I bet."

Edging around the bed, Daff made her way towards the dark patch on the floor. She crouched down beside it and hesitated. It was unlikely that she was about to disrupt some crucial piece of evidence, the room having already been dusted, but Lawrence had sent two officers back and the crime scene hadn't been cleaned yet. Maybe the department wasn't done collecting evidence. If she touched the carpet and contaminated the one thread of trace evidence that could link Henry to the crime, she would not only obstruct justice, but potentially put herself at risk as well.

She was about to stretch out her open palm when she realised it hadn't been washed since the incident at the clubhouse. Daff felt her nose wrinkle as she swiftly stood up, walked over to the bathroom and rinsed her hands. When she looked up at her reflection in the mirror, it was interrupted by the crude smear Melissa had drawn on the mirror. Despite what she'd seen earlier that day, Daff had to believe that the psychic's motivations for helping her were genuine. At any rate, she'd clearly kept her knowledge about Daff and the watch to herself, because neither Tramp nor Henry had made any mention of Liam returning from the dead.

"Did you find something else?" Liam's voice called out from the other room.

Daff stepped back out onto the thin pile carpet, drying her hands on her jeans. "Not yet."

The bloodstain lay in front of her like a welcome mat. She had to know. Sinking down, Daff stretched out her open palm and pressed it into the mark's crusty centre. Her head and stomach swirled as she felt herself pulled forward. Falling again, her mind raced as the tension in her limbs melted away, the muscles becoming heavy and lethargic, a fog settling over her senses.

Daff opened her eyes. Liam was gone, but she wasn't alone. A blonde woman dressed in a bra and denim skirt sat slack in a chair in the corner, her head limp as though she'd fallen asleep. *Sarah.*

Beth watched in confusion as Henry leered over Sarah, his grubby hands still wrapped around his dead wife's neck. Daff could feel her heart rate increasing, the adrenaline cutting a path through the drug haze. Despite Beth's doped-out state, alarm bells were starting to go off. Beth shook her head; something wasn't right—and yet she felt so *good.* She could keep this buzz going if she wanted to, and why wouldn't she? This was good stuff. All she had to do was relax, *chill Winston*, and then she could fly all night.

Henry straightened, rubbing a hand over his wide eyes as he turned towards her. Beth's breath hitched as the biker's face hardened and his hands curled into fists.

Run you, idiot! Daff screamed inside the girl's head, though she knew it was already too late. Beth took a step back and glanced over her shoulder towards the closed motel room door.

She could still feel Mikey's parting kiss on her lips. He said he'd only be a minute, and Mikey was one of the good ones. He always came back. He'd gone off for a puff with Mel and Tramp. Beth used to hate that Mikey constantly smelt of stale cigarette smoke, but now it was like his personal scent; a whiff of smoke and she'd think of him. She wished he was here now. Henry had always given her the creeps—the way his eyes would burrow into hers like she owed him something.

Henry mumbled.

"What?" Beth's words slurred as she looked up at him.

"You gonna say something?" Henry marched forward, his heavy boots causing the floor to vibrate. Daff tried to pull back and kick herself out of the memory; she knew what was coming next and she didn't need to see that again, but the memory wouldn't let her go.

"Where's Mikey?" Beth rubbed her head; sure that she knew the answer.

"You gonna squeal on me, bitch?" Henry spat the question and Beth stepped back.

"Huh?"

Henry grabbed her by the throat before Beth had a chance to scream. Daff felt the girl's weak and stoned hands slip over Henry's, trying to free herself from the stranglehold.

"Don't say a fuckin' word." Henry's eyes bulged as his grip tightened. "I'll shut you up, bitch."

Daff could feel Beth's larynx and carotid artery being crushed, cutting off the oxygen to her brain. Her face burned with the sudden lack of oxygen as her adrenaline increased with the threat. If she didn't get him off, her heart would go into arrhythmia. She reached out to claw him, but Henry quickly kicked the legs out from under her and pinned her to the ground with the full weight of his body.

"Bitch. Gonna end you."

Henry released his grip, replacing his hands with a forearm. Using his free hand, he slipped the blade free from the sheath on his hip.

"Quit wrigglin'." He pressed against her harder until Beth's vision became blotchy. The biker released his grip, pushed Beth over onto her stomach and pressed a knee into the centre of her back. Before Beth could draw enough breath to shout out, she felt the cold slice of metal pressing into her throat.

Daff snatched her hand back. Her face was hot and she was sweating in her jacket, but at least she could breathe. Sitting back on her haunches, Daff took in the stain that had signalled the end of Beth's life.

Henry Ernst had killed his wife and then Beth.

Did Lawrence know this? Had he found something in this room that linked the club with the murders? Is that why Lawrence was looking into the Road Dogs? Daff hoped so.

She looked up at Liam. "Did you see that?"

He nodded. "Yup. I think you got plenty. We need to go see your father."

Rising, Daff headed back to the bathroom. Flicking on the tap, she washed her hands and splashed cool water onto her face. Reminding herself she was still alive.

"You got your answers." Liam appeared in the bathroom door when she didn't reply, arms folded over his black shirt.

"I didn't see you in the memory." There were still too many questions.

"We'll find out the full story some other way. This is serious, and you need to get serious. You've seen what that Henry guy is capable of … There's no reason for you to keep at this alone. You gotta go back to your father, give him the knife and tell him what you know, let the chips fall where they may."

Daff looked up at Liam. Though his eyes were hard, his face was soft. There was no point in arguing with him and, if she was honest, she didn't have the energy for it. The sleep she'd had yesterday morning was long gone and she couldn't remember ever feeling this tired. It pained her to admit it, but she was out of ideas. Though Liam hadn't been in the memory, Beth had been thinking about him, or at least she'd been thinking about his undercover identity, Mikey. Liam must have been here on the night of the murders. Maybe he'd come back to the room after finishing his ciggie, found Henry and the two dead women and blown his cover.

It was a safe assumption … yet Liam was *still here.* What were they missing?

Daff's stomach tightened, despite the fatigue, like she was holding on to something she couldn't let go of. "I don't know if I'm ready."

"Ready for what?" Exasperation plain on his face.

"To give this up. I'm the only one who can see what really happened. If the cops stuff if up …" She couldn't meet his eye, fixing her gaze on a chipped bathroom tile instead.

"We've hit a dead end—no pun intended—and this has gotta go to the cops eventually, Daff. When they find my body, and compare the wound with Henry's knife, that murdering bastard will get locked up for sure."

Daff had heard Lawrence complain more than once about "sure-fire" cases being upended and crooks getting off, but Liam was right. The only way for Sarah, Beth and Liam to get justice was to turn this evidence over to the department.

With a quick nod that made her head spin, Daff crossed the small bathroom and walked through Liam's unmoving figure as she headed for the motel door, twisted the nob and stepped out into the cool of the night.

Daff heard herself gasp before she realised what was happening. One hand was clamped tight over her mouth while the other had looped around her neck in a headlock. For the second time that night, Daff felt the crush of a man's grip around her throat and rising panic as the oxygen was cut off from her brain. She dug her fingers into the leather-clad forearm and Henry laughed, encasing them in the stink of tobacco. She tried to pull free, but his hold tightened, crushing her windpipe until Daff thought her head may explode.

"Daff, stay calm! I'll fix—"

But Daff couldn't hear him. Will couldn't replace breath, and she felt her grip loosen. Darkness drew over her like a winter blanket.

CHAPTER 20

Daff

Sunday July 3, 2016

Daff's wrists ached. Her hands were tied and stretched above her, the full weight of her body suspended from those fragile joints. Pain ran down her arms in rivulets only to settle in the soft flesh of her underarm.

It was cold. So. Fucking. Cold. Yet, she could feel fat droplets of perspiration sitting on her upper lip and the delicate pads of her eyes. *Cold sweats*, she thought. *I'm entering fight or flight mode*. Loose strands of hair stuck to the back of her neck. In that moment, she'd do just about anything to knot it up and away. Anything would be better than that god-awful itch. They'd hung her high; she could feel the tip of her boots scraping the wooden floor, but not enough to find purchase. She opened her eyes.

"You're awake!" She could hear Liam, but she couldn't see him.

For a moment, Daff thought she was back at the clubhouse, but as her eyes adjusted to the slim strip of light that crept beneath a door, far in front of her, she knew that she wasn't. Blinking away the sweat that blurred her vision, Daff took in the space around her. The floor was covered in open and closed wooden crates, gleaming ride-on lawn mowers, cardboard boxes and a scattering of tools. Twisting to get a better look behind her, a ripple of renewed pain tore down her arms, and she muffled a scream. She looked up; the rope that tightly bound her hands was looped over the hook of a hoist. Pressing the tips of her toes into the floorboards, Daff stretched her body to its full extent. It wasn't enough. She couldn't slide the knot free of the hook; all she managed to do was send a fresh bolt of pins and needles over her upper body.

When the pain subsided, the brief memory of how she'd gotten here emerged. "Henry."

"He's not here. After he grabbed you at the motel, he brought you here and, well, you can guess the rest."

"Where am I?" Daff's eyes darted around the crates, but she couldn't see any identifying logos.

"Port of Brisbane."

Daff would have been relieved, if not for the searing pain in her shoulder. A port the size of Brisbane would be a twenty-four-hour, seven-day-a-week operation; someone would find her here, eventually. She was about to ask Liam if he'd seen any staff members when she realised, for the first time, that her mouth hadn't been gagged or taped up. "There's no one around here, is there?"

Liam shook his head, his eyes not quite meeting hers. "You're in a shipping container in the storage yard. The only thing around here is more empty shipping containers."

"Where did Henry go?"

He shrugged. "Don't know. After they grabbed you, they drove straight here to this storage yard, unlocked the container, dropped you and left."

"You should have followed them." At least then they would know what Henry was up to, what he may be planning to do to her.

"I couldn't. You're still wearing the watch, and even if I wasn't tied to that stupid thing, I wouldn't have left you alone anyway."

Daff imagined what it would have been like to wake up alone in this near pitch-black shipping container with no idea where she was, and the horror hit her like a punch in the guts. She'd never been so grateful to be wearing the watch.

"What now?" The area between Daff's shoulders ached. If Henry came back into the shipping container now, she'd have no way to defend herself. Liam could jump into her body again, but it wouldn't change the fact that she was strung up like a ham.

A metallic screech sounded from the other end of the shipping container. *He's coming,* Daff thought, unnecessarily. Two heavy clunks rattled the four metal walls as the handles of the locking bars smacked against the door.

"It'll be okay, just stay calm." Despite the attempt at reassurance, Liam's voice was strained.

The door opened with a stiff creak, letting in the blinding light of morning. Daff winced and pressed her face into the sleeve of her damp shirt; the screaming in her eyes briefly overriding the pain in her shoulders and wrists.

The floorboards shook as he approached her. Daff tried to look at him, but her eyes hadn't adjusted and she felt she'd reached the limit of her pain threshold.

"Wakey, wakey." Henry's hand shot up and loosely grabbed her throat. "Hope you feel like talking, girly." He squeezed and released, emphasising the threat.

The room shook again. "She talked yet?" Tramp pulled the door behind him, leaving it open a crack to let some light in.

"Not yet." Henry squeezed again.

Daff wheezed, her throat already throbbing from Henry's previous chokehold. In another day or two—provided she lived that long—the ruptured capillaries across her throat would become purple and red bruises.

"What the fuck were you doing at our clubhouse?" Henry released his grip. "How did you know about the watch? Why the fuck were you at the Sundowner Motel?"

Henry's face had scrunched into a fist; looking at it, Daff remembered the gutless way he'd killed Liam: hands bound together, unable to defend himself. Heat rose up in her belly as her face hardened. Rage could be potent—an energy intense enough to live off, but it wasn't the same as bravery. It was easy to be brave when you didn't have anything to lose.

"Drug dealing, plus three counts of murder, that's a sentence of up to fourteen years. You have no intention of letting me go, so why would I tell you anything?"

The biker's brows shot up and he glanced at Tramp. "Pig-cunt's kids, eh?" He spun around and slapped Daff across the face. The speed of the slap startled her more than the force, and her eyes welled. "Next time, it'll be a fist. Why the fuck were you at the clubhouse?"

"I'm Detective Lawrence's daughter."

"I know, darlin'. So, the old copper sent you after all."

"Yup." Daff stuck out her chin, hoping the false confidence would cover the lie.

"What are you doing?" Liam's gaze shifted from Henry to Tramp, as though he were weighing up who would be the bigger threat. "Don't egg 'em on. Just shut up or you'll make it worse."

Daff gave a dry bark. "How could this get worse?"

Henry turned towards Tramp who shrugged. "Pingers? Check her pupils."

Henry pried open her eye, then the other. "They're normal. She's a cop's daughter, no wonder she's fucked up. Well, love, if you aren't gonna talk, then I'll just have to send your dad another message."

Henry's hand reached out, popping the button at the waist of Daff's jeans.

Daff twisted away and felt a fresh cramp break across her shoulders. "I know you killed Liam!"

Henry looked up at her, brows furrowed. "Who the fuck is Liam?"

Fuck. "Mike, I mean Mike."

"Why did you call him Liam?" Henry seized her throat again. "Was that his real name? Too good to fuck an actual club member, but you had no problem moving from one dead copper boyfriend to another, eh?"

The fire that had burned in Daff's stomach suddenly went out. How did he know about Tom? "Go to hell."

"Oooo didn't like that did ya, love? Bit messed up, don't you think? Fucking the guy that killed your boyfriend? I knew Mikey had balls, but this shit is next level. Maybe I should have kept the lad around ..."

Daff tried to break away from his grip, but his hold was too tight. "What are you talking about? Tom died in a car accident."

Henry smiled, a genuine, gold-toothed smile. "You don't know."

"Know what?"

"Henry, we don't have time for this shit. The longer we're here the higher the risk of getting caught."

"What are you talking about? Answer me!" Daff raised her voice despite the strain on her throat.

"Mike told me you were driving. Said your pulse was good, can't remember if he checked the lad's ... really, it never occurred to you to ask Mikey why he had Tom's watch? Missed that clue, didn't ya? *Daphne*."

He sneered her name, making a ripple run up Daff's spine. "He was there?" She looked at Liam, but he was looking at Tramp.

"He's the bugger that forced you off the road. Black SUV, no number plate, right?"

Her body went limp. She could summon the memory of that SUV as easily as she could recall her own reflection. She remembered the black SUV, but in the chaos of the crash, she'd never seen the plates. Now, she knew why.

"That's why you're here. *I'm* your unfinished business." She glanced up at Liam, but his attention was still focussed on Tramp.

Henry's brow furrowed, but he shrugged off her comment and returned to the business of Daff's jeans. He pulled the zipper down.

The memory of the black SUV disappeared. "No!" Daff tried to kick out at the biker, but her wrists screamed as she swung from the hook above her.

"Daff! Get ready." Liam bolted across the container and merged into Tramp's body. For a moment, Daff thought he'd gone through Tramp—breaking the twenty-metre barrier that kept him fastened to her side—but the tall man shuddered and took a staggering step forward.

"Henry. Stop." The words were strained, forced out through tight lips.

Henry turned towards his mate. "You want first dibs, brother?"

Tramp marched forward and threw a punch deep into Henry's stomach. The bikie president gasped and instinctively clutched his belly, his eyes growing wide as he glared at his partner. "What the hell are you doing?"

Instead of answering, Tramp doubled up on him by aiming for the older man's jaw, but Henry dodged the blow and lunged for his number two's legs, tackling him to the ground and causing the shipping container to shudder.

"What the fuck are you doing, mate?" Henry whacked Tramp in the jaw as if he was a twenty-year-old boxer and not a sixty-year-old smoker.

While the two seasoned bikers were locked in fisticuffs, Daff pressed the tips of her toes hard into the floor and stretched her arms to the limit, but she still couldn't get enough height to lift her bound wrists over the hook. A fresh cramp pulsed between her shoulders and vision became spotty as she lost her breath. She lost her flimsy footing too, her wrists burning as the full weight of her body came down on them again, the rope growing tighter, rubbing her flesh raw.

"Daff, hold on." Tramp rolled, knocking Henry flat onto the floor. Swiftly punching the club president in the mouth, he sent a spray of blood across the exposed floor. Henry groaned and rolled onto his side, instinctively covering his face, as Tramp spun around and headed straight for Daff. Though she knew Liam had possessed him, the sight of Tramp's broad frame marching towards her caused an involuntary quiver.

"It's okkayyy." The words stammered through Tramp's pressed lips. His hands shook as he slipped an arm around Daff's waist, lifting her, while the other unhooked the rope from the hoist. The relief of having her arms lowered was sudden and euphoric, turning her mind dumb with bliss.

"He's fighting me." Tramp's fat fingers tugged at her ropes and she shuddered as the sawing motion brought her back into her body. "I can't hold him much longer. You're gonna have to run." The ropes loosened enough for Liam to quickly untie them and pull Daff's hands free. "Go!" He barked, pushing her towards the door.

Daff spun, clasped his hand and squeezed it. "Thank you."

"Go." Tramp suddenly sprung forward as Henry landed on top of him.

"Stop, you—"

"Go!" Liam suddenly appeared beside her. "I couldn't hold him. Run!"

Daff sprinted for the container door, the metal screeching as she pushed it open. The sudden hit of salty air stung her throat as she bolted across the storage yard's loose bitumen. Pins and needles coursed through her legs, but each step took her further away from Tramp and Henry's vicious shouts. The yard was filled with neatly stacked shipping containers, each row three high and five deep. Daff swerved to her left and bolted down a new row. She hoped she was heading *for* the exit and not *away* from it.

"How do we get out?" Liam raced beside her, his voice irritatingly normal.

I don't know. Don't you remember? Daff switched to telepathy, not having enough breath to run for her life and talk out loud.

"No, it was still dark when we came here. And I was more worried about you."

The pins and needles had started to disappear as her blood circulation returned to normal, and she could feel a tight pull at the back of her jeans. She slowed down, curled around another row of containers and pulled the mobile phone out of her pocket. She tried to catch her breath enough to talk as she punched in her lock code and opened the keypad. She still remembered her old man's number, and it was faster to key it in than scroll through her list of contacts.

"Daff!" Lawrence answered on the second ring. "Peta's here, she's told me what's going on. Where are you?"

"Port of Brisbane. Storage yard. Don't come alone." She gulped another mouthful of air and thanked the stars for Peta.

"I'm on the motorway. Stay on the line." She could hear Lawrence pick up the speaker on the police radio and redirect a squad car. "They're not at the clubhouse. Head to the port." His voice came back on the line. "Are you hurt?"

"Not bad," she whispered, unsure whether the bikers had stopped fighting or if she was just too far away to hear it. Either way, it was safer to be quiet, but she also had to keep moving. Slowly, she started to head south, walking parallel to a row of containers. Every footstep on the loose bitumen sounded as loud as a car crash. Daff tried to silence her ragged breath. Liam stayed close, his head jutting forward so he could hear what Lawrence was saying.

"Good. Where's Henry? Are you somewhere safe?"

She held the phone away for a moment, her ears pricked for the sound of a footstep or the rattle of a wallet chain, but there was nothing bar the lapping of waves and the odd bird call. "I don't know where he is. I'm in a storage yard full of shipping containers. But Henry knows things about me; he was talking about Tom."

Henry's word echoes in her mind, *He's the bugger that forced you off the road.* She glanced at Liam, her stomach churning with uncertainty. He'd looked just as shocked as she'd felt when Henry made that announcement. If Liam had been behind the accident that killed Tom, if he'd been the driver of that SUV, he truly didn't remember. She felt herself drowned in questions; his betrayal the cinder block that kept her sinking, down, down. *This isn't the time*, she thought, *I can't think about this, not now. Let me up, let me go.*

She circled around another square of stacked sea containers and stopped in front of a chain-link fence. A fence. Escape. Relief flooded her system as she slipped the phone into her pocket, the call still active, hooked a foot into the wired diamond and lifted, trying to ignore the gripping pain across her shoulders.

"Stop. You can't climb it." Liam pointed at the top of the six-foot fence that was wrapped in barbed wire.

Her chest fell as the crunch of gravel sounded behind her. She dropped from the fence and spun, but the corridor between the stacked containers was empty. Her heart rate picked up as she stepped around another row and pulled her phone back out of her pocket.

"Daff? Daff? Can you hear me? Are you there? What's happening?"" Lawrence's voice was so loud Daff was sure it could be heard from the other side of the storage yard.

"Hurry." She whispered, hung up and switched the phone onto silent before deciding off was better; Lawrence would only call her back.

"What are you doing?" Liam's eyes grew wide.

I can't risk Henry hearing me.

"If they catch you again," Liam's jaw clenched as he stared through the wire fence and out onto the channel that led to the Brisbane River, "I don't know if I have enough energy to stop them."

Lawrence is on his way. You won't have to. At least, she hoped he wouldn't have to. Lawrence said he was on the motorway; he *could* be here in under five minutes. She pushed up her sleeve and checked the time; it was just after eight-thirty. Peak hour traffic. Her heart sank. Even with sirens on, a squad car could only travel so fast through the morning gridlock.

Thank you, again, for what you did back there. Daff followed his gaze out onto the water and she saw the corner of his lip curl before quickly fading away.

"You're welcome."

There was another crackling of rocks, this time from her right. *I can't just stand here waiting for them. They'll expect me to come to the fence, follow its perimeter, it's the most obvious thing to do. They won't expect me to head back into the centre. Stick your head out around the corner, check that the coast is clear.* She pointed in the opposite direction.

Liam nodded, silently moving towards the end of the row before his head vanished around its edge. "We're right, come on."

Daff followed him around the corner, though trying to move both quickly and quietly was almost impossible, so she settled for the latter. She'd reached the end of another row when she thought she heard the distant intermittent whoop of a siren. She stopped, reached for the sound, but all she could hear was the industrial hum of the port. Liam stuck his head out, looked left then right and waved Daff forward. They'd reached the end of this block; they could either circle it again or cross the open corridor to the next block.

Daff couldn't remember where Henry's container had been, but it was the safest place in this whole damn yard. Before she had a chance to pick a direction, Liam marched out across the divide that separated the blocks of containers, and Daff followed.

"Stop right there, darlin'." Tramp stepped out behind her. "Henry! I got her!" Tramp reached forward, wrapping his hand around the exposed flesh of her wrist. She cried out as it sent a searing pain up the length of her arm and he struck her, quick and fierce, across the face. "You'll only make it worse for yourself if you keep that up." He pulled her towards him, locking an arm around her chest and pinning her against his.

Henry stepped out from behind a block of containers in front of them. His nose was bent at an unnatural angle, likely broken, and the blood from the break had dried over his mouth and beard. He glanced at Tramp, eyes suddenly weary. "You got yourself together, mate?"

"I don't know what the fuck happened," Tramp's voice wavered. "I couldn't stop. I … ah … fuck, Henry, I don't know. Let's just get this shit over with." He clamped a hand over Daff's mouth. "Don't fight me, girl, or you'll fucking regret it."

"Put a plug in her and throw her in the river." Henry stepped towards the chain-link fence. "There's a back gate further down this way."

Liam's face hardened and he quickly launched himself forward, passing through Daff and into Tramp. Daff felt the tall biker's frame shudder.

"Fuck off Mikey." Tramp uttered under his breath, shaking his shoulders before forcing Daff to follow the president. The biker shuddered again, but kept moving forward.

Liam curled around in front them, his eyes wide and disbelieving. "He knows. He keeps pushing me out. He's blocking me, I can't get a hold of him."

Melissa is his girlfriend; she's probably taught him a thing or two.

Daff's heart thrashed against her chest with every step. Tramp carted her along the chain-link fence that separated the storage yard from Moreton Bay. There was a metre's clearance outside the fence, and beyond that was a twenty-metre drop to the low icy grey tide.

Henry stopped in front of a gate and stuck his hand through the gap to twist the dummy lock free. He pushed the gate open and stepped out onto the narrow ledge. Daff pushed her heels into the bitumen, but resistance was pointless; Tramp simply shoved her forward, scattering the rocks beneath her, and she fell onto the thin edge outside the gate, her abused shoulders throbbing from the impact.

Henry stepped forward, grabbed her by the hair and forced her to look out over the bay. "Take a good fuckin' look girly, 'cos it's a decent drop."

The precipice was raw and slimy, worn down by years of incoming and outgoing tides. "If you scream now, I'll kick you over. No second chances." Daff was about to inform him that twenty metres was hardly enough to kill her, then she remembered Henry's brutal chokehold and the ease with which he'd cut Beth's throat. Henry released his grip and pulled her to her feet.

"It's gonna be okay, Daff." Liam came in beside her, but she kept her head turned towards that wet horizon.

"It's daylight, Henry, you really want to do this now?" Tramp's eyes cut to the left and right.

Daff could read his thoughts as they crossed that lined face. Though the storage yard was in a remote part of the port, it was still a highly populated work place. Any shift workers desperate for a morning camp or a couple of hours of quiet could slink in here and find them. Then there'd be two bodies floating.

"Girly here is gonna tell us what the fuck is going on."

"I told you," Daff's voice cut between her teeth. "I'm Detective Lawrence's daughter."

"Yeah, but what do you know?" Henry dug into her shoulder, his nails biting into the flesh.

Her mind motored through her options and their likely ramifications, but none guaranteed that she'd walk out of this yard. Henry was a rat on fire, and his actions were just as predictable; he'd chew through flesh if it meant he'd get away alive.

There was only one answer he'd believe. "I know you killed Mike." The name felt strange on her tongue. "Cops know it too. They also know you're importing coke into the port, hiding it inside lawn mowers that one of your members orders in for his outdoor power equipment business. They didn't have enough evidence for a warrant, so they sent me in to see what I could find."

"You think I'm fuckin' stupid, girly? They couldn't use anything found without a warrant."

"You think a judge would give a shit? You think you mob are the only ones who can bend the law?" She spat her question out, hoping the venom would make the accusation more plausible. When it came to police work, Lawrence was clean; no way would he risk having a case binned on a technicality. Hopefully, Henry saw all cops in the same light: mad do-gooders who did anything to serve their own egotistical sense of purpose.

Henry spun her around, locked an arm over her chest and forced her to look over the edge. "You lying to me, girly?"

"Fuck you."

"Daff, take it easy." Liam moved into her peripheral vision. "You don't have much to bargain with here."

I'll drag him down too. Daff clasped both hands over the arm that bound her to Henry's chest.

"Looks like you do know everything. Well, if the coppers are zeroing in, not much point keeping you around."

"Henry Ernst!"

Daff felt the old biker turn in response to her father's gruff voice.

"Step away from the edge immediately." Lawrence raised his Glock, aiming it at Henry's head.

"Careful, boss, you might miss me and shoot your daughter." Henry twisted around so that Daff stood between him and the detective. Lawrence's frame filled the narrow gate. Beside him was the redheaded cop—the one she'd seen sitting at Lawrence's desk—his gun pointed at Tramp.

"Backup is on the way. You're done, Henry."

"No. It's gonna work like this. Tramp and I are gonna leave here with your daughter. We'll drop her off on some highway and she can give you a ring once we're gone. We'll go and you'll never see me again. Or, I can slit your daughter's throat and drop her over the edge. Wadda you like the sound of, Lawrence? Option one or option two?"

"Neither. I've got your knife." Lawrence fired.

The bullet burst through Henry's shoulder and he howled. Daff felt the sudden release of his grip and she slipped.

The fall was quick.

She could hear the flurry of sounds above her, but the shouts and clips of bullets vanished as she smashed through the glass of an oncoming wave. The shock of the impact froze her, and she could feel herself sinking, her body a dropped stone. She willed her fingers to wriggle, her legs to kick into action, but neither worked, her muscles seizing in the icy water. She could feel the lack of oxygen burning in her lungs, urging her to swim, to break the surface, to survive. Only, she didn't know where the surface was. How much time had passed? Her lungs were on fire, burning her alive while she drowned. She couldn't see the light; she couldn't tell which way was up. She could feel her muscles twitching, her throat caught in another chokehold, the ocean forcing her temples together like attracting magnets.

There was a flicker of light. A glimmer. The buzzing in her ears grew louder. She could feel the fight seeping from her limbs as the ocean curled her hand around Daff's floating form. Hugging her tight. Taking her home.

CHAPTER 21

Jon and Ruth Lawrence

Saturday January 6, 1990

Ruth struggled to keep her eyes open.

The stories were true; it really was the worst pain imaginable. At least that's what she thought until she'd done a round of chemotherapy, followed by radiation—but that wouldn't come her way for another twenty-five years, and she'd trade that for childbirth any day. Besides, what good had that damn treatment done anyway? It hadn't saved her. But Daphne. Daphne *had* lived on.

She'd watched as Jon held their daughter for the first time, how the room melted away as he took the baby into his arms.

"What about Daphne?"

Jon didn't hear her at first, and after a moment she asked again.

"It's a bit of an oldie, but sure, darlin'. If you like it, Daphne, it is."

Jon caressed his newborn daughter's cheek. He'd been on the clock when Ruth went into labour. Dispatch gave him the news over the radio; he must have been on a good wicket, because he was already heading back to the station with a couple of amateur dealers in the back of the paddy wagon. Another ten minutes and he would have missed it.

It was a Saturday and the traffic along Ann Street was hell, but he'd burst onto the maternity ward of the Mater Hospital just in time.

He'd seen things on the job, awful things: junkies, murdered wives, dipshit husbands, forgotten kids. Over time, that stuff can really start to affect you. You pick the seat that faces the entry of a restaurant, you double-check the locks, you tell your mother to get a dog, and when she doesn't, you buy her one. The problem with the job is that you start to believe that you know what's really going on, that the real world is filled with murder and rape and theft and prejudice and hate. You can't even see how badly it's affecting you, but then you hold your newborn daughter and all that crap disappears and you feel terrified for an entirely different reason. It's not the outside world you gotta worry about, but yourself—because you could really screw this up.

*

Ruth could feel sleep creeping up on her. Just a little bit longer, she thought, this moment won't ever come again and I want to remember it exactly as it happened. And she did, though Jon's account changed over time. Before she'd passed, all those years later, she found herself thinking about that day at the Mater Hospital; the way the world had shrunk to a room and the minutes had stretched out into hours.

She hadn't known what was coming: the cancer, the affair, the splintering of her small family. She couldn't stop any of it. Then she transitioned and everything became different. From here, she could see events coming like a shark through clear water, but knowledge and forewarning aren't in themselves a solution. You can't always dodge the jaws of life, because some events are destined, fated, pre-selected. There are some malleable events; there are some opportunities you can bend. Within reason.

If someone threw a watch off the jetty at Redcliffe beach, the timepiece would likely sink and become lodged in the peninsula's sand. Were the watch lucky enough to get caught in the East Australian Current, it would likely travel south towards the temperate Tasman Sea. And yet, sometimes events occur in defiance of logic, reason and explanation.

Sometimes the watch travels north.

Of course, she hadn't done all of this alone. She had plenty of help.

But neither Ruth nor Tom thought the watch would lead to this.

CHAPTER 22

Daff

Sunday July 3, 2016

The buzzing increased. The rumbling high-pitched rattle of cicadas competed against a deeper, mechanical drone. The prickle of bitumen bit into her from head to toe, and her eyes flipped open as her heart sank. She should be drifting in the waters of Moreton Bay, not looking at a panoramic view of the Milky Way, the Big Dipper, the Southern Cross. It was so dark that even the smallest of stars shone as vibrantly as the moon. How peculiar that the night sky is black instead of white, she thought.

"You're awake." A warm familiar hand briefly touched her knee.

"Am I dead?" She wanted to sit up, to look Tom square in the face, but the stars wouldn't release her.

"Always so dramatic."

"Is this the only goddamn memory you can bring me back to?"

"Come on, sit up. You need to see this, little Miss Avoidance." Tom cupped Daff's hand as she shouldered herself up off the road. His Lancer was less than twenty metres away. She drew back and covered her eyes against the bright glow of the brake lights. There was the quiet click of a car door opening and she peeked through her fingers. A figure dressed in dark jeans and a white singlet slipped out of an SUV that was clumsily parked up on the shoulder of the road.

"Liam." Daff shot up and sprinted down the empty highway. She thought, idiotically, how strange it was to see him in something other than his worn black tee and blue jeans. Like she'd bumped into a co-worker out of uniform.

"He can't see you, Daff." Tom added, unnecessarily, as Liam jogged right through her, his mouth pulled down into a grimace.

Daff followed, peering over his shoulder as he snapped open the Lancer's door.

"Fuck, fuck, fuck!" Liam said as he leaned into the cab. "Please don't be fucking dead."

Daff's stomach tightened as she looked down at a younger version of herself. She was unconscious and suspended halfway between the car seat and the wheel by the taut seatbelt. Liam pushed her back gently, one hand braced against the back of her head, the other on her chest.

He pressed two fingers against Daff's jugular and his face relaxed instantly.

Spotting Tom on the other side, he ducked around the front of the car, wrenched the passenger door open and checked again for a pulse. A quiet chuckle escaped his lips. Daff could have slapped him—as useless as that would have been—until she remembered that Tom hadn't died on impact. Her face flushed with rage. She hadn't wanted to believe Henry's accusation, but there was no denying Liam's part in the accident now. Daff watched helplessly as Liam raised Tom's limp hand and carefully untied the watch's red silicon band.

"A souvenir?" Her voice was hard and she turned away as Liam pocketed the timepiece and headed back towards the SUV.

"Sorry, mate." Liam whispered, then turned to head back towards the SUV.

"It was the easiest way to prove to the club that he'd done it." Tom explained. "He received his first official patch, a bottom rocker, a week later."

Tom strolled back up to the highway, following Liam's steps.

"What are you, like all-knowing now?"

"No, just had nothing better to do. I was keeping an eye on things. Though, I did have some help."

"What do you mean, *help?*"

Tom pressed a finger to his lips and pointed at Liam, whose face was lit up with the blue glow of his mobile phone.

"No doubt he's calling Henry to brag." Daff felt her stomach heave and she wondered if it were possible to be sick in a memory.

You have dialled emergency Triple Zero. Your call is being connected. An automated voice echoed from the phone. A beat passed and she could hear an operator asking if Liam was calling for police, fire, rescue or an ambulance.

"Liam is the one who called in our accident?"

"He tried." Tom shrugged. "His phone died before he got a chance to say anything."

Sure enough, the small glow disappeared and the screen went black. "Fuck!" Liam smacked the side of the phone, tapping the screen furiously. "Fuck!" Looking up, his eyes fixed on the horizon and widened. He pocketed the dead phone and bolted for the SUV. Daff turned and spotted the distant glow of high beams.

"That's the woman who found us." Tom pointed down the highway. "Luckily, *her* phone was fully charged."

"This isn't fucking funny, Tom! I've spent the last week trying to help your murderer figure out who he is. Do you know what that feels like?"

"Don't you ever wonder how my watch wound up on Golden Beach? How, of all the people who could have found it, *you* did?"

Daff plonked down on the wet grass. She'd spent days denying Liam's existence, analysing the probability of life after death, the validity of Melissa's reading and her own peculiar visions. She'd hypothesised a hundred different scenarios for Liam's demise—a hundred identities, a hundred different lives he may have lived including his location, his family, his friends, his girlfriends or boyfriends. In some he had children, and in others, pets.

She'd thought of answers for everything, except the obvious: was it Tom's watch?

Why was Liam attached to the watch? Why was it on Golden Beach? Why did she pick it up?

"You ..." she paused, trying to think of the right words, "planted the watch? You wanted me to find it?"

Tom nodded. "First of all, the watch isn't *like* my watch, it *is* my watch. Only you were in too much denial to even notice." His playful grin disappeared as he crouched down and gripped her shoulders hard. "You haven't move on, Daff. You never dealt with the accident, you just buried it. You can't move forward without forgiveness."

She pushed off his hands. "That's easy for you to say, you've known about this for eighteen months, but for me this has only just happened. I can't snap my fingers and forgive Liam just like that."

"Not Liam." Tom cupped her face gently. His thumb smoothed her cheek. "You have to forgive yourself, Daff. There was nothing you could have done differently; I was supposed to die that night. You don't need to show your loyalty to the world by stalling your life." He leaned forward and Daff could feel the warmth of his breath as he kissed her forehead. "I mean really, you should know better. Life is for the living."

Daff reached up and grabbed his face, pulling him down towards her. His lips brushed hers. A sharp pain exploded in her chest. Click, crack, boom. The darkness was torn away and there were flashes of light. Her chest cracked as her ribs became kindling to the fire in her torso. Another crack and the water drew back out of her lungs and up her throat; who knew water could burn? There were people talking. So many that their voices muffled together, making it impossible to distinguish one from the other. Pins and needles prickled the tips of her fingers and her lip trembled compulsively.

"Get her a blanket!" She heard her father's voice call above her.

Her eyes stung from the saltwater and she was glad when Lawrence leaned over her and blocked out the rising sun.

"Daphne, can you hear me?"

"Yes," she croaked, her tender throat starting to throb. "Where's Henry?"

She came up onto her hands, and Lawrence swung an arm around her back to help her sit up.

"McPhee's dealing with him. You're safe. Ambulance is on its way. Them buggers will rip me a new one for not keeping you flat."

"I'm fine." She winced against the renewed pain in her throat. "You're wet."

He was soaked from head to toe; his uniform stuck to him in unflattering clumps and his hair was slick across his scalp. He nodded, patting her gently on the back. "That's what happens when you go swimming."

Daff looked around. The storage yard was a hundred metres away on the other side of the channel. The boundary's gate was still open, only now the perimeter was filled with cops. Lawrence had hauled her up onto a floating platform and she could hear the water lapping at its sides. A tug boat passed by, and the deck hands exchanged inquiring looks before shrugging and turning back to the task at hand: an incoming ship whose containers were stacked on board like Legos.

"How are you feeling, Daff?"

She swivelled and winced as the sudden movement caused a jar in her neck.

He'd been so damn quiet she hadn't even seen Liam sitting behind her. *I'm doing alright. Did you see…?*

And he nodded. He looked as disappointed as she had felt on discovering that Henry had been right, that Liam's attempt to 'scare' Daff and Tom had caused the fatal accident. She knew she should be pissed, but it took a lot of energy to be angry and she was already in short supply.

"I need to tell you some things." Daff was talking to Lawrence, but looking at Liam.

"Yeah, you do. But you don't have to tell me now."

"Yes, I do." The police in the storage yard started to drift back inside the gate, slipping phones and notebooks back into their pockets. An ambulance siren wailed in the distance. "I need to tell you now, while we're still alone."

Daff told her father everything, amazed at her ability to whittle down multiple days and events into tidy soundbites. The ambulance arrived soon after and recommended that Daff be transported to hospital immediately. She flatly refused. Lawrence knew the location of Liam's body. Within the hour a team would be dispatched to search the Boiler at Beerwah, and she *had* to be there.

It took fifteen minutes to convince Lawrence that she was going with him. He relented, not because he agreed, he said, but because he was sick of arguing with her. Lawrence also laid out two conditions: firstly, Daff couldn't occupy the scene for long—forensic was already out there and they had a job to do, and secondly, under no circumstances was she to touch the body.

"I know how crime scenes work, Dad." It felt weird to call him that, and she was so out of practice that the word came out slightly forced and wooden. Things weren't about to suddenly return to normal as though the past four years hadn't happened, but Daff could feel herself shifting and softening. She called shotgun while Liam sat on the edge of his seat in the back. McPhee, thankfully, opted to ride out with another cop, giving Daff and Lawrence the space to talk things through, though the ride out to Beerwah was mostly silent.

The Boiler was located inside Caralan Way Park. Lawrence drove down the street with the same name, rolled over the park's lush grass and through the already open gate: a metal fence so low and simple Daff wondered why the local council even bothered with it. The police-issue vehicle turned up the soft lawn as they travelled across the park, swung right at the near-empty garden bed and into the Boiler proper.

Neither of them had been here in years and yet it looked exactly the same. The shrubs weren't any denser and the eucalyptus trees that shrouded the watering hole weren't any higher or greater in number. It was an organic time capsule; a preserved fragment of their shared past.

She'd noticed that Lawrence had gained a little weight, most of it needed; the flesh beneath his jaw had loosened and his hair was more salt than pepper. Maybe he'd softened. Maybe he wasn't a monster; maybe he was just a man. Then she remembered his confession over their kitchen table and how her mother, after thirty years of marriage, had died alone. She shook her head and the vision of a shrunken Ruth disappeared. Daff watched as a line of peeling eucalyptus trees passed by her window and they pulled into the clearing. Though the Boiler was popular amongst locals, it wasn't the easiest place to get a park, since the clearing was barely big enough to fit three vehicles. A police car and a forensic van had already pulled up and there was a small crew busying themselves around a dense crop of bush away from the river. The photographer's camera flashed every few seconds as his gloved hands pulled aside tall grass and delicately manipulated the stiff sheets of hessian.

Lawrence sandwiched the car between the other two vehicles, noses to the river, switched off the ignition and held the fob in his hand. "Peta told me a hell of a yarn this morning. I'm not saying I believed it, but I don't know why she'd spin a tale that far-fetched, and you're certainly clever enough to have come up with an explanation more believable than haunted watches and amnesiac ghosts."

Daff wanted to say that it had taken her a while to believe it too, but she was too tired and her throat was too sore to crack open that can of worms.

"So, you knew—know this guy?"

She gave a short single nod, afraid that any exaggerated movements would reignite the fire in her inflamed oesophagus.

Lawrence pocketed the fob and sighed. "I know you see this kind of thing every day, kiddo, but I'm telling you it's different when you know them …" He stared out the windshield and into flat reflective river. "Do you really want to see your mate like this?"

Daff glanced over her shoulder at the back seat, but Liam had already slipped out, and she watched as he rounded the back of the car and disappeared from view. "I'm sure."

She opened the car door before Lawrence could make an argument out of it and slipped down the side of the forensics van.

Despite his soft knee, Lawrence managed to catch up with her before she reached the small crime scene crew. As they drew closer, she heard him give a brief, albeit vague, explanation to the crew, and told them to take ten. The team exchanged glances as they walked down the scrub and back to their vehicles. Clearly, it was an unusual request, but they did as instructed; Lawrence was a senior detective.

He passed her a set of blue plastic gloves and contradicting advice. "Don't touch anything."

She nodded, took the gloves and lifted her brow. He smirked and pointed at the parked vehicles. "I'll wait with the others. Don't abuse the privilege, alright?"

Daff wasn't sure how much of a privilege it was to identify a body, but she nodded and snapped on the gloves.

"Good." Lawrence brushed her arm before making his way down the small incline and down into the clearing.

Liam stood a few metres in front of her on the other side of the bundled hessian; the grass was so tall and dense that it concealed his legs and made him look like a floating torso.

He was looking down. As Daff approached, she had a better view of the human shape beneath the fabric. The forensics crew had already peeled back the top layer, revealing the contents within.

Daff's breath hitched and she knelt down; he was in better condition than she'd expected. The folds of heavy hessian had protected him from predators, both insects and mammals, and the cool dry air of a coastal winter had slowed down the natural process of decay. Ignoring her father's instructions, she gently drew up the bottom of Liam's black shirt, the fabric stiff with dried blood, and examined his abdomen. The body displayed the usual post-mortem signs of putrefaction: the abdomen was swollen, the tissue discoloured and the blood pooled beneath the hips. Had he been buried or set into the river, the tissues would have suffered even less damage.

Timelines adding up. At a guess, you've been here four days.

She looked up at the ghost of Liam, but his eyes were fixed on the swollen thorax and puffed cheeks of his own former face. Daff followed his gaze. This bloated bundle didn't look like the man standing in front of her. Though the body had suffered minimal damage, the natural inflammation of Liam's tissues and organs had made him unrecognisable. The examination of the wounds and the calculation of time of death were easy because it looked nothing like him.

She stood up, her eyes levelling with his. *I can fix this.* Her throat thickened and she was thankful that the crew's close proximity had forced her to speak telekinetically. *I'll be able to make you look like you again.*

His eyes moved down the puffed face to the bloodied shirt, the same one he wore now—only that one was clean. "I really am dead."

Daff's mind went blank the way it had when the doctor had said *we couldn't save him. Your mother has cancer.*

"Did you think …" the words sliced through her inflamed throat and she flinched.

"I knew that I was dead, but it's different …"

Seeing it? She offered.

His head dropped. "Your dad's coming back."

Daff turned as Lawrence approached, carefully placing each step as though a misplaced foot could damage some crucial piece of evidence.

"Boys got another call, they gotta wrap this one up ASAP. Time to go."

Daff nodded, falling into step as he helped her down the incline and back into the clearing. She wasn't ready to go, but the chances of convincing Lawrence to let her stay were slim at best.

They were halfway along Steve Irwin Way when Daff finally spoke up. "What Peta told you was true. He's my friend but he doesn't know who he is—who he was before he died. Can you help me with that?"

"*Is* your friend? I'm sorry Daphne, but your friend is gone."

She sighed and shifted her gaze out the passenger window.

Lawrence amended. "He was an undercover cop. I met his handler, a sergeant from the Goldie who I'll need to call and give the news to, poor fella. I'll see what info I can get off him. But you don't need to be worrying about that right now, we need to get you to the hospital and get you looked over proper."

Daff touched the watch wrapped around her wrist. Despite its hard life and multiple owners, the hands had kept on ticking. Time had continued to move forward. She looked over her shoulder towards Liam in the back. His eyes were glazed over; he hadn't said anything since they'd left the crime scene. Seeing him by the river had been awful, and she'd supposed she also held some quiet hope that the memory of Liam's stabbing had been false, but it seemed Liam had done more than hope. It was wrong to invade his thoughts like this, but she tried it anyway, stretching her mind towards him like a reaching hand.

He shuffled, though she knew his ethereal form was incapable of feeling physical discomfort. "Not now, Daff."

She twisted in her seat as the Sunshine Coast's newest hospital came into view.

CHAPTER 23

Detective Lawrence

Monday July 4, 2016

Lawrence offered to help Daff into Accident and Emergency, but she refused, though she felt like the living dead. So the short walk from the car park to the University Hospital's entrance took longer than they expected. When the doors didn't open, Lawrence waved his hands in front of the automatic door sensors and the pair were immediately greeted by Peta, who informed them that she'd been waiting for three hours, and where had they been, and what the hell happened, and was everyone okay?

Lawrence wasn't sure who 'everyone' was, but he said yes, minus the body they'd found at the Boiler. Lawrence had never been inside the new facility; not knowing any of the staff, he was afraid they'd be told to take a seat and wait their turn. Thankfully, Daff's pale complexion made the purple bruising around her neck look even more vivid and she was admitted immediately. Being a Monday, lunchtime, the ward was quiet and Peta was permitted to accompany Daff and Lawrence onto the floor. Which was good, because the grim line of Peta's lips suggested that she wasn't going anywhere, anyway. Lawrence had the same idea, planting his feet firmly by the gurney as Daff had her initial examination.

The doctor removed the tongue depressor from her mouth and Daff shot her father a dark look, croaking, "What are you doing?"

Lawrence's brows furrowed as he tried to figure out what he'd done wrong now.

"You should go back to the station. If something happens and Henry gets off, I'm going to hold you responsible."

A cocked eye took the edge of her words, but Lawrence could hear the warning beneath it; the little blighter.

In the car, she'd told him about the watch and what Henry had said about "Mikey". It sounded pretty far-fetched, an officer putting another officer's life in jeopardy, but then Tom's death had never sat well with him. In her statement, Daff said there'd been a second car, but forensics had only found one set of tread marks and they'd matched Tom's Lancer. Still, maybe what Henry had said was the truth.

"Daphne, I'm gonna need that watch."

She turned away from him, not with resentment, but as if she was looking for a second opinion. Then she nodded, undid the straps and handed him the watch. "I expect to get it back soon. Sooner than soon. I don't want it sitting in some evidence box for six months, okay?"

Lawrence examined the beat-up watch. Even if it was Tom's, the reaction seemed a bit much. "I'll be sure to make it a priority." He turned towards Peta. "You will call me with every update?"

"You bet. You're at the top of the contact list, Mr Lawrence." He tried to remember the last time someone had called him that and couldn't.

Marching down the hospital's brightly lit corridors, Lawrence made a mental note to call in a favour with Officer Amy Poy over at forensics; he'd give her a bell from the car park and tell her he had some priority testing to do. She'll be pissed at first, he thought, but she'll change her tune when I say the watch and knife are linked to the murder of a police officer.

Now he was on the move, Lawrence felt a smidge relieved. Though the biker had Buckley's chance of getting off—the coke filled ride-on mowers in the shipping container alone were enough to lock Henry up for twenty-five years, maybe even life—Lawrence still wanted to be in that interview room.

He hit the beeper for his car, slid into the front seat and pulled out his phone. One missed call.

Dialling message bank, he was met with the familiar chirp of McPhee. "Well, you're either a lousy shot or a really good one. That bullet you put in Henry? Nothing more than a skin graze. He's in the lock-up now. If you want first dibs over Sergeant O'Neil, you better call me back."

A skin graze? Lawrence smiled to himself. The ambos had probably bandaged Henry up at the scene. A superficial wound like that meant no hospitals, no wasted time. Lawrence hit the call back button and told McPhee he was on his way.

***

Lawrence was right, Officer Poy wasn't impressed with his request, but she did it anyway. With the evidence and forensic report in hand, Lawrence pushed open the glass door of the Valley Station while he downed what must have been his sixth coffee for the day.

The clock in the bullpen said it was nearly four, yet the place was alive with cops. He spotted a grim-looking Sergeant O'Neil on the other side of the room and gave him a nod, but there were other uniforms there he didn't recognise. They must be from the Goldie too, Lawrence thought. Probably came up when they heard about Henry's arrest. He stopped in front of his desk; a redheaded officer was already occupying his chair.

"You look … *stunning*," McPhee grinned, looking equally stunning himself.

"Stick with those midnight drive-through runs, and one day you can look this good." The line came out wearily and the detective tried to calculate how long he'd been awake. "Where's Henry?"

"In an interview room out the back. Paul Sinclair too. They've spoken to their lawyer, Graham Maston, who politely requests that we don't question his client until he arrives." McPhee fluttered his eyes.

"Did you ask Henry if he'd agree to an interview?"

"Yup, and on the fifteenth time he caved."

Lawrence's eyes widened; he never would have expected the biker to agree to an interview, no matter how much they pestered him.

"He said yes, but only *after* I mentioned the word bail." McPhee explained.

"And he believed you?"

"Either I'm a really convincing liar or Henry thinks that he is."

Lawrence shook his head, scarcely believing his luck. He was halfway out the bullpen when he stopped, turned and called back to his partner. "You want to come in and question Henry with me?"

McPhee's eyebrows just about touched his hairline. Lawrence figured that was a yes.

Lawrence wondered if he'd ever questioned this many people in one shift. Though, technically, he'd signed off four hours ago.

The detective pushed open the door to the interview room and, without preamble, pulled up stumps at the table opposite his suspect. Henry looked like shit. He'd washed the blood off his face, but dried red flakes were caught in his beard. He sat slack in the chair, sinewy arms folded over his chest, looking like he'd spent the last three hours fighting back sleep. McPhee took his seat by Lawrence, but sat back in a way that suggested he was just here to observe. Reaching over, Lawrence hit the recording device's red button, recited the mandatory warnings about Henry's right to remain silent. Standard housekeeping.

"Mr Ernst, can you tell me why you and a Miss Daphne Lawrence were at the port this morning?"

"Why don't you tell me, copper? Why don't you tell your little recorder there about how you were too fat and too lazy to get a warrant, so ya sent your kid in to do the snooping?" Henry spat the words out, loosening the dry blood in his beard so that it sprinkled over the table top.

"Are you suggesting that I sent an untrained civilian on an errand to illegally enter your property? Why would I put my own daughter in danger for inadmissible evidence?"

Henry scoffed. "It's not just outlaws that are above the law." His eyes flicked towards McPhee. "Hell, half the coppers in this building look like bikies."

McPhee brushed a hand over his orange handlebar moustache, cleared his throat and made a study of his notepad.

Ignoring the jab, Lawrence reached inside his jacket and produced an evidence bag, dropping it onto the table with a clunk. Officer Poy had lifted several prints from the blade and run them through the national fingerprint identification system; Lawrence assumed that the ones that didn't have a match in the database belonged to Daff and Peta. The remaining prints were linked to the man who sat across from him.

"Do you recognise this knife, Mr Ernst?"

Henry answered without even looking at the bag. "Never seen it before."

"The handle is covered in your prints, Henry, and forensics have confirmed that it's an exact match for the weapon that killed Beth Dawson."

The forensic pathologist was still examining the officer's fatal wounds, so it would be a day or more until that report crossed Lawrence's desk—not that he needed proof of something he already knew.

"So? Any bloody fella could have used that knife."

"The knife isn't everything. We found a body out at Beerwah, locals call it the Boiler, you ever heard of that place?"

"Nope."

"Yeah, I guess you wouldn't unless you were a local. Wait, did you grow up around that area? Peachester wasn't it? That's a little over ten minutes away." Lawrence mentally thanked the constable who discovered that tidbit of information.

Henry glared at the detective, but said nothing.

"When was the last time you saw Mikey Gallegan?" Henry maintained his silence, so Lawrence continued. "I understand that Mikey was a member of your club Road Dogs. Is that correct?" Still Henry said nothing. "I'm sorry to inform you, but Mikey Gallegan has been killed. We believe him to be the victim of a violent attack. Do you know anyone who would want to hurt Mikey?" Lawrence took a beat; still the bikie refused to answer. "Medical examiners estimated the time of death as four days ago. When was the last time you saw Mikey?"

"I haven't seen him in days. Going off what you said, officer, I'm gonna say it's been four or more."

"You don't seem very upset. Given that your late wife was also murdered four days ago, I'd say that's quite the coincidence." Lawrence paused, letting that comment sink in for dramatic effect. "When I interviewed you on Thursday, you told me that you'd spent the previous night at the clubhouse with your second-in-charge, Paul Sinclair, or as you prefer to call him, *Tramp*. Problem is, CCTV captured Paul's car heading down Queen Street at one a.m. on Thursday. The Sundowner is on Gotha Street, less than ten minutes away.

"We also got footage of you blokes coming back into North Lakes at around seven a.m. Sounds to me like you guys did a run up the Sunny Coast, and I'm guessing you left your mate out at Beerwah because someone—probably a prospect you set up to keep an eye on the motel—told you cops were crawling all over the Sundowner. You probably decided that you should get back to the clubhouse in case any questions got asked. Does that sound right to you?"

Lawrence leaned forward to get a better look at the old biker. "Maybe you remember things wrong, maybe you got a little confused. I know it happens to me from time to time. So, I'll tell you what, I'm going to give you the chance to provide us with a fresh statement. Where were you on Wednesday night and into the early hours of Thursday morning?"

Henry leaned back in his chair, eyes narrowing to slits.

Lawrence clicked off the recorder, reached into his jacket and pulled out a second evidence bag. "Does this look familiar to you?"

Henry flinched at the sight of the watch like he'd accidently looked into the midday sun. "Don't think so."

"Really? Because I have reason to believe that Mikey Gallegan was wearing this watch at the time of his death, and that it was removed, post mortem, by Paul Sinclair."

Henry shrunk back, his eyes widening before he quickly composed his face. "I don't know what you're talking about."

"What's really strange is that the late officer Thomas Pease had a watch just like this. He was in a fatal car accident eighteen months ago; do you know anything about that?"

"What are you getting at, Detective?" The question came in a whisper.

"My daughter was wearing this watch when you grabbed her. She said you recognised it. She said the club was behind Tom's accident."

"Bitch is lying."

"My daughter was in the car accident too. She said there'd been a second car there that night, that's what caused her to run off the road. I also remember you paying me a private visit, telling me to back off, threatening my daughter. Officer Pease was wearing his watch the night of the accident, but no watch was listed on the coroner's report. Now, mistakes happen, so I called Tom's family.

Turns out, he wasn't buried with it. I'd say that's pretty interesting, wouldn't you?"

The blood drained from Henry's face and he stammered, "Not … really."

"Forensics found a print on the watch, by the way." Lawrence picked up the evidence bag, flicked it for effect. "Perfect match for Paul Sinclair."

The bags beneath Henry's eyes had deepened, making his peepers look like they were ready to pop.

The interview room door opened and in walked a slim man wearing a pale grey suit, his face beetroot red. "I told you my client wasn't to participate in an interview until I'd arrived."

McPhee shrugged, speaking up for the first time. "He agreed."

Henry's lawyer firmly told him to not say another word and immediately requested a private room in which to advise his client. With the interrogation coming to a halt, Lawrence returned to the bullpen and collapsed into his chair. The adrenaline and caffeine were wearing off and the only thing the detective felt was knackered.

"I've got something I have to tell you." McPhee dragged a chair over from behind an empty computer desk.

Lawrence sat up as the possibility of some shut-eye disappeared. "You're leaving me to partner up with Gibbs?"

McPhee released a slight chuckle, though it didn't reach his eyes; his hands two birds huddled together before him.

"You remember at the start of this investigation, how you'd told me you'd nearly booked the Road Dogs back in 2014?"

"Mmmmmm?" Lawrence nodded, tight-lipped.

"You said you'd caught a teenager for a B and E. When you realised he was high, you cut him a deal. If he squealed on who sold him the stuff, you wouldn't charge him. When he ratted on the Road Dogs, you got him to organise another meet-up, only the Dogs never showed."

Lawrence leaned forward, his hands on his knees. "Yeah, I know. I was there."

McPhee flopped back in his chair, his eyes falling to the floor, and took a deep breath. "The reason why they never showed is because I told them it was a set-up."

The detective rocked back in the chair like he'd been slapped. "You …"

But he couldn't finish that sentence; his scattered mind scrabbled to fit the pieces together. When Lawrence had made that arrest, McPhee had been at the station for barely a month. How had the Road Dogs bribed him that quickly? Lawrence's eyes ran over his partner's brilliant red hair, ruddy skin, handlebar moustache. Henry's words echoed in his ears. *Hell, half the coppas in this building look like bikies.*

"Are you one of them or an affiliate member?"

McPhee's jaw clenched and he searched his superior's face. "No," he stammered. "I'm not a member, *shit*, nothing like that."

The image of Henry showing up at his door, threatening his daughter, melded with the memory of a late-night New Year's Eve phone call. *Mr Lawrence, your daughter's been in a car accident.*

Lawrence shook his head; despite the rage that burned dirty through his blood, he tried to speak calmly. "What was it then? Did they threaten you or did they have something on you?"

Looking as though he were about to step on a leghold trap, McPhee released a heavy exhale. "Neither. It wasn't like that. I'd been here about a week when I got a call from this fella I'd been at the academy with. He knew I'd been relocated to the Valley and that I was working with you. We got along during training, but I thought it was kinda weird he'd kept tabs on me. Then he said he was going undercover, investigating a local bikie gang, the Road Dogs, and he knew you were hot on 'em. He said I'd be doing him a solid if I could keep him in the loop, pass on whatever it is we got on the Dogs."

"Why?" Though Lawrence suspected he knew the answer.

"He didn't want our investigation to pull the plug. He wanted to be the one to bring them in, said he had a promotion riding on it."

Bingo. "So, some fella you went to the academy with calls you out of the blue and asks this great big favour and you just said yes?"

McPhee shrugged, though he had the good sense to look embarrassed. "I figured it was more important that *someone* bring them in; it didn't much matter who. You know how much work goes into an undercover investigation, the expense .... The Queensland Police Service wasn't just going after the Road Dogs, but specifically Henry and all his associates and contacts. If we arrested some low-level member for the supplying of dangerous drugs, Henry may have quietened down or become increasingly suspicious of new members …" McPhee released another heavy breath, "Look, this is gonna make me sound like a fuck-up, but in around about way, it almost felt like we were jeopardising *their* case."

"Well, a lot of good it did anyone. If we'd busted the club two years ago, your friend might still be alive. Your friend being Mike Gallegan, I assume?"

McPhee nodded. "Yup, that was the name he was working under."

A part of Lawrence wished McPhee had told him all this two years ago, but he knew why he hadn't. Undercover operations *were* expensive and they asked a lot of the UC: abandoning their lives and their homes, sometimes for years. Maintaining that persona and the confidentiality of the investigation was paramount. By calling McPhee, that UC had broken the terms of his contract, and McPhee wasn't about to blow the whistle on him. Lawrence's eyes narrowed. "Why are you telling me this?"

McPhee's eyes dropped towards a hole in the threadbare carpet. "I saw that there was a mobile listed on the evidence report at the Beerwah scene. I called him on Wednesday when we found the bodies, left a message."

"Right-o." Lawrence dragged an open palm over his face and tried to decide what the hell he was going to do with this confession.

Apparently, McPhee was wondering too. "Will you have me suspended or …"

Lawrence scanned the now empty bullpen. “I can’t do anything with the phone—”

“I understand—”

“No,” Lawrence held up a hand to stop him. “What I mean is, I don’t know how to delete anything off the phone. If I get it for you, do you think you can do it?”

McPhee looked dumbfounded for a second, his jaw a fly trap.

“Don’t get too excited. If I can’t pull the phone out of evidence and your link to the UC is found out, the best you can hope for is suspension. If the station sergeant gets wind of it, I’ll do what I can to stop a termination.”

McPhee looked grim, thanked him anyway and offered to get them both a coffee.

“Sure, but make it a big one. I’m gonna need all the charm I can muster to pry that phone out of evidence.”

Looking as weary as Lawrence felt, McPhee dragged his feet, making his way towards the staff room at the opposite end of the station. Once he was out of sight, Lawrence pulled out his phone and checked to see if he had any missed calls from Peta. There were none, but she had sent a text.

Docs keeping Daff for a few more hours said her neck injuries are minimal but they want to be sure. Will send another update soon.

The detective switched off his phone when Graham Maston, Henry’s lawyer, reappeared in the bullpen. “My client said one of your officers offered bail if he agreed to an interview."

Lawrence noticed that the lawyer hadn't framed it as a question. "I have no idea what you're talking about. Perhaps your client misunderstood the situation."

He shrugged, shaping his reply around a smile.

***

Luckily, Lawrence's charm increased with fatigue. He managed to slip McPhee the phone while chatting to the constable responsible for photographing and documenting the evidence collected at the Boiler scene. As the detective well knew, parents love showing off pictures of their kids. Constable Jones scrolled through about fifty pictures of her two-year-old son on her phone, and when Lawrence pulled the single creased photo of Daphne from his wallet, she said it was *cute.* An actual photograph. McPhee erased his calls from the phone's history, and Lawrence sent his partner home, hoping there'd be no more surprises.

A few hours later, Lawrence knocked on thirty-four Willow Drive, though he doubted she'd be home. When Heather opened the door, she was dressed in a grey skirt and a delicate white button-up blouse. She looked fresh, like she was going to work, even though it was four in the arvo.

"I just got home." She explained when Lawrence commented on the outfit.

"I have some news, can I come in?"

"I don't see why not." She pushed the door back and gestured towards the lounge room behind her. "I was surprised you didn't call yesterday, that would have been the courteous thing to do, given our date."

Lawrence wanted to correct her—Saturday night had definitely not been a date—but he chose to ignore the comment instead. "I arrested Henry Ernst this morning. We found the knife that killed Beth Dawson; it was covered in Henry's finger prints. I wanted to tell you in person, though I haven't been able to link him directly with Sarah's death—yet. Our forensic physicians are busy comparing Henry's hands to the finger-marks left on your sister's neck. Once the results are in, I'll let you know."

Heather perched on the edge of her white leather lounge, her face composed. Lawrence thought surely she would have felt some relief or sense of justice. Maybe even a *thanks very much, detective.*

"I found that yesterday," Heather point towards a yellow spiral-bound notebook on the coffee table. It was the kind high-school and university students used, broken into sections by white tabs. Daff's desk had been covered in them when she'd been in school.

Lawrence sank into the single-seat recliner on the other side of the coffee table, picked up the notebook and opened it to the first page.

The words "Sleeping with Dogs" were scrawled on the top and underlined three times.

The detective feathered the pages between his thumbs; every page was full of blue looping cursive writing. "Is this—"

"Sarah's manuscript? Yes. She had beautiful penmanship didn't she? I remember her winning a class award when we were in primary school. I should have known she'd handwrite her manuscript rather than type it. I don't think she was much of a wizard when it came to computers."

That was something Lawrence knew plenty about. "Can I take this, Heather? I'd like to run it for prints, see if Henry ever touched it." If he did, Lawrence thought, we'd not only have enough physical evidence to lock him up, but a solid motive too.

"Oh yes, take it." Heather waved a hand. "It's not very good anyway. She could spin a good yarn in person—oh I'll miss that! She was so very funny—but I don't think she had the gift for writing."

"Ah-huh." Lawrence agreed, though he wasn't really paying attention. "Thank you, Heather. I'll keep you updated."

"Yes, yes." Heather stood, waving her hand again.

Lawrence heaved himself out of the soft chair and followed her to the door.

"You look very tired, Detective, would you like a coffee?"

Lawrence assumed the offer was just a courtesy, especially given that they were now standing in her entryway and the front door was open. McPhee was right; Heather was a little out of the ordinary. But after a lifetime's worth of drama, the truth was Lawrence found her cool, calm frankness refreshing.

"Thank you, but no. I better head back to the station and get the crew onto this notebook."

Heather smiled, and in the warmth of the setting winter sun her blonde wispy hair took on an ethereal glow. "Well, perhaps you'll let me buy you a coffee tomorrow. I know a place in the city. The décor is just awful, but the coffee's magnificent."

In the afternoon light, and in that white shirt, Lawrence could have said the same about her. "Heather, it's a date."

CHAPTER 24

Daff

Saturday July 16, 2016

Daff grabbed her long-sleeve denim button-up off the coat rack and checked her reflection in the stand's mirror. The swelling in her neck had eased after a few days and her vocal chords had healed, but the bruising was only just starting to fade. Somehow, she'd avoided breaking any bones. Which was a very good thing, because the two days spent on her back at the University Hospital had nearly driven her mad and if she'd been confined to bed rest at home, that would have tipped her over the edge.

Daff pushed back the sleeve of her top and checked her wrist for the time; it was nearly ten. Lawrence had returned the watch a week after he'd taken it and whatever tests forensics had run, it was still in good working order. That week without the timepiece and its ghost had been uncomfortably silent.

"Heading out, are you?" Liam appeared beside her.

"If I start now, I can get a few hours in before Melissa and Peta arrive."

Liam's face hardened at the mention of Melissa's name. After what had happened at the Sundowner Motel, he was still suspicious of the psychic; and if Daff were honest, she wasn't totally over the betrayal either. Melissa had tried to visit Daff at the hospital, but Peta had turned her away. Family only. Which wasn't true, but it sounded legit. For two days, Daff's phone had buzzed every twenty minutes and she'd let all the calls go through to voicemail.

Four days ago, the psychic had simply shown up at Daff's door.

Melissa had dressed in her usual attire: black jeans, a dark grey Misfits t-shirt and a jewellery rack's worth of bracelets on each arm. "You avoiding me, hon?"

The image of Melissa's bloody fingertips had flashed before Daff's eyes. "I've had a lot going on."

"Really? 'Cos I was starting to think that maybe you found out some things about me that you didn't like. Peta mentioned that you went on a little joy ride to the Sundowner, so I know that you know what happened that night. You want to talk out here, or are you gonna invite me in?"

Wordlessly, Liam stepped between them—a senseless gesture. A moment later, Melissa walked through him, pulling up a seat at the dining table as Daff went through the motions of scooping loose-leaf tea into a pot.

Liam lingered beside the psychic, unwilling to take his eyes off her. "Why is she here?"

For everyone's benefit, Daff repeated his question.

"I figured you'd appreciate knowing a few more details about everything that happened, and even if you didn't, I'd like to tell you my side of the story anyway."

"Alright." Daff dragged out the word as she slid the pot and accompanying cups onto the table.

Melissa exhaled, unsteadily, and closed her eyes. "First of all, I wanted to say that I'm so sorry for everything that happened to you, hon. That shit's on me."

"How is it your fault? You didn't strangle me."

The psychic flinched at the verb. "No, but I did give Liam's address to Tramp."

The idea of Melissa confiding anything to Tramp about Daff or Liam made Daff feel uncomfortably exposed. At the same time, Daff wasn't sure why passing on the address was such a big deal. "Are you saying that the club didn't know where Liam was living? How's that possible?"

"They *thought* they knew where he was living. As it turns out though, Mikey—*Liam*—had two addresses. They didn't know about the demountable. Maybe there were some things Liam wanted to keep to himself? Maybe he wanted a second bunker in case the club started to become suspicious." Melissa shrugged. "Anyway, Tramp was trying to make it look like Mikey had split from the club, disappeared in the middle of the night. After they killed Mikey, they knew they wouldn't have long until the cops came bangin' on the clubhouse door. So, Mikey's 'split' had to look real, or at least plausible. I mean, obviously, the cops would never believe that an undercover agent just got up and split, but they'd have to *prove* it, and Henry and Tramp were gonna do their best to make it look like that was the case."

"I still don't understand why you gave Tramp the address. You wanted to leave him, wouldn't you want him to get arrested?"

"And dob me in? Look, hon, I don't want to spend the rest of my days in jail more than anyone else. *I was there* that night; I drew the symbol. I couldn't risk Tramp getting arrested and ratting me out too, but at the same time, I was the only one besides Henry who knew what went down at the Sundowner. I was a loose end ..."

"And you didn't want to wind up dead in a motel room." Daff repeated the thought Melissa had had in the bathroom that night.

"Yeah, that's right. So, I told Tramp that I had a vision—he believes in all this stuff you know." Daff thought back to the storage yard, the way Tramp had resisted Liam's possession, even telling *Mikey* to fuck off. "I gave him the address as a way to prove my loyalty; they had to believe I wasn't gonna rat them out."

"Why would you want to show loyalty to him? At the motel, you were afraid—disgusted—by what happened."

"I wanted to leave Tramp, still do, but you don't get to the top of an outlaw club 'cos you're a good guy. You can't always just leave; especially when your partner's shared club business with you. I mean shit, Sarah tried to leave and look what happened to her."

"Okay?" Daff ran a hand through her hair as she tried to understand Melissa's conflicted motivations. "I assume then, that you knew Liam when he was alive? When he was Mikey?"

Melissa leaned forward, clasped her hands together on the table. Bracelets jiggling against each other and the wood. "Yeah, hon, I knew him. He'd been in the club two years and a full patch member for one. He was a pretty good guy, respectful. They aren't all that way."

"I don't care about that."

Liam's eyebrow shot up in a gesture that said *oh really?*

Daff deserved that. After all, it had been her need to redeem his character that had nearly caused her own death. Twice. "I'm asking because I want to know if you helped me because you wanted to help *me* or because you knew who Liam was."

"Both, hon." Melissa broke her gaze and filled the two cups. "I had no idea that you were Detective Lawrence's daughter. When Peta called to make an appointment, I thought you were just another client and that this was just another reading. Then, when I saw Liam in my mind's eyes during your reading, I realised what was going on. There are no accidents, Daff. There's a reason why Ange recommended me to Peta and why Peta decided to call me that day; of all the damn psychics on the coast, she called *me*. It was an opportunity for repentance, hon, the universe was giving me a chance to set things right."

Daff sipped her tea while craving a stronger amber drink.

"Have you told anyone what you saw? Your dad, maybe?" Melissa's fingers tapped the side of her cup, though she'd yet to drink any.

"No." It was a truth Daff remained conflicted about.

"Thank you." Melissa returned the cup to the table, her face relaxing slightly. "Tramp and Henry haven't said anything to the cops about me being there either. And as far as I know, the cops haven't found any evidence to show I was. At any rate, they haven't shown up at my apartment, so I figure …" she finished with a shrug.

Thinking back on that night, there'd been another one of Mel's thoughts that bothered Daff. "After you drew the symbol on the mirror that night, you thought, *I've touched her blood. We're connected.* What did you mean by that?"

Melissa's eye widened slightly. "Geez, hon, your abilities have improved. Yeah, I did think that, and I meant *just* that. When I used Beth's own blood to help the man who murdered her get away with it, I created a karmic bond. A seriously bad one. It's the kinda of bad juju that leaves you with only two options." She held up her index finger. "One: you gotta right your wrong," she raised her middle finger in the peace sign, "or two: wait to see what the consequences are and hope you can live with them."

Remembering the small glittering vial Melissa kept in her pocket, Daff counted. "I thought you were protecting against karma?"

Melissa smiled, "Some things aren't worth risking. That's why I didn't tell you who I was, what I knew. I needed you to trust me. If I'd told you what had happened when I first met you, you wouldn't have believed me and you'd probably have kicked me outta your house. And even if you did believe me, you'd always be wondering if I were double-crossing you." Leaning across the table, she took Daff's hands in her own. "Believe me, I didn't know that Liam was undercover and I definitely didn't know that he was the one behind the accident."

Daff's eyes shot towards Liam involuntarily. His memories hadn't returned, but he wore the guilt as if they had. But memory is a trickster, distorting events, heightening emotions, changing what people said and when, exaggerating their motivations. Daff's vision of that night was more painful than her memories of it because it was a non-biased, 360-degree home movie complete with surround sound. The only thing it lacked was a stream of consciousness voice over. According to her father, Henry had admitted in the interview he'd told Liam to give Daff a scare, but they'd never really know what Liam was thinking that night he'd driven her off the road.

She could live with that mystery; it was the other one she couldn't let go of. "Hey Mel, do you remember that first day you came over for a reading, and how Peta told you we'd been to *Circle* the night before?"

"Yeah?" Melissa's head tilted to the side, eyes narrowing silently in question.

Daff took a steadying breath. Despite all that had happened, she hadn't shared this experience with anyone. "During the meditation, I saw this white circular light. There was the silhouette of a figure standing in front of it, and the first thing I thought of was my mum. Do you think ... maybe ..."

"Do I think it was really her?"

Daff nodded, eyes dropping to the table.

"If you think it was your mum, hon, chances are it probably was." Melissa squeezed her hand as the one around Daff's heart loosened.

"Earth to Daphne," Liam waved his hands in front of her eyes. "Hello?"

Daff blinked and the memory of her conversation with Melissa melted away.

"Sorry." She shook her head, opened the front door and stepped out onto the verandah, determined to enjoy the day despite the circumstances.

Though another cold snap was inevitable, for now, the mornings were unseasonably warm. Looking across her lawn, Daff thought it'd never looked better for this time of year. She'd been generous with the fertiliser, and daily watering had encouraged the blades of carpet grass to become fat and vibrant green. It was a good project. She'd needed to do something after Liam's funeral; something that required focus, calculation and heavy lifting. Pruning the red robins and mock oranges; shifting full bags of blood and bone, dolomite and manure; carefully transplanting geranium clippings and selecting herbs for the oncoming winter had proved a decent distraction, and Liam seemed happy enough to indulge her as they both ignored the topic of his departure.

Slipping on her set of gardening gloves, Daff thought of Lawrence and promised herself to give him a call later. Four years of hurt couldn't be repaired within a month, but they'd made a start. They were talking, mostly awkwardly and cautiously, but they were talking. Daff squatted by the garden bed in front of the verandah and proceeded to pull the weeds out, roots and all. Liam dropped down on the stairs in silence. The sun was hitting him full on, but his floppy hair didn't shine and his skin didn't turn golden with it. He looked exactly the same. He would always look exactly the same.

Two days ago, she travelled down to the Gold Coast for Liam's funeral. Actually, it was Chris Bain's funeral, but Daff was never going to call him that. Lawrence kept his promise; when he'd given her back the watch, he also handed her a manila folder containing Liam's history and his graduation photo. He looked weird, dressed in the uniform she'd seen her father wear on only the most formal of police occasions. According to his profile, Liam was thirty-three years old, 183cm tall (that she already knew) and 82kgs.

His name was Christopher Anthony Bain. She supposed the name suited him. He'd been raised on the Gold Coast, the file told her, then relocated to Townsville in his teens where he graduated from the academy in 2011 before returning home. Given his age, good scores and tattoos—a panther on his back and eagle wings across his chest (neither of which Daff had seen)—he'd been selected for the undercover investigation of the Road Dogs. Though the Bain family had returned to the Gold Coast, he hadn't spoken to them for the two years prior to his death.

The forensic physician had positively ID'd the body within an hour. Lawrence, along with Sergeant O'Neil,

Liam's handler, had delivered the death message together. The Bains took the news as expected.

Most of the Surfers Paradise Department was at the funeral. A verbal invitation had been extended to Detective Lawrence, and Daff went under the guise that she was keeping her father company. She thought Liam's memories might come back at the funeral, when he saw the grieving faces of friends and family. They didn't. The knowledge that he had belonged to someone brought Liam some relief, but he also found the strangers' distressed faces unsettling. They were grieving for a man who didn't know them. After the service broke and before the wake started, she ducked into an alcove, alone, and asked Liam if he'd like her to hand the watch over to his mother and father. At least then he'd be able to spend some time with his family.

"Who knows, maybe that will make the memories come back."

But he'd shaken his head. He'd rather stay with her.

There was the sharp snap of a car door closing.

"The hippie is here," Liam smirked, then the light fell from his face. "Time to get on with it, then."

"Sorry I'm late. Apparently, all of Brisbane would rather be on the coast today," Peta rolled her eyes, but smiled broadly as she thrust a handful of wildflowers at her host and headed towards the front door. Daff followed a moment later to the banging of cupboard doors and the whoosh of running water as Peta filled the kettle and went about her usual ritual of making tea.

"I thought you said the bruises were getting better?" Peta called out from the kitchen. "They look even worse than last time. Is Melissa on her way?"

Peta placed the steaming pot of tea onto the well-worn table top and immediately filled the two cups without leaving it to steep. Though there were six empty seats at the table, both women remained standing. "You sure you don't want to do this on your own?"

She's worried, Daff thought. *She's worried I'll go back to the way I was before.* "If I have to do it on my own, I won't do it." Daff slipped her fingers through the handle of her cup, tactfully avoiding Liam's gaze. They'd talked about it a few mornings ago as she moved around the yard, watering the hedges and herbs.

"Are you sure you're ready?" Daff asked Liam.

"It's time. We know who I was, the trial is set, the funeral is over."

"Yes, but are you ready?"

He shrugged. "I'm … nervous. I don't know what to expect, but I also can't stay here. A nonentity."

"Nice pun."

He smiled briefly, but it didn't reach his eyes. "It's not good for you either. You need to get on with your life. Are you ready?"

She would have laughed, but the question wasn't actually absurd. "I'm not looking forward to being alone … again."

"Maybe we can still see each other sometimes? Do you still see Tom?"

She shook her head, dropping her gaze. "You're right, though. It's time."

"Daff, Daff, Daff?" Peta shook her friend's shoulder, breaking Daff from her reverie. "Melissa's here."

"Hey hon, you doing okay?" Melissa walked through the still-open door, and Daff tried to reassemble her face into a pleasant smile. It didn't work.

"You know, we don't have to do this today. There's no rush, hon."

Liam flopped into Daff's armchair, shot for a jovial tone and missed. "Bit of a space cadet today, eh, Daff?"

"I guess so," she mumbled. "I appreciate your concern, but we need to do this."

Saying goodbye isn't easy, even when you get to pick the day.

The ceremony was simple. Melissa lit some sage and a single candle. "Are you sure you want to do this, hon? I can make the portal if you'd rather."

Daff shook her head as she shrunk into a cross-legged position on the floor. "No, I want to do it, it should be me, but can you walk me through it again?"

"Your confidence is so reassuring." Liam stood by the wall that Daff faced. He swayed side to side, looking more concerned by the minute.

Melissa pulled out a chair and took her seat beside Peta at the dining table. "It's all about intention. Look at the wall, focus on it, and imagine opening a white light, like a gate, to the other side."

"And if it doesn't work?"

"Then I can do it for you."

Are you ready? Daff locked eyes with Liam and he nodded.

I'll try to come back and see you … if I can.

"Okay." Her vision blurred, but she pushed her shoulders back and kept her eyes down, focussing on the wall. Remembering her vision of the circular light, Daff tried to imagine the white-hot glow of the rising sun, a perfect sphere of burning light, in the centre of the blank wall. It started first as a pin-prick, as small and distant as a star, and then she plucked at its corners, her mind stretching the light until it grew to the size of a door.

Can you see it, Liam? Can you help me make it bigger?

Wordlessly, she could feel his *yes* as the light suddenly expanded. Its shine filling the room, so that soon it was all she could see.

"Daff, Daff!"

She could hear Liam call, but his form was lost in the brilliant void. "Where are you?"

"I remember." His voice broke. "All of it. I remember my childhood, what oranges taste like. I hated winter and living in cities. I always wanted to be a cop, but then things changed. I remember brushing back your hair to check your pulse and taking Tom's watch. I remember dying. I remember all of it."

Daff's chest tightened; she could see it all too. A three-year-old Liam playing with his dog in the grass, an older Liam biting into a too-hot cookie fresh from the oven. She felt the soft memory of his first kiss, the speed of his first car, the first time he'd fired a gun and the first time it hit someone. She felt all of it. A life time of experience, mundane and extraordinary. All at once. And then it was gone. She felt him drift from her, moving towards the light, and though he hadn't said anything, she had felt the depth of his gratitude and the regret that she could not follow him now.

Slowly, the light drew back and folded in on itself.

Daff blew out the candle and slowly undid the straps of the watch. Peta's arms were around her before she even realised she was crying.

CHAPTER 25

Daff

Saturday August 20, 2016

Daff thought she'd caught the whiff of lemon myrtle as she stepped onto the footpath outside Toowong Cemetery. She'd spotted Lawrence's silver Honda a couple of blocks back, and as she approached the gate she could see him leaning against one of the four fat concrete pillars that guarded the front entrance, two take-away coffees in hand. Daff preferred tea, but the early morning commute from the Sunshine Coast meant she'd gone without—a particularly cruel sacrifice given the morning chill.

He was wearing the burgundy button-up she'd bought him for a birthday years before. It hadn't faded with time, so it was either seldom worn or handled with care. She wondered if he'd picked it intentionally, the way she had, knowing the colour would make his blue eyes pop. He looked better today, fresher. Daff hopped it was the result of a decent night's sleep and not a bottomless coffee mug.

"Been waiting long?" Though they'd maintained regular contact since that day at the port, the embrace was awkward; admittedly the take-away cups didn't help.

"Not for long." He released his hold and handed her a coffee.

She accepted, wishing she'd brought her own thermos of tea, and thanked him. Taking a cautious sip, she was surprised by the sweet, tart flavour of orange peel. Bergamot. Earl Grey. He remembered.

Lawrence guided her through the wrought iron entryway, one hand on her back, and towards a park bench. "Can we talk for a minute?"

Daff nodded into her disposable cup, taking another sip, as they navigated the bitumen walkway. The cemetery was leafy, its border marked by well-established trees that cast the grounds in a dappled light. Besides the odd jogger or dog-walker, the grounds were empty. They stopped at a bench beneath a fig tree, Lawrence brushing off a scatter of dead leaves, and took a seat.

"Thanks for coming with me." Daff slid into position beside him. "I didn't want to do this alone."

Lawrence snorted lightly. "Thanks for calling me. It means a lot that you … that you don't mind me being here."

"You knew him too." She shrugged, though the gesture wasn't intended as dismissive. "How long until the trial?"

"Be a good while yet. The magistrate is backed up, may have to wait as long as a year. Forensics are still doing their thing, be at least a month until those reports hit my desk. They may not even show up until after …"

"Until after you retire?"

"Yeah." Lawrence took a sip of his triple-shot long black. She remembered too. "You could really see that fella, couldn't you? Christopher Bain."

It was about the twentieth time he'd asked. "Yeah, I could see him, but I called him Liam."

"Right. And you could see Tom too?"

She nodded. "Yes, but that was different. I could only see him in dreams or visions. Liam, I could see all the time."

Lawrence shook his head, looking baffled, and changed the subject. "When was the last time you visited him?"

Not needing to ask who he meant, she replied, "Oh, I guess about eighteen months ago."

"You never came back?"

Her eyes dropped towards her booted feet. "No. I've never been back to see Mum either."

"It's a bit of a commute."

Daff's mouth lifted in a smirk. It was a generous comment. "It's not the drive that stopped me. I'm in the city every couple of weeks visiting Peta."

Lawrence flinched and she immediately regretted her confession; no doubt he was mentally calculating all the times she'd visited the city in the past eighteen months and not seen him.

"I guess I just figured, why? What good would coming back here do? There's some things you'd rather not remember," she recoiled from her own comment. "Not that I had to come back here to remember them … I don't think I'm explaining this right. I guess what I'm trying to say is that it hurt."

"Yeah," his eyebrows lifted and he sighed. "I know."

Daff stared out across the still and peaceful park; the rows of dearly departed. She wondered what lives they had lived and what loved ones remained behind, if any. She wondered if they were missed—if their loved ones were *brave enough* to miss them. She wondered if anyone ever visited them, laying tokens and wreaths beside their timeless faces; and if they were visited, did they know it? A month had passed since Liam went into the light. She hadn't seen him or Tom since.

"Do you ever visit Mum?"

Lawrence nodded, silent for a moment, his eyes tracing the park. When he spoke again, his voice was unsteady. "I hurt her in so many ways and I didn't mean any of it."

"I know," she replied too quickly, dispensing her own generosity. "Sometimes things just happen."

"It didn't *just* happen," his words came out harsh, then softened. "But it did happen and I regret it."

Daff wasn't sure if he meant the affair, the separation or their own estrangement.

"We could go visit her after here. Maybe get some flowers from Rocklea."

"You want to spend your Saturday morning on a cemetery crawl with your old man?"

She stood, smoothing her jacket. "I think my reputation can handle it."

Finishing their drinks, they dumped the disposables in a nearby bin and cut across the park. Lawrence offered to direct her, but there was no need. Daff remembered exactly where Tom was buried.

The memorabilia that decorated his grave had faded severely beneath the harsh Queensland sun. There was an American-inspired sheriff's badge, a plastic gun (which Daff thought horribly distasteful), toy cars and an old birthday card depicting the classic AC/DC logo. Her hands were steady as she removed the watch from her pocket, tucking it between the weathered plastic flowers and a photo frame of Tom and his mother.

"Don't you think you should keep it? Someone might come along and nick it."

Daff shrugged. "You can't stop everything. I don't want to keep it, but I don't want to give it away either. Tom should have it back, at least for a little while."

Lawrence huffed, checked his left then right before crouching down and digging a small hole in front of the headstone. He picked up the watch, dropped it into the hollow and covered it up again. "Now he can have it a little bit longer."

Standing up, it took the detective a moment to catch his breath. "You know, they do ghost tours in this cemetery."

"I don't really need help in that department, thanks," she laughed, burying her hands into the pocket of her jacket.

They stood there for a while—Daff wasn't sure how long exactly, not that it mattered. Re-reading the plaque until it ceased to make sense, she cast out a silent apology, hoping the channels would catch it and carry it to him unchanged.

She was about to pull on Lawrence's sleeve and say that it was time to go when Melissa's words echoed in her ears, *you need to forgive yourself.* She wasn't sure if that was possible, not yet; some thoughts are too deep-seated, but at least now she was willing to try. They stood together, father and daughter, as the sun continued to rise and the day grew warmer. People came, paid their respects and left. Birds sang, then stopped. The wind kicked up, giving dry leaves a new life as they danced over the lawn. Eventually, Daff knew that it was time.

EPILOGUE

Daff pushed open the doors to the morgue. It was early; she'd have at least an hour until the others arrived. Even though her control over the visions had improved, she never really knew what was going to happen, so she preferred to exercise her abilities in private. She examined the work plan that hung from its runner opposite the wash bays. It was going to be a busy day. The first name on her list was Clarisse Newton. Sliding open the fridge door, Daff checked the racks one by one, which took a while—it was a full house. Eventually she found her, the name on the wrist band matching both the folder and run sheet. Daff started up the forklift and carefully carried Mrs Newton back into the morgue, looped the hoist around her and manoeuvred her onto the steel wash table.

Mrs Newton was small, with a narrow nose, a deeply lined face and thin, straight grey hair. Daff flipped open the folder, examining the supplied photograph and information sheet. At the time of death, Mrs Newton was ninety-three. It seemed a good age. Now that things were settling in, Daff introduced herself and explained that they'd be spending the next hour or so together. She propped the folder open on the bench, pulled a set of plastic gloves from their box and tucked them into the empty pocket of her scrubs. She didn't need them just yet.

Standing beside the table, she felt her stomach tighten with anticipation. It still felt like a violation, like reading someone's diary or picking through their underwear drawer.

"I hope you don't mind," she whispered, leaning forward. "It's just that I need the practice." She jumped as the phone in her other pocket started buzzing. Gulping a mouthful of air, she tried to slow her heart down as she pulled out her phone. There were only two people who would call her this early in the morning, and one of them had retired two months ago.

"Hey, Dad."

"Can you just get a transfer to Brisbane already?"

Daff wasn't in the mood to explain, again, that Dean & Clayton's didn't have any funeral homes in Brisbane—so no, she couldn't get a transfer. Though, she had checked out a couple of funeral homes with vacancies and filled out the occasional application.

"Why, what's happened?"

"McPhee got a call out yesterday morning, woman in her forties, that looks suspicious. You reckon you can get down here this afternoon?"

"Maybe," Daff looked at the clock on the wall, even though her shift had just started and she knew exactly what the time was. "Can you give me a few more details?"

"She was found in her home and there were drugs present, but she has a DVO out on her ex-husband who has a history of dealing—"

"The same drugs found at her house, got ya. I've got a big day here, but I can probably get in around six. Will McPhee be expecting me?"

A month ago, she met McPhee at the coroner's office to help out with a possible murder/suicide. It wasn't an enjoyable experience for either of them, and Daff got the impression that she gave McPhee the creeps.

"Yeah, I'll tell him."

"*Dad*—"

"I'll tell him, I will!"

Daff sighed and ran a hand over her brows. Sliding in and out of the visions had become easier, but the visions themselves weren't always fantastic. She'd explained to her father how terrifying it was sometimes, to feel yourself on the verge of death—even knowing that you weren't going to die. He shrugged and maintained his stance. Her gift could really help people; wasn't that worth a little discomfort?

"I'll meet you at the station tonight, we'll go in together."

"Alright, kiddo. I'll see you then."

She hit the 'end call' button, slipped the phone back into her pocket and returned to the patient Mrs Newton. "Sorry."

Daff stepped forward and gently lay her open hand over the deceased woman's cheek: so hard, so cold.

Her head spun with a gentle dizziness similar to intoxication, and her stomach tightened. She opened her eyes. The room was dark and the bed warm. She'd left the curtains open, so that she could look out onto the stars and have them look in on her.

There was a strange rumbling sound beside her and she shifted, scratching Mr Tinkers behind the ear in the way that he liked best. The cat flopped on his side, curling against her stroking hand with pleasure. She could feel her eyes growing heavy as a tight pressure built in her chest. There was a sensation of falling backwards, only slower and more gentle, until suddenly she could feel nothing at all but the expanse of an endless and infinite light.

The vision faded and Daff withdrew her hand from the woman's cheek.

Natural causes.

"Lucky you," Daff whispered.

Pulling the gloves from her pocket, Daff snapped them on, flipped open Mrs Newton's folder and began calculating the volume of embalming fluid required for a woman of her weight. A small smile tugged at her lips.

ACKNOWLEDGEMENTS

Writing is a solitary activity, yet many hands have been involved in the making of *Every Time He Dies.*

To my partner Ashley, thank you, thank you, thank you. Your unrelenting support is the reason this book exists. You sacrificed a lot to make my dream happen and yet you've never resented me or this project. That is love.

Mum, thanks for answering all my medical and mechanical questions. You are a wonder. To Bob, thank you for the inventive nicknames and colloquialisms which added much needed colour to Lawrence and Henry's story.

Thank you to my gifted and insightful beta readers, Sharon Green (who prefers double ticks) and Sara Land (who favours hearts and smiley faces).

To crime author Greg Lamney, thank you for answering my *many* questions about police procedure and providing feedback on early drafts.

To the staff at Gregson and Weight Funerals. Your industry knowledge added a level of detail to Daff's work day that Google could not!

Endless thanks to Samantha Schragg and that one *particularly* productive phone call (many moons ago) where you offered marvellous solutions for every plothole.

To my mentor and friend Kate Goldsworthy whose keen eye and expert advice transformed a messy manuscript into a neat novel.

Jane Smith, thank you for your kind words, sharp skills and for catching every typo. You gave this work its final polish.

Special thanks go to Dr Paul Williams who convinced me to enrol in USC's Master's program—a decision that *literally* changed my life—and to Dr Sarah Kanake for saying that the only difference between a published writer and an unpublished one is persistence. You guys rock! Thanks to the USC Master's Class of 2017, your feedback and advice helped me figure out what the heck I was doing.

To my brilliant supervisor Nike Sulway, thank you. You are a prime example of what it means to live a creative life and my studies and writing have been enriched by our exchanges.

Deb and Andy, thank you for opening your home and hearts to me and Sadie. I would not have a Master's degree without your generosity.

To Ele. I owe you … a lot … I wish you could have been here to celebrate the completion of this manuscript's journey. I fucking miss you. And to April, your friendship meant the world to me. I fucking miss you too.

And finally, to you, dear reader. Without you, this book would be nothing but words. Thanks for bringing Daff's story to life.

CPSIA information can be obtained
at www.ICGtesting.com
Printed in the USA
BVHW031048260919
559511BV00001B/86/P

9 780648 581505